Ten Years of the Caine Prize for African Writing

Ten Years of the Caine Prize for African Writing

Ten Years of the Caine Prize for African Writing

First published in the UK in 2009 by
New Internationalist™ Publications Ltd
Oxford OX4 1BW
www.newint.org
New Internationalist is a registered trademark.

Individual contributions © The Authors. For permissions information on the stories by Nadine Gordimer, J.M. Coetzee and Ben Okri, see the notes at the end of each section.

Cover photograph from Senegal by Chris Keulen / Panos Pictures.

Edited by Chris Brazier and designed by Andrew Kokotka for New Internationalist.

 Printed on recycled paper by TJ International Limited, Cornwall, UK, who hold environmental accreditation ISO 14001.

British Library Cataloguing-in-Publication Data.
A catalogue record for this book is available from the British Library.

Library of Congress Cataloguing-in-Publication Data.
A catalogue record for this book is available from the Library of Congress.

ISBN: 978-1-906523-24-4

Contents

Preface

The Caine Prize for African Writing

Founded in 1999, the Caine Prize was named in celebration of the late Sir Michael Caine, former Chairman of Booker plc, who for nearly 25 years chaired the Booker Prize management committee. Shortly before he died he was working on the idea of a prize to encourage the growing recognition of the worth of African writing in English, its richness and diversity, by bringing it to a wider audience. His friends and colleagues decided to carry this idea forward and establish a prize of £10,000 to be awarded annually in his memory. They asked his widow Emma, Baroness Nicholson of Winterbourne, to be its President.

In the ten years since it was founded, the Caine Prize has won widespread recognition throughout Africa, in the UK and increasingly in the US. It is the only literary prize open to all African writers from whatever part of the continent, and the only African literary prize awarded exclusively for short stories, the medium in which budding African fiction writers find it easiest to express themselves and attract attention, given the difficulties they face in devoting time to creative writing and in getting their work published. It is Africa's leading prize for literature published in English; and its winners and shortlisted candidates have seen their careers immeasurably enhanced, typically by attracting the interest of leading literary agents, having their books published by mainstream publishers, and winning further prizes with them.

In addition to awarding the Prize, for the past seven years we have held an annual Caine Prize Workshop for African Writers, gathering in an African location 12 writers from African countries, including our shortlisted candidates and others, to work together and each produce a short story, with guidance from more experienced writers. These stories are then published in the annual Caine Prize anthology, alongside those shortlisted for the Prize.

In a new development, since 2007 Caine Prize winners are invited to spend a month's residence at Georgetown University, Washington DC, as guests of the Department of English Literature, an extremely valuable stimulus to their writing careers.

That the Prize has been awarded regularly over the past ten years is thanks to the generosity of the donors who have contributed funds, most notably the Oppenheimer Memorial Trust, whose ninth year of generous support approaches in 2010, and the Gatsby Charitable Foundation, which provided similarly valuable support from 2002 to 2007. And Celtel BV International – latterly Zain Africa – have sponsored three of the Caine Prize Workshops for African Writers.

We are especially grateful to the African winners of the Booker Prize, Nadine Gordimer, J.M. Coetzee and Ben Okri, who have graciously contributed stories of their own to this anthology.

Jonathan Taylor   **Nick Elam**
Chairman   Administrator

"I believe that a literary prize for African writers both honours Michael's work for Africa and will show the creative spirit of Africa and her humanity more globally."
Archbishop Desmond Tutu June 1999

"This Prize is the result of a love story. Of Emma Nicholson's love for Michael Caine, and Michael Caine's love for Africa. It is the result of fidelity to their shared ideals. A translation of grief into a dream, and a dream into the reality of this Prize, which we celebrate in this volume. It has successfully helped the renaissance of a new African literature – and in just ten years."
Ben Okri July 2009

Introduction by Ben Okri

O ye who invest in futures

1

It is easy to dismiss Africa. It is easy to patronise Africa. It is easy to profess to like Africa. It is easy to exploit Africa. And it is easy to insult Africa.

But it is difficult to see Africa truly. It is difficult to see its variety, its complexity, its simplicity, its individuals. It is difficult to see its ideas, its contributions, its literature. It is difficult to hear its laughter, understand its cruelties, witness its spirituality, withstand its suffering, and grasp its ancient philosophies.

Africa is difficult to see because it takes heart to see her. It takes simplicity of spirit to see her without confusion. And it takes a developed human being to see her without prejudice.

2

Africa is a challenge to the humanity and sleeping wisdom of the world. It is an eyeball-challenging enigma. Africa reveals what most hides in people. It reveals their courage or cowardice, their complacency or their conscience, their smallness or their generosity. Faced with Africa, nothing of what you truly are can hide. Africa brings to light the true person beneath their politeness, their diplomacy, or their apparent good intentions.

Africa is the challenge of the human race in the 21st century because, through her, humanity can begin to feel at peace with itself. Africa is our conscience. There can be no true progress for humanity till the sufferings of our brother and sister continents are overcome, till people everywhere live reasonably good lives, free from vile diseases, undernourishment, illiteracy and tyranny.

3

There is another sense in which Africa is difficult to see. To see Africa one must first see oneself.

The laziness of the eyes has to go. It won't do any more to let our hearts and minds be affected by the colour of someone's skin. This problem, amazingly, is still here. It is one of the silent tragedies of our times. It prevents people making true friends. It prevents them reading the literature of others. It hinders the flow of ideas and the mutual enrichment of our lives. More often than not culture is colour-biased. We are still primitives in the art of being human.

4

This is what gives literature its sublime importance. Literature makes it possible to encounter others in the mind first. Literature is the encounter of possibilities, the encounter of the work and the heart. It is the true ambassador of the unity of humankind.

5

When I visit the houses of acquaintances a cursory glance at their bookshelves reveals everything I need to know, regardless of what they profess.

It is easy enough to have bookshelves weighed down with formidable rows of Shakespeare, Dickens, Jane Austen, Thomas Hardy, or Henry James, and all else that has acquired the patina of the classical. It is easy enough to have a fashionable collection of Toni Morrison, Rushdie, Marquez, and all else that displays a progressive tendency, alongside the popular books of the day.

But to have novels by Ukrainians, Iranians, Indians, Egyptians, poems by an unknown Samoan, a Dutch collection of stories, works by Kenyan, Nigerian, Jamaican novelists, plays from Portugal, Japanese elegies, all mixed in with books that reveal a healthy interest in what the human spirit is dreaming, now that is something special. For here would be a person that Goethe might have thought a citizen of the world. Here would be a person one would hope to have as a friend, a person keen on humanity, fascinated by its varied genius.

6

That's what the Caine Prize is about: celebrating the genius of human diversity. The idea is to enrich the world through its greater contact with Africa, and to enrich Africa through its greater contact with the world. The dream is to create a bridge of the imagination. The hope is to share in the fun and the marvel of the creative spirit.

7

But it is not enough to just pass one's eyes over the words, to merely read literature. That would be like what Mozart said about his mother-in-law: "She would see the opera, but not hear it." We should read this literature with an open mind, an intelligent heart.

True literature tears up the script of what we think humanity to be. It transcends the limitations we impose on the possibilities of being human. It dissolves preconceptions. True literature makes us deal with something partly new and partly known. That is why we can't ask new literature to be like the old, to give us the same pleasures as those that have gone before. That wouldn't be living literature, which surprises and redefines. That would be mere repetition.

Literature mirrors, reveals, liberates.

8

Literature from Africa has long been in the margins. One of the benefits of this is that it has much to do. It has so many new moods, possibilities, philosophies to bring into being. This literature will bring many unsuspected gifts and wonderful surprises to the world in the fullness of time.

9

O ye who invest in futures, pay heed to Africa. Today she is wounded and is somewhat downcast. But tomorrow she will flower and bear fruit, like the Nile once flowered into the pyramids, or like the savannahs after the rains.

10

Africa has a weird resilience. Her future bristles with possibilities. When she heals, Africa will amaze. I should know.

The Ultimate Safari

Nadine Gordimer – winner of the 1974 Booker Prize

The African Adventure Lives On... You can do it!
The ultimate safari or expedition
With leaders who <u>know</u> Africa.

– TRAVEL ADVERTISEMENT,
Observer, LONDON, 27/11/88

That night our mother went to the shop and she didn't come back. Ever. What happened? I don't know. My father also had gone away one day and never come back; but he was fighting in the war. We were in the war, too, but we were children, we were like our grandmother and grandfather, we didn't have guns. The people my father was fighting – the bandits, they are called by our government – ran all over the place and we ran away from them like chickens chased by dogs. We didn't know where to go. Our mother went to the shop because someone said you could get some oil for cooking. We were happy because we hadn't tasted oil for a long time; perhaps she got the oil and someone knocked her down in the dark and took that oil from her. Perhaps she met the bandits. If you meet them, they will kill you. Twice they came to our village and we ran and hid in the bush and when they'd gone we came back and found they had taken everything; but the third time they came back there was nothing to take, no oil, no food, so they burned the thatch and the roofs of our houses fell in. My mother found some pieces of tin and we put those up over part of the house. We were waiting there for her that night she never came back.

We were frightened to go out, even to do our business, because the bandits did come. Not into our house – without a roof it must have looked as if there was no one in it, everything gone – but all through the village. We heard people screaming and running. We were afraid even to run, without our mother to tell us where. I am the middle one, the girl, and my little brother clung against my stomach with his arms round my neck and his legs round my waist like a baby monkey to its mother. All night my first-born brother kept in his hand a broken piece of wood from one of our burnt house-poles. It was to save himself if the bandits found him.

We stayed there all day. Waiting for her. I don't know what day it was; there was no school, no church any more in our village, so you didn't know whether it was a Sunday or a Monday.

When the sun was going down, our grandmother and grandfather came. Someone from our village had told them we children were alone, our mother had not come back. I say 'grandmother' before 'grandfather' because it's like that: our grandmother is big and strong, not yet old, and our grandfather is small, you don't know where he is, in his loose trousers, he smiles but he hasn't heard what you're saying, and his hair looks as if he's left it full of soap suds. Our grandmother took us – me, the baby, my first-born brother, our grandfather – back to her house and we were all afraid (except the baby, asleep on our grandmother's back) of meeting the bandits on the way. We waited a long time at our grandmother's place. Perhaps it was a month. We were hungry. Our mother never came. While we were waiting for her to fetch us our grandmother had no food for us, no food for our grandfather and herself. A woman with milk in her breasts gave us some for my little brother, although at our house he used to eat porridge, same as we did. Our grandmother took us to look for wild spinach but everyone else in her village did the same and there wasn't a leaf left.

Our grandfather, walking a little behind some young men, went to look for our mother but didn't find her. Our grandmother cried with other women and I sang the hymns with them. They brought a little food – some beans – but after two days there was nothing again. Our grandfather used to have three sheep and a cow and a vegetable garden but the bandits had long ago taken the sheep and the cow, because they were hungry, too; and when planting time came our grandfather had no seed to plant.

So they decided – our grandmother did; our grandfather made little noises and rocked from side to side, but she took no notice – we would go away. We children were pleased. We wanted to go away from where our mother wasn't and where we were hungry. We wanted to go where there were no bandits and there was food. We were glad to think there must be such a place; away.

Our grandmother gave her church clothes to someone in exchange for some dried mealies and she boiled them and tied them in a rag. We took them with us when we went and she thought we would get water from the rivers but we didn't come to any river and we got so thirsty we had to turn back. Not all the way to our grandparents' place but to a village where there was a pump. She opened the basket where she carried some clothes and the mealies and she sold her shoes to buy a big plastic container for water. I said, *Gogo*, how will you go to church now even without shoes, but she said we had a long journey and too much to carry. At that village we met other people who were also going away. We joined them because they seemed to know where that was better than we did.

To get there we had to go through the Kruger Park. We knew about the Kruger Park. A kind of whole country of animals – elephants, lions, jackals, hyenas, hippos, crocodiles, all kinds of animals. We had some of them in our own country, before the war (our grandfather remembers; we children weren't born yet) but the bandits kill the elephants and sell their tusks, and the bandits and our soldiers have eaten all the buck. There was a man in our village without legs – a crocodile took them off, in our river; but all the same our country is a country of people, not animals. We knew about the Kruger Park because some of our men used to leave home to work there in the places where white people come to stay and look at the animals.

So we started to go away again. There were women and other children like me who had to carry the small ones on their backs when the women got tired. A man led us into the Kruger Park; are we there yet, are we there yet, I kept asking our grandmother. Not yet, the man said, when she asked him for me. He told us we had to take a long way to get round the fence, which he explained would kill you, roast off your skin the moment you touched it, like the wires high up on poles that give electric light in our towns. I've seen that sign of a head without eyes or skin or hair on an iron box at the mission hospital we used to have before it was blown up.

When I asked the next time, they said we'd been walking in the Kruger Park for an hour. But it looked just like the bush we'd been walking through all day, and we hadn't seen any animals except the monkeys and birds which live around us at home, and a tortoise that, of course, couldn't get away from us. My first-born brother and the other

13

boys brought it to the man so it could be killed and we could cook and eat it. He let it go because he told us we could not make a fire; all the time we were in the Park we must not make a fire because the smoke would show we were there. Police, wardens, would come and send us back where we came from. He said we must move like animals among the animals, away from the roads, away from the white people's camps. And at that moment I heard – I'm sure I was the first to hear – cracking branches and the sound of something parting grasses and I almost squealed because I thought it was the police, wardens – the people he was telling us to look out for – who had found us already. And it was an elephant, and another elephant, and more elephants, big blots of dark moved wherever you looked between the trees. They were curling their trunks round the red leaves of the Mopane trees and stuffing them into their mouths. The babies leant against their mothers. The almost grown-up ones wrestled like my first-born brother with his friends – only they used trunks instead of arms. I was so interested I forgot to be afraid. The man said we should just stand still and be quiet while the elephants passed. They passed very slowly because elephants are too big to need to run from anyone.

The buck ran from us. They jumped so high they seemed to fly. The warthogs stopped dead, when they heard us, and swerved off the way a boy in our village used to zigzag on the bicycle his father had brought back from the mines. We followed the animals to where they drank. When they had gone, we went to their water-holes. We were never thirsty without finding water, but the animals ate, ate all the time. Whenever you saw them they were eating, grass, trees, roots. And there was nothing for us. The mealies were finished. The only food we could eat was what the baboons ate, dry little figs full of ants that grow along the branches of the trees at the rivers. It was hard to be like the animals.

When it was very hot during the day we would find lions lying asleep. They were the colour of the grass and we didn't see them at first but the man did, and he led us back and a long way round where they slept. I wanted to lie down like the lions. My little brother was getting thin but he was very heavy. When our grandmother looked for me, to put him on my back, I tried not to see. My first-born brother stopped talking; and when we rested he had to be shaken to get up again, as if he was just like our grandfather, he couldn't hear. I saw flies crawling on our grandmother's face and she didn't brush them off; I was frightened. I picked a palm leaf and chased them.

We walked at night as well as by day. We could see the fires where the white people were cooking in the camps and we could smell the smoke and the meat. We watched the hyenas with their backs that slope as if they're ashamed, slipping through the bush after the smell. If one turned its head, you saw it had big brown shining eyes like our own, when we looked at each other in the dark. The wind brought voices in our own language from the compounds where the people who work in the camps live. A woman among us wanted to go to them at night and ask them to help us. They can give us the food from the dustbins, she said, she started wailing and our grandmother had to grab her and put a hand over her mouth. The man who led us had told us that we must keep out of the way of our people who worked at the Kruger Park; if they helped us they would lose their work. If they saw us, all they could do was pretend we were not there; they had seen only animals.

Sometimes we stopped to sleep for a little while at night. We slept close together. I don't know which night it was – because we were walking, walking, any time, all the time – we heard the lions very near. Not groaning loudly the way they did far off. Panting, like we do when we run, but it's a different kind of panting: you can hear they're not running, they're waiting, somewhere near. We all rolled closer together, on top of each other, the ones on the edge fighting to get into the middle. I was squashed against a woman who smelled bad because she was afraid but I was glad to hold tight on to her. I prayed to God to make the lions take someone on the edge and go. I shut my eyes not to see the tree from which a lion might jump right into the middle of us, where I was. The man who led us jumped up instead, and beat on the tree with a dead branch. He had taught us never to make a sound but he shouted. He shouted at the lions like a drunk man shouting at nobody, in our village. The lions went away. We heard them groaning, shouting back at him from far off.

We were tired, so tired. My first-born brother and the man had to lift our grandfather from stone to stone where we found places to cross the rivers. Our grandmother is strong but her feet were bleeding. We could not carry the basket on our heads any longer, we couldn't carry anything except my little brother. We left our things under a bush. As long as our bodies get there, our grandmother said. Then we ate some wild fruit we didn't know from home and our stomachs ran. We were in the grass called elephant grass because it is nearly as tall as an elephant, that day we had those pains, and our grandfather couldn't just get down in front of people like my little brother, he went off into the grass to be on his own. We had to keep up, the man who led us always kept telling us, we must catch up, but we asked him to wait for our grandfather.

So everyone waited for our grandfather to catch up. But he didn't. It was the middle of the day; insects were singing in our ears and we couldn't hear him moving through the grass. We couldn't see him because the grass was so high and he was so small. But he must have been somewhere there inside his loose trousers and his shirt that was torn and our grandmother couldn't sew because she had no cotton. We knew he couldn't have gone far because he was weak and slow. We all went to look for him, but in groups, so we too wouldn't be hidden from each other in that grass. It got into our eyes and noses; we called him softly but the noise of the insects must have filled the little space left for hearing in his ears. We looked and looked but we couldn't find him. We stayed in that long grass all night. In my sleep I found him curled round in a place he had tramped down for himself, like the places we'd seen where the buck hide their babies.

When I woke up he still wasn't anywhere. So we looked again, and by now there were paths we'd made by going through the grass many times, it would be easy for him to find us if we couldn't find him. All that day we just sat and waited. Everything is very quiet when the sun is on your head, inside your head, even if you lie, like the animals, under the trees. I lay on my back and saw those ugly birds with hooked beaks and plucked necks flying round and round above us. We had passed them often where they were feeding on the bones of dead animals, nothing was ever left there for us to eat. Round and round, high up and then lower down and then high again. I saw their necks poking to this side and that. Flying round and round. I saw our grandmother, who sat up all the time with my little brother on her lap, was seeing them, too.

In the afternoon the man who led us came to our grandmother and told her the other people must move on. He said, If their children don't eat soon they will die.

Our grandmother said nothing.

I'll bring you water before we go, he told her.

Our grandmother looked at us, me, my first-born brother, and my little brother on her lap. We watched the other people getting up to leave. I didn't believe the grass would be empty, all around us, where they had been. That we would be alone in this place, the Kruger Park, the police or the animals would find us. Tears came out of my eyes and nose onto my hands but our grandmother took no notice. She got up, with her feet apart the way she puts them when she is going to lift firewood, at home in our village, she swung my little brother onto her back, tied him in her cloth – the top of her dress was torn and her big breasts were showing but there was nothing in them for him. She said, Come.

So we left the place with the long grass. Left behind. We went with the others and the man who led us. We started to go away, again.

There's a very big tent, bigger than a church or a school, tied down to the ground. I didn't understand that was what it would be, when we got there, away. I saw a thing like that the time our mother took us to the town because she heard our soldiers were there and she wanted to ask them if they knew where our father was. In that tent, people were praying and singing. This one is blue and white like that one but it's not for praying and singing, we live in it with other people who've come from our country. Sister from the clinic says we're two hundred without counting the babies, and we have new babies, some were born on the way through the Kruger Park.

Inside, even when the sun is bright it's dark and there's a kind of whole village in there. Instead of houses each family has a little place closed off with sacks or cardboard from boxes – whatever we can find – to show the other families it's yours and they shouldn't come in even though there's no door and no windows and no thatch, so that if you're standing up and you're not a small child you can see into everybody's house. Some people have even made paint from ground rocks and drawn designs on the sacks.

Of course, there really is a roof – the tent is the roof, far, high up. It's like a sky. It's like a mountain and we're inside it; through the cracks paths of dust lead down, so thick you think you could climb them. The tent keeps off the rain overhead but the water comes in at the sides and in the little streets between our places – you can only move along then one person at a time – the small kids like my little brother play in the mud. You have to step over them. My little brother doesn't play. Our grandmother takes him to the clinic when the doctor comes on Mondays. Sister says there's something wrong with his head, she thinks it's because we didn't have enough food at home. Because of the war. Because our father wasn't there. And then because he was so hungry in the Kruger Park. He likes just to lie about on our grandmother all day, on her lap or against her somewhere, and he looks at us and looks at us. He wants to ask something but you can see he can't. If I tickle him he may just smile. The clinic gives us special powder to make into porridge for him and perhaps one day he'll be all right.

When we arrived we were like him – my first-born brother and I. I can hardly remember. The people who live in the village near the tent took us to the clinic, it's where you have to sign that you've come – away, through the Kruger Park. We sat on the grass and everything was muddled. One Sister was pretty with her hair straightened and beautiful high-heeled shoes and she brought us the special powder. She said we must mix it with water and drink it slowly. We tore the packets open with our teeth and licked it all up, it stuck round my mouth and I sucked it from my lips and fingers. Some other children who had walked with us vomited. But I only felt everything in my belly moving, the stuff going down and around like a snake, and hiccups hurt me. Another Sister called us to stand in line on the verandah of the clinic but we couldn't. We sat all over the place there, falling against each other; the Sisters helped each of us up by the arm and then stuck a needle in it. Other needles drew our blood into tiny bottles. This was against sickness, but I didn't understand, every time my eyes dropped closed I thought I was walking, the grass was long, I saw the elephants, I didn't know we were away.

But our grandmother was still strong, she could still stand up, she knows how to write and she signed for us. Our grandmother got us this place in the tent against one of the sides, it's the best kind of place there because although the rain comes in, we can lift the flap when the weather is good and then the sun shines on us, the smells in the tent go out. Our grandmother knows a woman here who showed her where there is good grass for sleeping mats, and our grandmother made some for us. Once every month the food truck comes to the clinic. Our grandmother takes along one of the cards she signed and when it has been punched we get a sack of mealie meal. There are wheelbarrows to take it back to the tent; my first-born brother does this for her and then he and the other boys have races, steering the empty wheelbarrows back to the clinic. Sometimes he's lucky and a man who's bought beer in the village gives him money to deliver it – though that's not allowed, you're supposed to take that wheelbarrow straight back to the Sisters. He buys a cold drink and shares it with me if I catch him. On another day, every month, the church leaves a pile of old clothes in the clinic yard. Our grandmother has another card to get punched, and then we can choose something: I have two dresses, two pants and a jersey, so I can go to school.

The people in the village have let us join their school. I was surprised to find they speak our language; our grandmother told me, That's why they allow us to stay on their land. Long ago, in the time of our fathers, there was no fence that kills you, there was no Kruger Park between them and us, we were the same people under our own king, right from our village we left to this place we've come to.

Now that we've been in the tent so long – I have turned eleven and my little brother is nearly three although he is so small, only his head is big, he's not come right in it yet – some people have dug up the bare ground around the tent and planted beans and mealies and cabbage. The old men weave branches to put up fences round their gardens. No one is allowed to look for work in the towns but some of the women have found work in the village and can buy things. Our grandmother, because she's still strong, finds work where people are building houses – in this village the people build nice houses with bricks and cement, not mud like we used to have at our home. Our grandmother carries bricks for these people and fetches baskets of stones on her head. And so she has money to buy sugar and tea and milk and soap. The store gave her a calendar she has hung up on our flap of the tent. I am clever at school and she collected advertising paper people throw away outside the store and covered my schoolbooks with it. She makes my first-born brother and me do our homework every afternoon before it gets dark because there is no room except to lie down, close together, just as we did in the Kruger Park, in our place in the tent, and candles are expensive. Our grandmother hasn't been able to buy herself a pair of shoes for church yet, but she has bought black school shoes and polish to clean them with for my first-born brother and me. Every morning, when people are getting up in the tent, the babies are crying, people are pushing each other at the taps outside and some children are already pulling the crusts of porridge off the pots we ate from last night, my first-born brother and I clean our shoes. Our grandmother makes us sit on our mats with our legs straight out so she can look carefully at our shoes to make sure we have done it properly. No other children in the tent have real school shoes. When we three look at them it's as if we are in a real house again, with no war, no away.

Some white people came to take photographs of our people living in the tent – they said they were making a film, I've never seen what that is though I know about it. A white woman squeezed into our space and asked our grandmother questions which were told to us in our language by someone who understands the white woman's.

How long have you been living like this?

She means here? our grandmother said. In this tent, two years and one month.

And what do you hope for the future?

Nothing. I'm here.

But for your children?

I want them to learn so that they can get good jobs and money.

Do you hope to go back to Mozambique – to your own country?

I will not go back.

But when the war is over – you won't be allowed to stay here? Don't you want to go home?

I didn't think our grandmother wanted to speak again. I didn't think she was going to answer the white woman. The white woman put her head on one side and smiled at us.

Our grandmother looked away from her and spoke – There is nothing. No home.

Why does our grandmother say that? Why? I'll go back. I'll go back through that Kruger Park. After the war, if there are no bandits any more, our mother may be waiting for us. And maybe when we left our grandfather, he was only left behind, he found his way somehow, slowly, through the Kruger Park, and he'll be there. They'll be home, and I'll remember them.

Nadine Gordimer is a South African who won the 1974 Booker Prize for her novel *The Conservationist*. She has published 14 novels and 17 volumes of short stories. She was awarded the Nobel Prize for literature in 1991. 'The Ultimate Safari' was originally published in *Jump*, Bloomsbury, London 1991, and is reprinted with permission of A P Watt Ltd on behalf of Felix Licensing BV.

Nietverloren

J.M. Coetzee – winner of the Booker Prize in 1983 and 1999

F or as long as he could remember, from when he was first allowed to roam by himself out in the veld, out of sight of the farmhouse, he was puzzled by it: a circle of bare, flat earth ten paces across, its periphery marked with stones, a circle in which nothing grew, not a blade of grass.

He thought of it as a fairy circle, a circle where fairies came at night to dance by the light of the tiny sparkling rods that they carried in the picturebooks he read, or perhaps by the light of glowworms. But in the picturebooks the fairy circle was always in a clearing in a forest, or else in a glen, whatever that might be. There were no forests in the Karoo, no glens, no glowworms; were there even fairies? What would fairies do with themselves in the daytime, in the stunned heat of summer, when it was too hot to dance, when even the lizards took shelter under stones? Would the fairies have enough sense to hide under stones too, or would they lie panting among the thornbushes, longing for England?

He asked his mother about the circle. Is it a fairy circle? he demanded. It can only be a fairy circle, she replied. He was not convinced.

They were visitors on the farm, though not particularly welcome visitors. They visited because they were family, and family were always entitled to visit. This particular visit had stretched on month after month: his father was away in the war, fighting the Italians, and they had nowhere else to go. He could have asked his grandmother what the circle was, but his grandmother never went into the veld, saw no sense in walking for the sake of walking. She would never have laid eyes on the circle, it was not the kind of thing that interested her.

The war ended, his father returned with a stiff little military moustache and a dapper, upright stride. They were back on the farm; he was walking with his father in the veld. When they came to the circle, which he no longer called a fairy circle since he no longer believed in fairies, his father casually remarked, "Do you see that? That's the old threshing floor. That's where they used to thresh, in the old days."

Thresh: not a word he knew, but whatever it meant, he did not like it. Too much like *thrash*. *Get a thrashing*: that was what happened to boys when they were naughty. *Naughty* was another word he drew back from. He did not want to be around when words like that were spoken.

Threshing turned out to be something one did with flails. There was a picture of it in the encyclopedia: men in funny old-fashioned clothes beating the ground with sticks with what look like bladders tied to them.

"But what are they *doing*?" he asked his mother.

"They are flailing the wheat," she replied.

"What is flailing?"

"Flailing is threshing. Flailing is beating."

"But *why*?"

"To separate the kernels of wheat from the chaff," she explained.

Flailing the wheat: it was all beyond him. Was he being asked to believe that once upon a time men used to beat wheat with bladders out in the veld? What wheat? Where did they get wheat to beat?

He asked his father. His father was vague. The threshing happened when he was small, he said, he was not paying attention. He was small, then he went away to boarding school; when he came back they were no longer threshing, perhaps because the drought killed the wheat, the drought of 1929 and 1930 and 1931, on and on, year after year.

That was the best his father could offer: not a fairy circle but a threshing floor, until the great drought came; then just a patch of earth where nothing grew. There the story rested for 30 years. After 30 years, back on the farm on what turned out to be his final visit, the story came up again, or if not the story in full then enough of it for him to be able to fill in the gaps. He was paging through photographs from the old days when he came upon a photograph of two young men with rifles, off on a hunt. In the background, not supposed to be part of the photograph, were two donkeys yoked together, and a man in tattered clothes, also not supposed to be in the picture, one hand on the yoke, squinting toward the camera from under his hat.

He peered more closely. Surely he recognized the site! Surely that was the threshing floor! The donkeys and their leader, captured in mid-stride sometime in the 1920s, were on the threshing floor, treading the wheat with their hooves, separating the grains from the chaff. If the photograph could come to life, if the two grinning young men were to pick up their rifles and disappear over the rim of the picture, he would at last have it before him, the whole mysterious business of threshing. The man with the hat, and the two donkeys, would resume their tread round and round the threshing floor, a tread that would, over the years, compact the earth so tightly that nothing would ever grow there. They would trample the wheat, and the wind – the wind that always blows in the Karoo, from horizon to horizon – would lift the chaff and whirl it away; the grain that was left behind would be gathered up and picked clean of straw and pebbles and ground small, ground to the finest flour, so that bread could be baked in the huge old wood-burning oven that used to dominate the farm kitchen.

But where did the wheat come from that the donkeys so patiently trod, donkeys dead now these many years, their bones cast out and picked clean by ants?

The wheat, it turned out (this was the outcome of a long investigation, and even then he could not be sure if what he heard was true), was grown right here, on the farm, on what in the old days must have been cultivated land but has now reverted to bare veld. An acre of land had been given over to the growing of wheat, just as there had been an acre given over to pumpkin and squash and watermelon and sweetcorn and beans. Every day, from a dam that was just a pile of stones now, farmhands used to irrigate the acres; when the kernels turned brown, they reaped the wheat by hand, with sickles, bound it in sheaves, carted it to the threshing-floor, threshed it, then ground it to flour (he searched everywhere for the grinding-stones, without success). From the bounty of those two acres the table was stocked not only of his grandfather but of all the families who worked for him. There were even cows kept, for milk, and pigs to eat the scraps.

So all those years ago this had been a self-sufficient farm, growing all its needs; and all the other farms in the neighbourhood, this vast, sparsely peopled neighbourhood, were self-sufficient too, more or less – farms where nothing grows any more, where no ploughing or sowing or tilling or reaping or threshing takes place, farms which have turned into vast grazing grounds for sheep, where farmers sit huddled over computers in darkened rooms calculating their profit and loss on sheepswool and lambsflesh.

Hunting and gathering, then pastoralism, then agriculture: those, he had been taught as a child, were the three stages in the ascent of man from savagery, an ascent whose end was not yet in sight. Who would have believed that there were places in the world where in the space of a century or two man would graduate from stage one to stage two to stage three and then regress to stage two. This Karoo, looked upon today as a desert on which flocks of ungulates barely clung to life, was not too long ago a region where hopeful farmers planted in the thin, rocky soil seeds brought from Europe and the New World, pumped water out of the artesian basin to keep them alive, subsisted on their fruits: a region of small, scattered peasant farmers and their labourers, independent, almost outside the money economy.

What put an end to it? No doubt the Great Drought disheartened many and drove them off the land. And no doubt, as the artesian basin was depleted over the years, they had to drill deeper and deeper for water. And of course who would want to break his back growing wheat and milling flour and baking bread when you had only to get in a car and drive for an hour to find a shop with racks and racks of ready-baked bread, to say nothing of pasteurized milk and frozen meat and vegetables?

Still, there was a larger picture. What did it mean for the land as a whole, and the conception the land had of itself, that huge tracts of it should be sliding back into prehistory? In the larger picture, was it really better that families who in the old days lived on the land by the sweat of their brow should now be mouldering in the windswept townships of Cape Town? Could one not imagine a different history and a different social order in which the Karoo was reclaimed, its scattered sons and daughters reassembled, the earth tilled again?

Bill and Jane, old friends from the United States, have arrived on a visit. Starting in the north of the country, they have driven in a hired car down the east coast; now the plan is that all four of them will drive from Cape Town to Johannesburg. The route, which runs for hundreds of miles through the Karoo, is not one that he likes. For reasons of his own he finds it depressing. But these are special friends, this is what they want to do, he does not demur.

"Didn't you say your grandfather had a farm in the Karoo?" says Bill. "Do we pass anywhere near there?"

"It's not in the family any more," he replies. It is a lie. The farm is in the hands of his cousin Constant. Furthermore it does not take much of a detour off the Cape Town-Johannesburg road to get there. But he does not want to see the farm again, and what it has become, not in this life.

They leave Cape Town late in the day, spend the first night in Matjiesfontein at the Lord Milner Hotel, where they are served dinner by waitresses in floral dresses and frilled Victorian caps. He and his wife sleep in the Olive Schreiner Room, their friends in the Baden Powell Room. On the walls of the Olive Schreiner Room are watercolours of Karoo scenes ('Crossing the Drift', 'Karoo Sunset'), photographs of cricketers: the Royal Fusiliers team of 1899, burly, moustachioed young Englishmen, come to die for their queen in a far-off land, some of them buried not far away.

The next morning they leave early. For hours they drive through empty scrubland ringed by flat-topped hills. Outside Richmond they stop for gas. Jane picks up a pamphlet. "NIETVERLOREN," it says. "Visit an old-style Karoo farm, experience old-style grace and simplicity. Only 15 km from Richmond on the Graaff-Reinet road. Luncheons 12-2."

They follow the signs to Nietverloren. At the turnoff a young man in a beret and khaki shirt scrambles to open the gate for them, stands to attention and salutes as they drive through.

The farmhouse, gabled in Cape Dutch style, brilliantly whitewashed, stands on an outcrop of rock overlooking fields and orchards. They are greeted at the door by a smiling young woman. "I'm Velma, I'm your hostess," she says, with a light, pleasing Afrikaans accent. They are the only guests thus far.

For lunch they are served leg of lamb and roast potatoes, braised baby carrots with raisins, roast pumpkin with cinnamon, followed by custard pie, *melktert*. "It's what we call *boerekos*," explains Velma, their hostess, "farm cuisine. Everything grown on the farm."

"And the bread?" he asks. "Do you grow your own wheat, and thresh it and all the rest?"

Velma laughs lightly. "Good heavens no, we don't go as far back

25

as that. But our bread is baked here in our kitchen, in our wood-fired oven, just like in the old days, as you will see on the tour."

They exchange glances. "I'm not sure we have time for a tour," he says. "How long does it take?"

"The tour is in two parts. First my husband takes you around the farm in the four-wheel drive. You see sheep-shearing, you see wool-sorting; if there are children they get to play with the lambs, the lambs are very cute. Then we've got a little museum, you can see all the grades of wool and the sheep-shearing instruments from the old days and the clothes people wore. Then I take you on a tour of the house, you see everything – the kitchen, which we have restored just as it used to be, and the bathroom, the old bathroom with the hip bath and the furnace, all just like in the old days, and everything else. Then you can relax, and at four o'clock we offer you tea."

"And how much is that?"

"For the tour and the tea together it is 75 rands per person."

He glances at Bill, at Jane. They are the guests, they must decide. Bill shakes his head. "It sounds fascinating, but I just don't think we have the time. Thank you, Velma."

They drive back through the orchard – grapevines, oranges, apricots heavy on the bough – past a pair of languid-eyed Jersey cows with calves by their side.

"Remarkable what they grow, considering how dry it is," says Jane.

"The soil is surprisingly fertile," he says. "With enough water you could grow anything here. It could be a paradise."

"But...?"

"But it makes no economic sense. The only crop it makes sense to farm nowadays is people. The tourist crop. Places like Nietverloren are the only farms, if you can call them that, left in the Karoo: time-bubble, theme-park farms. The rest are just sheep ranches. There is no reason for the owners to live on them. They might as well be managed out of the cockpit of a helicopter. As in some cases they are. More enterprising landowners have gone back even further in time. They have got rid of the sheep and re-stocked their farms with game – antelope, zebra – and brought in hunters from overseas, from Germany and the US. A thousand rand for an eland, two thousand for a kudu. You shoot the animal, they mount the horns for you, you take them home with you on the plane. Trophies. The whole thing is called the safari experience, or sometimes just the African experience."

"You sound bitter."

"The bitterness of defeated love. I used to love this land. Then it fell into the hands of the entrepreneurs, and they gave it a makeover and a face-lift and put it on the market. This is the only future you have in South Africa, they told us: to be waiters and whores to the rest of the world. I want nothing to do with it."

A look passes between Bill and Jane. "I'm sorry," murmurs Jane.

Jane is sorry. He is sorry. All of them are a bit sorry, and not only for his outburst. Even Velma back on Nietverloren must be sorry for the charade she has to go through day after day, and the girls in their Victorian getup back in the hotel in Matjiesfontein: sorry and ashamed. A light grade of sorriness sits over the whole country, like cloud, like mist. But there is nothing to done about it, nothing he can think of.

J.M. Coetzee is a South African who has won the Booker Prize twice: in 1983 for his novel *Life & Times of Michael K*; and in 1999 for *Disgrace*. He was awarded the Nobel Prize for Literature in 2003. 'Nietverloren' is a new story, published with the kind permission of J.M. Coetzee and his agents, David Higham Associates in Britain and Peter Lampack Agency in the US.

Incidents at the Shrine

Ben Okri – winner of the 1991 Booker Prize

Anderson had been waiting for something to fall on him. His anxiety was such that for the first time in several years he went late to work. It was just his luck that the Head of Department had chosen that day for an impromptu inspection. When he got to the museum he saw that his metal chair had been removed from its customary place. The little stool on which he rested his feet after running endless errands was also gone. His official messenger's uniform had been taken off the hook. He went to the main office and was told by one of the clerks that he had been sacked, and that the supervisor was not available. Anderson started to protest, but the clerk got up and pushed him out of the office.

He went aimlessly down the corridors of the Department of Antiquities. He stumbled past the visitors to the museum. He wandered amongst the hibiscus and bougainvillea. He didn't look at the ancestral stoneworks in the museum field. Then he went home, dazed, confused by objects, convinced that he saw many fingers pointing at him. He went down streets he had never seen in his life and he momentarily forgot where his compound was.

When he got home he found that he was trembling. He was hungry. He hadn't eaten that morning and the cupboard was empty of food. He couldn't stop thinking about the loss of his job. Anderson had suspected for some time that the supervisor had been planning to give his job to a distant relation. That was the reason why the supervisor was always berating him on the slightest pretext. Seven years in the city had begun to make Anderson feel powerless because he didn't belong to the important societies, and didn't have influential relatives. He spent the afternoon thinking about his condition in the world. He fell asleep and dreamt about his dead parents.

He woke up feeling bitter. It was late in the afternoon and he was hungry. He got out of bed and went to the market to get some beef and tripe for a pot of stew. Anderson slid through the noise of revving motors and shouting traders. He came to the goatsellers. The goats stood untethered in small corral. As Anderson went past he had a queer feeling that the goats were staring at him. When he stopped and looked at them the animals panicked. They kicked and fought backwards. Anderson hurried on till he found himself at the meat stalls.

The air was full of flies and the stench was overpowering. He felt ill. There were intestines and bones in heaps on the floor. He was haggling the price of tripe when he heard confused howls from the section where they sold generators and videos. The meat-seller had just slapped the tripe down on the table and was telling him to go somewhere else for the price he offered, when the fire burst out with an explosion. Flames poured over the stalls, Waves of screaming people rushed in Anderson's direction. He saw the fire flowing behind them, he saw black smoke. He started to run before the people reached him.

He heard voices all around him. Dry palm fronds crackled in the air. Anderson ducked under the bare eaves of a stall, tripped over a fishmonger's basin of writhing eels, and fell into a mound of snailshells. He struggled back up. He ran past the fortune-tellers and the amulet traders. He was shouldering his way through the bamboo poles of the lace-sellers when it struck him with amazing clarity that the fire was intent upon him because he had no power to protect himself. And soon the fire was everywhere. Suddenly, from the midst of voices in the smoke, Anderson heard someone calling his names. Not just the one name, the ordinary one which made things easier in the city – Anderson; he heard all the others as well, even the ones he had forgotten: Jeremiah, Ofuegbu, Nutcracker, Azzi. He was so astonished that when he cut himself, by brushing his thigh against two rusted nails, he did not know how profusely he bled till he cleared out into the safety of the main road. When he got home he was still bleeding. When the bleeding ceased, he felt that an alien influence had insinuated itself into his body, and an illness took over.

He became so ill that most of the money he had saved in all the years of humiliation and sweat went into the hands of the quack chemists of the area. They bandaged his wound. They gave him tetanus injections with curved syringes. They gave him pills in squat, silvery bottles. Anderson was reduced to creeping about the compound, from room to toilet and back again, as though he were terrified of daylight. And then, three days into the illness, with the taste of alum stale in his mouth, he caught a glimpse of himself in the mirror. He saw the gaunt face of a complete stranger. Two days later, when he felt he had recovered sufficiently, Anderson packed his box and fled home to his village.

The Image-maker

Anderson hadn't been home for a long time. When the lorry driver dropped him at the village junction, the first things he noticed were the ferocity of the heat and the humid smell of rotting vegetation. He went down the dirt track that led to the village. A pack of dogs followed him for a short while and then disappeared. Cowhorns and the beating of drums sounded from the forest. He saw masks, eaten by insects, along the grass verge.

He was sweating when he got to the obeche tree where, during the war, soldiers had shot a woman thought to be a spy. Passing the well which used to mark the village boundary, he became aware of three rough forms running after him. They had flaming red eyes and they shouted his names.

"Anderson! Ofuegbu!"

He broke into a run. They bounded after him.

"Ofuegbu! Anderson!"

In his fear he ran so hard that his box flew open. Scattered behind him were his clothes, his medicines, and the modest gifts he had brought to show his people that he wasn't entirely a small man in the world. He discarded the box and sped on without looking back. Swirls of dust came towards him. And when he emerged from the dust, he saw the village.

It was sunset. Anderson didn't stop running till he was safely in the village. He went on till he came to the pool office with the signboard that read: MR ABAS AND CO. LICENSED COLLECTOR. Outside the office, a man sat in a depressed cane chair. His eyes stared divergently at the road and he snored gently. Anderson stood panting. He wanted to ask direction to his uncle's place, but he didn't want to wake the owner of the pool office.

Anderson wasn't sure when the man woke up, for suddenly he said: "Why do you have to run into our village like a madman?"

Anderson struggled for words. He was sweating.

"You disturb my eyes when you come running into our village like that."

Anderson wiped his face. He was confused. He started to apologize, but the man looked him over once, and fell back into sleep, with his eyes still open. Anderson wasn't sure what to do. He was thirsty. With sweat dribbling down his face, Anderson tramped on through the village.

Things had changed since he'd been away. The building had lost their individual colours to that of the dust. Houses had moved several yards from where they used to be. Roads ran diagonally to how he remembered them. He felt he had arrived in a place he had almost never known.

Exhausted, Anderson sat on a bench outside the market. The roadside was full of ants. The heat mists made him sleepy. The market behind him was empty, but deep within it he heard celebrations and arguments. He listened to alien voices and languages from the farthest reaches of the world. Anderson fell asleep on the bench and dreamt that he was being carried through the village by the ants. He woke to find himself inside the pool office. His legs itched.

The man whom he had last seen sitting in the cane chair, was now behind the counter. He was mixing a potion of local gin and herbs. There was someone else in the office: a stocky man with a large forehead and a hardened face.

He stared at Anderson and then said: "Have you slept enough?"

Anderson nodded. The man behind the counter came round with a tumbler full of herbal mixtures.

Almost forcing the drink down Anderson's throat, he said: "Drink it down. Fast!"

Anderson drank most of the mixture in one gulp. It was very bitter and bile rushed up in his mouth.

"Swallow it down!"

Anderson swallowed. His head cleared a little and his legs stopped itching.

The man who had given him the drink said: "Good." Then he pointed to the other man and said: "That's your uncle. Our Image-maker. Don't you remember him?"

Anderson stared at the Image-maker's face. The lights shifted. The face was elusively familiar. Anderson had to subtract seven years from the awesome starkness of the Image-maker's features before he could recognize his own uncle.

Anderson said: "My uncle, you have changed."

"Yes, my son, and so have you," his uncle said.

"I'm so happy to see you," said Anderson.

Smiling, his uncle moved into the light at the doorway. Anderson saw that his left arm was shrivelled.

"We've been expecting you," his uncle said.

Anderson didn't know what to say. He looked from one to the other. Then suddenly he recognized Mr Abas, who used to take him fishing down the village stream.

"Mr Abas! It's you!"

"Of course it's me. Who did you think I was?"

Anderson stood up.

"Greetings, my elders. Forgive me. So much has changed."

His uncle touched him benevolently on the shoulder and said: "That's all right. Now, let's go."

Anderson persisted with his greeting. Then he began to apologize for his bad memory. He told them that he had been pursued at the village boundary.

"They were strange people. They pursued me like a common criminal."

The Image-maker said: "Come on. Move. We don't speak of strange things in our village. We have no strange things here. Now, let's go."

Mr Abas went outside and sat in his sunken cane chair. The Image-maker led Anderson out of the office.

They walked through the dry heat. The chanting of worshippers came from the forest. Drums and jangling bells sounded faintly in the somnolent air.

"The village is different," Anderson said.

The Image-maker was silent.

"What has happened here?"

"Don't ask questions. In our village we will provide you with answers before it is necessary to ask questions," the Image-maker said with some irritation.

Anderson kept quiet. As they went down the village Anderson kept looking at the Image-maker: the more he looked, the more raw and godlike the Image-maker seemed. It was as though he had achieved an independence from human agencies. He looked as if he had been cast in rock, and left to the wilds.

"The more you look, the less you see," the Image-maker said.

It sounded, to Anderson, like a cue. They had broken into a path.

Ahead of them were irregular rows of soapstone monoliths. Embossed with abstract representations of the human figure, the monoliths ranged from the babies of their breed to the abnormally large ones. There were lit candles and varied offerings in front of them. There were frangipani and iroko trees in their midst. There were also red-painted poles which had burst into flower.

The uncle said: "The images were originally decorated with pearls, lapis lazuli, amethysts and magic glass which twinkled wonderful philosophies. But the pale ones from across the seas came and stole them. This was whispered to me in a dream."

Anderson gazed at the oddly elegant monoliths and said: "You resemble the gods you worship."

His uncle gripped him suddenly.

Anderson nodded. His uncle relaxed his grip. They moved on.

After a while his uncle said: "The world is the shrine and the shrine is the world. Everything must have a centre. When you talk rubbish, bad things fly into your mouth."

They passed a cluster of huts. Suddenly the Image-maker bustled forward. They had arrived at the main entrance to a circular clay shrinehouse. The Image-maker went to the niche and brought out a piece of native chalk, a tumbler and a bottle of herbs. He made a mash which he smeared across Anderson's forehead. On a nail above the door, there was a bell which the Image-maker rang three times.

A voice called from within the hut.

The Image-maker sprayed himself forth in a list of his incredible names and titles. Then he requested permission to bring to the shrine an afflicted 'son of the soil'.

The voices asked if the 'son of the soil' was ready to come in.

The Image-maker was silent.

A confusion of drums, bells, cowhorns, came suddenly from within. Anderson fainted.

Then the Image-maker said to the voices: "He is ready to enter!"

They came out and found that Anderson was light. They bundled him into the shrinehouse and laid him on a bed of congealed palm oil.

The Image

When Anderson came to he could smell burning candles, sweat and incense. Before him was the master Image, a hallucinatory warrior monolith decorated in its original splendour of precious stones and twinkling glass. At its base were roots, kola nuts and feathers. When Anderson gazed at the master Image he heard voices that were not spoken and he felt drowsiness come over him.

Candles burned in the mist of blue incense. A small crowd of worshippers danced and wove Anderson's names in songs. Down the corridors he could hear other supplicants crying out in prayer for their heart's desires, for their afflictions and problems. They prayed like people who are ill and who are never sure of recovering. It occurred to Anderson that it must be a cruel world to demand such intensity of prayer.

Anderson tried to get up from the bed, but couldn't. The master Image seemed to look upon him with a grotesque face. The ministrants closed in around him. They praised the master Image in songs. The Image-maker gave a sudden instruction and the ministrants rushed to Anderson. They spread out their multiplicity of arms and embraced Anderson in their hard compassions. But when they touched Anderson he screamed and shouted in hysteria. The ministrants embraced him with their remorseless arms and carried him through the corridors and out into the night. They rushed him past the monoliths outside. They took him past creeks and waterholes. When they came to a blooming frangipani tree, they dumped him on the ground. Then they retreated with flutters of their smocks, and disappeared as though the darkness were made of their own substance.

Anderson heard whispers in the forest. He heard things falling among the branches. Then he heard footsteps that seemed for ever approaching. He soon saw that it was Mr Abas. He carried a bucket in one hand and a lamp in the other. He dropped the bucket near Anderson.

"Bathe of it," Mr Abas said, and returned the way he had come.

Anderson washed himself with the treated water. When he finished the attendants came and brought him fresh clothes. Then they led him back to the shrine-house.

The Image-maker was waiting for him. Bustling with urgency, his bad arm moving restlessly like the special instrument of his functions, the Image-maker grabbed Anderson and led him to an alcove.

He made Anderson sit in front of a door. There was a hole greased with palm oil at the bottom of the door. The Image-maker shouted an instruction and the attendants came upon Anderson and held him face down. They pushed him towards the hole; they forced his head and shoulders through it.

In the pain Anderson heard the Image-maker say: "Tell us what you see!"

Anderson couldn't see anything. All he could feel was the grinding pain. Then he saw a towering tree. There was a door on the tree trunk. Then he saw a thick blue pall. A woman emerged from the pall. She was painted over in native chalk. She had bangles all the way up her arms. Her stomach and waist were covered in beads.

"I see a woman," he cried.

Several voices asked: "Do you know her?"

"No."

"Is she following you?"

"I don't know."

"Is she dead?"

"I don't know."

"Is she dead?"

"No!"

There was the merriment of tinkling bells.

"What is she doing?"

She had come to the tree and opened the door. Anderson suffered a fresh agony. She opened a second door and tried the third one, but it didn't open. She tried again and when it gave way with a crash Anderson finally came through – but he lost consciousness.

Afterwards, they fed him substantially. Then he was allowed the freedom to move round the village and visit some of his relations. In the morning the Image-maker sent for him. The attendants made him sit on a cowhide mat and they shaved off his hair. They lit red and green candles and made music around him. Then the Image-maker proceeded with the extraction of impurities from his body. He rubbed herbal juices into Anderson's shoulder. He bit into the flesh and pulled out a rusted little padlock which he spat into an enamel bowl. He inspected the padlock. After he had washed out his mouth, he bit into Anderson's shoulder again and pulled out a crooked needle. He continued like this till he had pulled out a piece of broken glass, a twisted nail, a cowrie, and a small key. There was some agitation as to whether the key would fit the padlock, but it didn't.

When the Image-maker had finished he picked up the bowl, jangled the objects, and said: "All these things, where do they come from? Who sent them into you?"

Anderson couldn't say anything.

The Image-maker went on to cut light razor strokes on Anderson's arm and he rubbed protective herbs into the bleeding marks. He washed his hands and went out of the alcove. He came back with a pouch, which he gave to Anderson with precise instructions of its usage.

Then he said: "You are going back to the city tomorrow. Go to your place of work, collect the money they are owing you, and look for another job. You will have no trouble. You understand?"

Anderson nodded.

"Now, listen. One day I went deep into the forest because my arm hurt. I injured it working in a factory. For three days I was in the forest praying to our ancestors. I ate leaves and fishes. On the fourth day I forgot how I came there. I was lost and everything was new to me. On the fifth day I found the Images. They were hidden amongst the trees and tall grasses. Snakes and tortoises were all around. My pain stopped. When I found my way back and told the elders of the village what I had seen they did not believe me. The Images had been talked about in the village for a long time but no one had actually seen them. That is why they made me the Image-maker."

He paused, then continued.

"Every year, around this time, spirits from all over the world come to our village. They meet at the marketplace and have heated discussions about everything under the sun. Sometimes they gather round our Images outside. On some evenings there are purple mists round the iroko tree. At night we listen to all the languages, all the philosophies, of the world. You must come home now and again. This is where you derive power. You hear?"

Anderson nodded. He hadn't heard most of what was said. He had been staring at the objects in the enamel bowl.

The Image-eaters

Anderson ate little through the ceremonies that followed the purification of his body. After all the dancing and feasting to the music of cowhorns and tinkling bells, they made him lie down before the master Image. Then the strangest voice he had ever heard thundered the entire shrinehouse with its full volume.

"ANDERSON! OFUEGBU! YOU ARE A SMALL MAN. YOU CANNOT

RUN FROM YOUR FUTURE. GOVERNMENTS CANNOT EXIST WITHOUT YOU. ALL THE DISASTERS OF THE WORLD REST ON YOU AND HAVE YOUR NAME. THIS IS YOUR POWER."

The ministrants gave thanks and wept for joy.

Anderson spent the night in the presence of the master Image. He dreamt that he was dying of hunger and that there was nothing left in the world to eat. When Anderson ate of the master Image he was surprised at its sweetness. He was surprised at its sweetness. He was surprised also that the Image replenished itself.

In the morning Anderson's stomach was bloated with an imponderable weight. Shortly before his departure the Image-maker came to him and suggested that he contribute to the shrine fund. When Anderson made his donation, the Image-maker gave his blessing. The ministrants prayed for him and sang of his destiny.

Anderson had just enough money to get him back to the city. When he was ready to leave, Anderson felt a new heaviness come upon him. He thanked his uncle for everything and made his way through the village.

He stopped at the pool office. Mr Abas was in his sunken cane chair, his eyes pursuing their separate lines of vision. Anderson wasn't sure if Mr Abas was asleep.

He said: "I'm leaving now."

"Leaving us to our hunger, are you?"

"There is hunger where I am going," Anderson said.

Mr Abas smiled and said: "Keep your heart pure. Have courage. Suffering cannot kill us. And travel well."

"Thank you."

Mr Abas nodded and soon began to snore. Anderson went on towards the junction.

As he walked through the heated gravity of the village Anderson felt like an old man. He felt that his face had stiffened. He had crossed the rubber plantation, had crossed the boundary, and was approaching the junction, when the rough forms with blazing eyes fell upon him. He fought them off. He lashed out with his stiffened hands and legs. They could easily have torn him to pieces, because their ferocity was greater than his. There was a moment in which he saw himself dead. But they suddenly stopped and stared at him. Then they pawed him, as though he had become allied with them in some way. When they melted back into the heat mists, Anderson experienced the new simplicity of his life, and continued with his journey.

Ben Okri is a Nigerian who won the 1999 Booker Prize for his novel *The Famished Road*. His most recent book is *Tales of Freedom* (Rider, London 2009). 'Incidents at the Shrine' originally appeared in the collection *Incidents at the Shrine*, published by William Heinemann. It is reprinted by permission of The Random House Group Ltd and The Marsh Agency.

The Museum

Leila Aboulela – winner of the 2000 Caine Prize

At first Shadia was afraid to ask him for his notes. The earring made her afraid. And the straight long hair that he tied up with a rubber band. She had never seen a man with an earring and such long hair. But then she had never known such cold, so much rain. His silver earring was the strangeness of the West, another culture-shock. She stared at it during classes, her eyes straying from the white scribbles on the board. Most times she could hardly understand anything. Only the notation was familiar. But how did it all fit together? How did *this* formula lead to *this*? Her ignorance and the impending exams were horrors she wanted to escape. His long hair, a dull colour between yellow and brown, different shades. It reminded her of a doll she had when she was young. She had spent hours combing that doll's hair, stroking it. She had longed for such straight hair. When she went to Paradise she would have hair like that. When she ran it would fly behind her, if she bent her head down it would fall over like silk and sweep the flowers on the grass. She watched his ponytail move as he wrote and then looked up at the board. She pictured her doll, vivid suddenly after years, and felt sick that she was day-dreaming in class, not learning a thing.

The first days of term, when the classes started for the MSc in Statistics, she was like someone tossed around by monstrous waves. Battered, as she lost her way to the different lecture rooms, fumbled with the photo-copying machine, could not find anything in the library. She could scarcely hear or eat or see. Her eyes bulged with fright, watered from the cold. The course required a certain background, a background she didn't have. So she floundered, she and the other African students, the two Turkish girls, and the men from Brunei. Asafa, the short, round-faced Ethiopian, said, in his grave voice, as this collection from the Third World whispered their

41

anxieties in grim Scottish corridors, the girls in nervous giggles, "Last year, last year a Nigerian on this very same course committed suicide. *Cut his wrists.*"

Us and them, she thought. The ones who would do well, the ones who would crawl and sweat and barely pass. Two predetermined groups. Asafa, generous and wise (he was the oldest) leaned and whispered to Shadia, "The Spanish girl is good. Very good." His eyes bulged redder than Shadia's. He cushioned his fears every night in the university pub, she only cried. Their countries were next-door neighbours but he had never been to Sudan, and Shadia had never been to Ethiopia. "But we meet in Aberdeen!" she had shrieked when this information was exchanged, giggling furiously. Collective fear had its euphoria.

"That boy Bryan," said Asafa, "is excellent."

"The one with the earring?"

Asafa laughed and touched his own unadorned ear. "The earring doesn't mean anything. He'll get the Distinction. He did his undergraduate here, got First Class Honours. That gives him an advantage. He knows all the lecturers, he knows the system."

So the idea occurred to her of asking Bryan for the notes of his graduate year. If she strengthened her background in stochastic processes and time series, she would be better able to cope with the new material they were bombarded with every day. She watched him to judge if he was approachable. Next to the courteous Malaysian students, he was devoid of manners. He mumbled and slouched and did not speak with respect to the lecturers. He spoke to them as if they were his equal. And he did silly things. When he wanted to throw a piece of paper in the bin, he squashed it into a ball and from where he was sitting he aimed it at the bin. If he missed, he muttered under his breath. She thought that he was immature. But he was the only one who was sailing through the course.

The glossy handbook for overseas students had explained about the "famous British reserve" and hinted that they should be grateful, things were worse further south, less "hospitable". In the cafeteria, drinking coffee with Asafa and the others, the picture of 'hospitable Scotland' was something different. Badr, the Malaysian, blinked and whispered, "Yesterday our windows got smashed, my wife today is afraid to go out."

"Thieves?" asked Shadia, her eyes wider than anyone else's.

"Racists," said the Turkish girl, her lipstick chic, the word tripping out like silver, like ice.

Wisdom from Asafa, muted, before the collective silence, "These people think they own the world..." and around them the aura of the dead Nigerian student. They were ashamed of that brother they had never seen. He had weakened, caved in. In the cafeteria, Bryan never sat with them. They never sat with him. He sat alone, sometimes reading the local paper. When Shadia walked in front of him he didn't smile. "These people are strange... One day they greet you, the next day they don't."

On Friday afternoon, as everyone was ready to leave the room after Linear Models, she gathered her courage and spoke to Bryan. He had spots on his chin and forehead, was taller than her, restless, as if he was in a hurry to go somewhere else. He put his calculator back in its case, his pen in his pocket. She asked him for his notes and his blue eyes behind his glasses took on the blankest look she had ever seen in her life. What was all the surprise for? Did he think she was an insect, was he surprised that she could speak?

A mumble for a reply, words strung together. So taken aback, he was. He pushed his chair back under the table with his foot.

"Pardon?"

He slowed down, separated each word, "Ah'll have them for ye on Monday."

"Thank you." She spoke English better than him! How pathetic. The whole of him was pathetic. He wore the same shirt every blessed day. Grey and white stripes.

*   *   *

On the weekends, Shadia never went out of the halls and unless someone telephoned long distance from home, she spoke to no-one. There was time to remember Thursday nights in Khartoum, a wedding to go to with Fareed, driving in his red Mercedes. Or the club with her sisters. Sitting by the pool drinking lemonade with ice, the waiters all dressed in white. Sometimes people swam at night, dived in the water dark like the sky above. Here, in this country's weekend of Saturday and Sunday, Shadia washed her clothes and her hair. Her hair depressed her. The damp weather made it frizz up after she straightened it with hot tongs. So she had given up and now wore it in a bun all the time, tightly pulled back away from her face, the curls held down by pins and Vaseline Tonic. She didn't like this style, her corrugated hair, and in the mirror her eyes looked too large. The mirror in the public bathroom, at the end of the corridor to her room, had printed on it "This is the face of someone with HIV". She had written about this mirror to her sister, something foreign and sensational like hail and cars driving on the left. But she hadn't written that the mirror made her feel as if she had left her looks behind in Khartoum.

On the weekends, she made a list of the money she had spent, the sterling enough to keep a family alive back home. Yet she might fail her exams after all that expense, go back home empty-handed without a degree. Guilt was cold like the fog of this city. It came from everywhere. One day she forgot to pray in the morning. She reached the bus-stop and then realised that she hadn't prayed. That morning folded out like the nightmare she sometimes had, of discovering that she had gone out into the street without any clothes.

In the evening, when she was staring at multidimensional scaling, the telephone in the hall rang. She ran to answer it. Fareed's cheerful greeting. "Here Shadia, Mama and the girls want to speak to you." His mother's endearments, "They say it's so cold where you are…"

Shadia was engaged to Fareed. Fareed was a package that came with the 7Up franchise, the paper factory, the big house he was building, his sisters and widowed mother. Shadia was going to marry them all. She was going to be happy and make her mother happy. Her mother deserved happiness after the misfortunes of her life. A husband who left her for another woman. Six girls to bring up. People felt sorry for her mother. Six girls to educate and marry off. But your Lord is generous, each of the girls, it was often said, was lovelier than the other. They were clever too; dentist, pharmacist, architect, and all with the best of manners.

"We are just back from looking at the house," Fareed's turn again to talk. "It's coming along fine, they're putting the tiles down…"

"That's good, that's good," her voice strange from not talking to anyone all day.

"The bathroom suites. If I get them all the same colour for us and the girls and Mama, I could get them on a discount. Blue, the girls are in favour of blue," his voice echoed from one continent to another. Miles and miles.

"Blue is nice. Yes, better get them all the same colour." He was building a block of flats, not a house. The ground floor flat for his mother and the girls until they married, the first floor for him and Shadia. The girls' flats on the two top floors would be rented out. When Shadia had first got engaged to Fareed, he was the son of rich man. A man with the franchise for 7Up and the paper factory which had a monopoly in ladies' sanitary towels. Fareed's sisters never had to buy sanitary towels, their house was abundant with boxes of Pinky, fresh from the production line. But Fareed's father died of an unexpected heart attack soon after the engagement party (500 guests at the Hilton). Now Shadia was going to marry the rich man himself. You are a lucky, lucky girl, her mother said and Shadia rubbed soap in her eyes so that Fareed would think she had been weeping about his father's death.

There was not time to talk about her course on the telephone, no space for her anxieties. Fareed was not interested in her studies. He had said, "I am very broad-minded to allow you to study abroad. Other men would not have put up with this..." It was her mother who was keen for her to study, to get a postgraduate degree from Britain and then have a career after she got married. "This way," her mother had said, "you will have your in-laws' respect. They have money but you will have a degree. Don't end up like me. I left my education to marry your father and now..." Many conversations ended with her mother bitter, with her mother saying, "No-one suffers like I suffer," and making Shadia droop. At night her mother howled in her sleep, noises that woke Shadia and her sisters.

No, on the long-distance line, there was no space for her worries. Talk about the Scottish weather. Picture Fareed, generously perspiring, his stomach straining the buttons of his shirt. Often she had nagged him to lose weight, with no success. His mother's food was too good, his sisters were both overweight. On the long-distance line listen to the Khartoum gossip as if listening to a radio play.

*　　*　　*

On Monday, without saying anything, Bryan slid two folders across the table towards her as if he did not want to come near her, did not want to talk to her. She wanted to say, "I won't take till you hand them to me politely." But, smarting, she said, "Thank you very much." She had manners. She was well brought up.

Back in her room, at her desk, the clearest handwriting she had ever seen. Sparse on the pages, clean. Clear and rounded like a child's, the tidiest notes. She cried over them, wept for no reason. She cried until she wet one of the pages, stained the ink, blurred one of the formulas. She dabbed at it with a tissue but the paper flaked and became transparent. Should she apologise about the stain, say that she was drinking water, say that it was rain? Or should she just keep quiet, hope he wouldn't notice? She chided herself for all that concern. He wasn't concerned about wearing the same shirt every day. She was giving him too much attention thinking about him. He was just an immature and closed-in sort of character. He probably came from a small town, his parents were probably poor, low-class. In Khartoum, she never mixed with people like that. Her mother liked her to be friends with people who were higher up. How else were she and her sisters going to marry well? She must study the notes and stop crying over this boy's handwriting. His handwriting had nothing to do with her, nothing to do with her at all.

Understanding after not understanding is fog lifting, is pictures swinging into focus, missing pieces slotting into place. It is fragments gelling, a sound vivid whole, a basis to build on. His notes were the knowledge she needed, the gaps. She struggled through them, not skimming them with the carelessness of incomprehension, but taking them in, making them a part of her, until in the depth of concentration, in the late hours of the nights, she lost awareness of time and place and at last when she slept she became epsilon and gamma and she became a variable making her way through discrete space from state i to state j.

*   *   *

It felt natural to talk to him. As if now that she had spent hours and days with his handwriting she knew him in some way. She forgot the offence she had taken when he had slid his folders across the table to her, all the times he didn't say hello.

In the computer room, at the end of the Statistical Packages class, she went to him and said, "Thanks for the notes. They are really good. I think I might not fail, after all. I might have a chance to pass." Her eyes were dry from all the nights she had stayed up.

She was tired and grateful.

He nodded and they spoke a little about the Poisson distribution, queuing theory. Everything was clear in his mind, his brain was a clear pane of glass where all the concepts were written out boldly and neatly. Today, he seemed more at ease talking to her, though he still shifted about from foot to foot, avoided her eyes.

He said, "Do ye want to go for a coffee?"

She looked up at him. He was tall and she was not used to speaking to people with blue eyes. Then she made a mistake. Perhaps because she had been up late last night, she made that mistake. Perhaps there were other reasons for that mistake. The mistake of shifting from one level to another.

"I don't like your earring."

The expression in his eyes, a focusing, no longer shifting away. He lifted his hand to his ear and tugged the earring off. His earlobe without the silver looked red and scarred.

She giggled because she was afraid, because he wasn't smiling, wasn't saying anything. She covered her mouth with her hand then wiped her forehead and eyes. A mistake was made and it was too late to go back. She plunged ahead, careless now, reckless, "I don't like your long hair."

He turned and walked away.

* * *

The next morning, Multivariate Analysis, and she came in late, dishevelled from running and the rain. The professor whose name she wasn't sure of (there were three who were McSomething), smiled unperturbed. All the lecturers were relaxed and urbane, in tweed jackets and polished shoes. Sometimes she wondered how the incoherent Bryan, if he did pursue an academic career, was going to transform himself into a professor like that. But it was none of her business.

Like most of the other students, she sat in the same seat in every class. Bryan sat a row ahead which was why she could always look at his hair. But he had cut it, there was no ponytail today! Just his neck and the collar of the grey and white striped shirt.

Notes to take down. *In discriminant analysis, a linear combination of variables serves as the basis for assigning cases to groups...*

She was made up of layers. Somewhere inside, deep inside, under the crust of vanity, in the untampered-with essence, she would glow and be in awe, and be humble and think, this is just for me, he cut his hair for me. But there other layers, bolder, more to the surface. Giggling. Wanting to catch hold of a friend. Guess what? You wouldn't *believe* what this idiot did!

Find a weighted average of variables... The weights are estimated so that they result in the best separation between the groups.

After the class he came over and said very seriously, without a smile. "Ah've cut my hair."

A part of her hollered with laughter, sang, you stupid boy, you stupid boy, I can see that, can't I?

She said, "It looks nice." She had said the wrong thing and her face felt hot and she made herself look away so that she would not know his reaction. It was true, though, he did look nice; he looked decent now.

*   *   *

She should have said to Bryan, when they first held their coffee mugs in their hands and were searching for an empty table, "Let's sit with Asafa and the others." Mistakes follow mistakes. Across the cafeteria, the Turkish girl saw them together and raised her perfect eyebrows, Badr met Shadia's eyes and quickly looked away. Shadia looked at Bryan and he was different, different without the earring and the ponytail, transformed in some way. If he would put lemon juice on his spots... but it was none of her business. Maybe the boys who smashed Badr's windows looked like Bryan, but with fiercer eyes, no glasses. She must push him away from her. She must make him dislike her.

He asked her where she came from and when she replied, he said, "Where's that?"

"Africa," with sarcasm. "Do you know where *that* is?"

His nose and cheeks, under the rim of his glasses, went red. Good, she thought, good. He will leave me now in peace.

He said, "Ah know Sudan is in Africa, I meant where exactly in Africa."

"North-east, south of Egypt. Where are *you* from?"

"Peterhead. It's north of here. By the sea."

It was hard to believe that there was anything north of Aberdeen. It seemed to her that they were on the northernmost corner of the world. She knew better now than to imagine suntanning and sandy beaches for his 'by the sea'. More likely dismal skies, pale bad-tempered people shivering on the rocky shore.

"Your father works in Peterhead?"

"Aye, he does."

She had grown up listening to the proper English of the BBC World Service only to come to Britain and find people saying 'yes' like it was said back home in Arabic, aye.

"What does he do, your father?"

"He looked surprised, his blue eyes surprised, "Ma dad's a joiner."

Fareed hired people like that to work on the house. Ordered them about.

"And your mother?" she asked.

He paused a little, stirred sugar in his coffee with a plastic spoon. "She's a lollipop lady."

Shadia smirked into her coffee, took a sip.

"My father," she said proudly, "is a doctor, a specialist." Her father was a gynaecologist. The woman who was his wife now had been one of his patients. Before that, Shadia's friends had teased her about her father's job, crude jokes that made her laugh. It was all so sordid now.

"And my mother," she blew the truth up out of proportion, "comes from a very big family. A ruling family. If you British hadn't colonised us, my mother would have been a princess now."

"Ye walk like a princess," he said.

What a gullible, silly boy! She wiped her forehead with her hand, said, "You mean I am conceited and proud?"

"No, Ah didnae mean that, no..." The packet of sugar he was tearing open tipped from his hand, its contents scattered over the table. "Ah shit... sorry..." He tried to scoop up the sugar and knocked against his coffee mug, spilling a little on the table.

She took out a tissue from her bag, reached over and mopped up the stain. It was easy to pick up all the bits of sugar with the damp tissue.

"Thanks," he mumbled and they were silent. The cafeteria was busy, full of the humming, buzzing sound of people talking to each other, trays and dishes. In Khartoum, she avoided being alone with

49

Fareed. She preferred it when they were with others; their families, their many mutual friends. If they were ever alone, she imagined that her mother or her sister was with them, could hear them, and spoke to Fareed with that audience in mind.

Bryan was speaking to hear, saying something about rowing on the River Dee. He went rowing on the weekends, he belonged to a rowing club.

To make herself pleasing to people was a skill Shadia was trained in. It was not difficult to please people. Agree with them, never dominate the conversation, be economical with the truth. Now here was someone whom all these rules needn't apply to.

She said to him, "The Nile is superior to the Dee. I saw your Dee, it is nothing, it is like a stream. There are two Niles, the Blue and the White, named after their colours. They come from the south, from two different places. They travel for miles, over countries with different names, never knowing they will meet. I think they get tired of running alone, it is such a long way to the sea. They want to reach the sea so that they can rest, stop running. There is a bridge in Khartoum and under this bridge the two Niles meet and if you stand on the bridge and look down you can see the two waters mixing together."

"Do ye get homesick?" he asked and she felt tired now, all this talk of the river running to rest in the sea. She had never talked like that before. Luxury words, and the question he asked.

"Things I should miss I don't miss. Instead I miss things I didn't think I would miss. The *azan*, the Muslim call to prayer from the mosque, I don't know if you know about it. I miss that. At dawn it used to wake me up. I would hear *prayer is better than sleep* and just go back to sleep, I never got up to pray." She looked down at her hands on the table. There was no relief in confessions, only his smile, young, and something like wonder in his eyes.

"We did Islam in school," he said, "Ah went on a trip to Mecca." He opened out his palms on the table.

"What!"

"In a book."

"Oh."

The coffee was finished. They should go now. She should go to the library before the next lecture and photocopy previous exam papers. Asafa, full of helpful advice, had shown her where to find them.

"What is your religion?" she asked.

"Dunno, nothing I suppose."

"That's terrible! That's really terrible!" Her voice was too loud, concerned.

His face went red again and he tapped his spoon against the empty mug.

Waive all politeness, make him dislike her. Badr had said, even before his windows got smashed, that here in the West they hate Islam. Standing up to go, she said flippantly, "Why don't you become a Muslim then?"

He shrugged, "Ah wouldnae mind travelling to Mecca, I was keen on that book."

Her eyes filled with tears. They blurred his face when he stood up. In the West they hate Islam and he… She said, "Thanks for the coffee" and walked away but he followed her.

"Shadiya, Shadiya," he pronounced her name wrong, three syllables instead of two, "there's this museum about Africa. I've never been before. If you'd care to go, tomorrow…"

* * *

No sleep for the guilty, no rest, she should have said no, I can't go, no I have too much catching up to do. No sleep for the guilty, the memories come from another continent. Her father's new wife, happier than her mother, fewer worries. When Shadia visits she offers fruit in a glass bowl, icy oranges and guava, soothing in the heat. Shadia's father hadn't wanted a divorce, hadn't wanted to leave them, he wanted two wives not a divorce. But her mother had too much pride, she came from fading money, a family with a 'name'. Of the new wife her mother says, bitch, whore, the dregs of the earth, a nobody.

Tomorrow, she need not show up at the museum, even though she said that she would. She should have told Bryan she was engaged to be married, mentioned it casually. What did he expect from her? Europeans had different rules, reduced, abrupt customs. If Fareed knew about this… her secret thoughts like snakes… Perhaps she was like her father, a traitor. Her mother said that her father was devious. Sometimes Shadia was devious. With Fareed in the car, she would deliberately say, "I need to stop at the grocer, we need things at home." At the grocer he would pay for all her shopping and she would say, "No, you shouldn't do that, no, you are too generous, you are embarrassing me." With the money she saved, she would buy a blouse for her mother, nail varnish for her mother, a magazine, imported apples.

* * *

It was strange to leave her desk, lock her room and go out on a Saturday. In the hall the telephone rang. It was Fareed. If he knew where she was going now... Guilt was like a hard-boiled egg stuck in her chest. A large cold egg.

"Shadia, I want you to buy some of the fixtures for the bathrooms. Taps and towel hangers. I'm going to send you a list of what I want exactly and the money..."

"I can't, I can't."

"What do you mean you can't? If you go into any large department store..."

"I can't, I wouldn't know where to put these things, how to send them."

There was a rustle on the line and she could hear someone whispering, Fareed distracted a little. He would be at work this time in the day, glass bottles filling up with clear effervescent, the words 7Up written in English and Arabic, white against the dark green.

"You can get good things, things that aren't available here. Gold would be good. It would match..."

Gold. Gold toilet seats!

"People are going to burn in Hell for eating out of gold dishes, you want to sit on gold!"

He laughed. He was used to getting his own way, not easily threatened, "Are you joking with me?"

"No."

In a quieter voice, "This call is costing..."

She knew, she knew. He shouldn't have let her go away. She was not coping with the whole thing, she was not handling the stress. Like the Nigerian student.

"Shadia, gold-coloured, not gold. It's smart."

"Allah is going to punish us for this, it's not right..."

"Since when have you become so religious!"

* * *

Bryan was waiting for her on the steps of the museum, familiar-looking against the strange grey of the city, streets where cars had their headlamps on in the middle of the afternoon. He wore a different shirt, a navy-blue jacket. He said, not looking at her, "Ah was beginning to think you wouldnae turn up."

There was no entry fee to the museum, no attendant handing out tickets. Bryan and Shadia walked on soft carpets, thick blue carpets that made Shadia want to take off her shoes. The first hing they saw was a Scottish man from Victorian times. He sat on a chair surrounded with possessions from Africa, overflowing trunks, an ancient map strewn on the floor of the glass cabinet. All the light in the room came from this and other glass cabinets, gleamed on the wax. Shadia turned away, there was an ugliness in the lifelike wispiness of his hair, his determined expression, the way he sat. A hero who had gone away and come back, laden, ready to report.

Bryan began to conscientiously study every display cabinet, read the posters on the wall. She followed him around and thought that he was studious, careful and studious, that was why he did so well in his degree. She watched the intent expression on his face as he looked at everything. For her the posters were an effort to read, the information difficult to take in. It had been so long since she had read anything outside the requirements of the course. But she persevered, saying the words to herself, moving her lips... *During the 18th and 19th centuries, northeast Scotland made a disproportionate impact on the world at large by contributing so many skilled and committed individuals... In serving an empire they gave and received, changed others and were themselves changed and often returned home with tangible reminders of their experiences.*

The tangible reminders were there to see, preserved in spite of the years. Her eyes skimmed over the disconnected objects out of place and time. Iron and copper, little statues. Nothing was of her, nothing belonged to her life at home, what she missed. Here was Europe's vision, the clichés about Africa; cold and old.

She had not expected the dim light and the hushed silence. Apart from Shadia and Bryan, there was only a man with a briefcase, a lady who took down notes, unless there were others out of sight on the second floor. Something electrical, the heating or the lights, gave out a humming sound like that of an air conditioner. It made Shadia feel as if they were in an aeroplane without windows, detached from the world outside.

"He looks like you, don't you think?" she said to Bryan. They stood in front of a portrait of a soldier who died in the first year of this century. It was the colour of his eyes and his hair. But Bryan did not answer her, did not agree with her. He was preoccupied with reading the caption. When she looked at the portrait again, she saw that she was mistaken. That strength in the eyes, the purpose, was something Bryan didn't have. They had strong faith in those days long ago.

Biographies of explorers who were educated in Edinburgh; doctors, courage, they knew what to take to Africa: Christianity, commerce, civilisation. They knew what they wanted to bring back; cotton watered by the Blue Nile, the Zambezi River. She walked after Bryan, felt his concentration, his interest in what was before him and thought, "In a photograph we would not look nice together."

She touched the glass of a cabinet showing papyrus rolls, copper pots. She pressed her forehead and nose against the cool glass. If she could enter the cabinet, she would not make a good exhibit. She wasn't right, she was too modern, too full of mathematics.

Only the carpet, its petroleum blue, pleased her. She had come to the museum expecting sunlight and photographs of the Nile, something to appease her homesickness, a comfort, a message. But the messages were not for her, not for anyone like her. A letter from West Africa, 1762, an employee to his employer in Scotland. An employee trading European goods for African curiosities. *It was difficult to make the natives understand my meaning, even by an interpreter, it being a thing so seldom asked of them, but they have all undertaken to bring something and laughed heartily at me and said I was a good man to love their country so much...*

Love my country so much. She should not be here, there was nothing for her here. She wanted to see minarets, boats fragile on the Nile, people. People like her father. Times she had sat in the waiting room of his clinic, among pregnant women, the pain in her heart because she was going to see him in a few minutes. His room, the air conditioner and the smell of his pipe, his white coat. When she hugged him, he smelled of Listerine mouthwash. He could never remember how old she was, what she was studying, six daughters, how could he keep track? In his confusion, there was freedom for her, games to play, a lot of teasing. She visited his clinic in secret, telling lies to her mother. She loved him more than she loved her mother. Her mother who did everything for her, tidied her room, sewed her clothes from *Burda* magazine. Shadia was 25 and her mother washed everything for her by hand, even her pants and bras.

"I know why they went away," said Bryan, "I understand why they travelled." At last he was talking. She had not seen him intense before. He spoke in a low voice, "They had to get away, to leave here..."

"To escape from the horrible weather..." she was making fun of him. She wanted to put him down. The imperialists who had humiliated her history were heroes in his eyes.

He looked at her. "To escape..." he repeated.

"They went to benefit themselves," she said, "people go away because they benefit in some way..."

"I want to get away," he said.

She remembered when he had opened his palms on the table and said, "I went on a trip to Mecca." There had been pride in his voice.

"I should have gone somewhere else for the course," he went on, "a new place, somewhere down south."

He was on a plateau, not like her. She was punching and struggling for a piece of paper that would say she was awarded an MSc from a British university. For him the course was a continuation.

"Come and see," he said, and he held her arm. No one had touched her before, not since she had hugged her mother goodbye. Months now in this country and no one had touched her.

She pulled her arm away. She walked away, quickly up the stairs. Metal steps rattled under her feet. She ran up the stairs to the next floor. Guns, a row of guns aiming at her. They had been waiting to blow her away. Scottish arms of centuries ago, gunfire in the service of the empire.

Silver muzzles, a dirty grey now. They must have shone prettily once, under a sun far away. If they blew her away now, where would she fly and fall? A window that looked out at the hostile sky. She shivered in spite of the wool she was wearing, layers of clothes. Hell is not only blazing fire, a part of it is freezing cold, torturous ice and snow. In Scotland's winter you live a glimpse of this unseen world, feel the breath of it in your bones.

There was a bench and she sat down. There was no one here on this floor. She was alone with sketches of jungle animals, words on the wall. The dead speaking out, not of what they know now but their ignorance of old. A diplomat away from home, in Ethiopia in 1903, Asafa's country long before Asafa was born. *It is difficult to imagine anything more satisfactory or better worth taking part in than a lion drive. We rode back to camp feeling very well indeed. Archie was quite right when he said that this was the first time since we have started that we have really been in Africa – the real Africa of jungle inhabited only by game, and plains where herds of antelope meet your eye in every direction.*

"Shadiya, don't cry." He still pronounced her name wrong because she had not shown him how to say it properly.

He sat next to her on the bench, the blur of his navy jacket blocking the guns, the wall-length pattern of antelope herds. She should explain that she cried easily, there was no need for the alarm on his face. His awkward voice, "Why are you crying?" He didn't know, he didn't understand. He was all wrong, not a substitute...

"They are telling you lies in this museum," she said, "Don't believe them. It's all wrong. It's not jungles and antelopes, it's people. We have things like computers and cars. We have 7Up in Africa and some people, a few people, have bathrooms with golden taps... I shouldn't be here with you. You shouldn't talk to me..."

He said, "Museums change, I can change..."

He didn't know it was a steep path she had no strength for. He didn't understand. Many things, years and landscapes, gulfs. If she was strong she would have explained and not tired of explaining. She would have patiently taught him another language, letters curved like the epsilon and gamma he knew from mathematics. She would have showed him that words could be read from right to left. If she was not small in the museum, if she was really strong, she would have made his trip to Mecca real, not only in a book.

Leila Aboulela was born in Cairo, Egypt, and grew up in Khartoum, Sudan. She is the author of two novels, *The Translator* (1999) and *Minaret* (2005), published by Bloomsbury. She is currently living and lecturing in Abu Dhabi. 'The Museum' was originally published in *Opening Spaces*, Heinemann, Oxford 1999.

Love Poems

Helon Habila – winner of the 2001 Caine Prize

In the middle of his second year in prison, Lomba got access to pencil and paper and he started a diary. It was not easy. He had to write in secret, mostly in the early mornings when the night warders, tired of peeping through the door bars, waited impatiently for the morning shift. Most of the entries he simply headed with the days of the week; the exact dates, when he used them, were often incorrect. The first entry was in July 1997, a Friday.

Friday, July 1997

Today I begin a diary, to say all the things I want to say, to myself, because here in prison there is no one to listen. I express myself. It stops me from standing in the centre of this narrow cell and screaming at the top of my voice. It stops me from jumping up suddenly and bashing my head repeatedly against the wall. Prison chains not so much your hands and feet as it does your voice.

I express myself. I let my mind soar above these walls to bring back distant, exotic bricks with which I seek to build a more endurable cell within this cell. Prison. Misprison. Dis. Un. Prisoner. See? I write of my state in words of derision, aiming thereby to reduce the weight of these walls from my shoulders, to rediscover my nullified individuality. Here in prison loss of self is often expressed as anger. Anger is the baffled prisoner's attempt to recrystallise his slowly dissolving self. The anger creeps on you, like twilight edging out the day. It builds in you silently until one day it explodes in violence, surprising you. I saw it happen in my first month in prison. A prisoner, without provocation, had attacked an unwary warder at the toilets. The prisoner had come out of a bath-stall and there was the warder before him, monitoring the morning ablutions. Suddenly the prisoner leaped upon him, pulling him by the neck to the ground, grinding him into the black, slimy water that ran in the gutter from the toilets. He pummelled the surprised face repeatedly until other warders came and dragged him away. They beat him to a pulp before throwing him into solitary.

Sometimes the anger leaves you as suddenly as it appeared; then you enter a state of tranquil acceptance. You realise the absolute puerility of your anger: it was nothing but acid, cancer, eating away your bowels in the dark. You accept the inescapability of your fate; and with that, you learn the craft of cunning. You learn ways of surviving – surviving the mindless banality of the walls around you, the incessant harassment from the warders; you learn to hide money in your anus, to hold a cigarette inside your mouth without wetting it. And each day survived is a victory against the jailor, a blow struck for freedom.

My anger lasted a whole year. I remember the exact day it left me. It was a Saturday, a day after a failed escape attempt by two convicted murderers. The warders were more than usually brutal that day; the inmates were on tenterhooks, not knowing from where the next blow would come. We were lined up in rows in our cell, waiting for hours to be addressed by the prison superintendent. When he came his scowl was hard as rock, his eyes were red and singeing, like fire. He paced up and down before us, systematically flagellating us with his harsh, staccato sentences. We listened, our heads bowed, our hearts quaking.

When he left, an inmate, just back from a week in solitary, broke down and began to weep. His hands shook, as if with a life of their own. "What's going to happen next?" he wailed, going from person to person, looking into each face, not waiting for an answer. "We'll be punished. If I go back there I'll die. I can't. I can't." Now he was standing before me, a skinny mass of eczema inflammations, and ringworm, and snot. He couldn't be more than twenty. I thought, what did he do to end up in this dungeon? Then, without thinking, I reached out and patted his shoulder. I even smiled. With a confidence I did not feel I said kindly, "No one will take you back."

He collapsed into my arms, soaking my shirt with snot and tears and saliva. "Everything will be all right," I repeated over and over. That was the day the anger left me.

* * *

In the over two months that he wrote before he was discovered and his diary seized, Lomba managed to put in quite a large number of entries. Most of them were poems, and letters to various persons from his by now hazy, pre-prison life – letters he can't have meant to send. There were also long soliloquies and desultory interior monologues. The poems were mostly love poems; fugitive lines from poets he had read in school: Donne, Shakespeare, Graves, Eliot, etc. Some were his original compositions rewritten from memory; but a lot were fresh creations – tortured sentimental effusions to women he had known and admired, and perhaps loved. Of course they might be imaginary beings, fabricated in the smithy of his prison-fevered mind. One of the poems reads like a prayer to a much doubted, but fervently hoped for God:

> *Lord, I've had days black as pitch*
> *And nights crimson as blood*
>
> *But they have passed over me, like water*
> *Let this one also pass over me, lightly,*
> *Like a smooth rock rolling down the hill,*
> *Down my back, my skin, like soothing water.*

That, he wrote, was the prayer on his lips the day the cell door opened without warning and the superintendent, flanked by two baton carrying warders, entered.

Monday, July

I had waited for this; perversely anticipated it with each day that passed, with each surreptitious sentence that I wrote. I knew it was me he came for when he stood there, looking bigger than life, bigger than the low, narrow cell. The two dogs with him licked their chops and growled menacingly. Their eyes roved hungrily over the petrified inmates caught sitting, or standing, or crouching; laughing, frowning, scratching – like figures in a movie still.

"Lomba, step forward!" his voice rang out suddenly. In the frozen silence it sounded like glass breaking on concrete, but harsher, without the tinkling. I was on my mattress on the floor, my back propped against the damp wall. I stood up. I stepped forward.

He turned the scowl on me. "So, Lomba. You are."

"Yes. I am Lomba," I said. My voice did not fail me. Then he nodded, almost imperceptibly, to the two dogs. They bounded forward eagerly, like game hounds scenting a rabbit, one went to a tiny crevice low in the wall, almost hidden by my mattress. He threw aside the mattress and poked two fingers into the triangular crack. He came out with a thick roll of papers. He looked triumphant as he handed it to the superintendent. Their informer had been exact. The other hound reached unerringly into a tiny hole in the sagging, rain-designed ceiling and brought out another tube of papers.

"Search. More!" the superintendent barked. He unrolled the tubes. He appeared surprised at the number of sheets in his hands. I was. I didn't know I had written so much. When they were through with the holes and crevices the dogs turned their noses to my personal effects. They picked my mattress and shook and sniffed and poked. They ripped off the tattered cloth on its back. There were no papers there. They took the pillow-cum-rucksack (a jeans trouser-leg cut off at mid-thigh and knotted at the ankle) and poured out the contents onto the floor. Two threadbare shirts, one trouser, one plastic comb, one toothbrush, one half-used soap, and a pencil. This is the sum of my life, I thought, this is what I've finally shrunk to; the detritus after the explosion: a comb, a toothbrush, two shirts, one trouser, and a pencil. They swooped on the pencil before it had finished rolling on the floor, almost knocking heads in their haste.

"A pencil!" the superintendent said, shaking his head, exaggerating his amazement. The prisoners were standing in a tight, silent arc. He walked the length of the arc, displaying the papers and pencil, clucking his tongue. "Papers. And pencil. In prison. Can you believe that? In my prison!"

I was sandwiched between the two hounds, watching the drama in silence. I felt removed from it all. Now the superintendent finally turned to me. He bent a little at the waist, pushing his face into mine. I smelt his grating smell; I picked out the white roots beneath his carefully dyed moustache. "I will ask. Once.

Who gave you. Papers?" He spoke like that, in jerky, truncated sentences. I shook my head. I did my best to meet his red hot glare. "I don't know."

Some of the inmates gasped, shocked; they mistook my answer for reckless intrepidity. They thought I was foolishly trying to protect my source. But in a few other eyes I saw sympathy. They understood that I had really forgotten from where the papers came.

"Hmm," the superintendent growled. His eyes were on the papers in his hands, he kept folding and unfolding them. I was surprised he had not pounced on me yet. Maybe he was giving me a spell to reconsider my hopeless decision to protect whoever it was I was protecting. The papers. They might have blown in through the door bars on the sentinel wind that sometimes patrolled the prison yard in the evenings. Maybe a sympathetic warder, seeing my yearning for self-expression emblazoned like neon on my face, had secretly thrust the roll of papers into my hands as he passed me in the yard. Maybe – and this seems more probable – I bought them from another inmate (anything can be bought here in prison: from marijuana to a gun). But I had forgotten.

In prison, memory short-circuit is an ally to be cultivated at all costs.

"I repeat. My question. Who gave you the papers?" he thundered into my face, spraying me with spit. I shook my head. "I have forgotten."

I did not see it, but he must have nodded to one of the hounds. All I felt was the crushing blow on the back of my neck, where it meets the head. I pitched forward, stunned by pain and the unexpectedness of it. My face struck the door bars and I fell before the superintendent's boots. I saw blood where my face had touched the floor. I waited. I stared, mesmerized, at the reflection of my eyes in the high gloss of the boots' toecaps. One boot rose and descended on my neck, grinding my face into the floor.

"So, you won't. Talk. You think you are. Tough," he shouted. "You are. Wrong. Twenty years! That is how long I have been dealing with miserable bastards like you. Let this be an example to all of you. Don't. Think you can deceive me. We have our sources of information. You can't. This insect will be taken to solitary and he will be properly dealt with. Until. He is willing to. Talk."

I imagined his eyes rolling balefully round the tight, narrow cell, branding each of the sixty inmates separately. The boot pressed down harder on my neck; I felt a tooth bend at the root.

"Don't think because you are political. Detainees you are untouchable. Wrong. You are all rats. Saboteurs. Anti-government rats. That is all. Rats."

But the superintendent was too well versed in the ways of torture to throw me into solitary that very day. I waited two days before they came and blindfolded me and took me away to the solitary section. In the night. Forty-eight hours. In the first 24 hours I waited with my eyes fixed to the door, bracing myself whenever it opened; but it was only the cooks bringing the meal, or the number-check warders come to count the inmates for the night, or the slop-disposal team. In the second 24 hours I bowed my head into my chest and refused to look up. I was tired. I refused to eat or speak or move.

I was rehearsing for solitary.

They came, around ten in the night. The two hounds. Banging their batons on the door bars, shouting my name, cursing and kicking at anyone in their path. I hastened to my feet before they reached me, my trouser-leg rucksack clutched like a shield in my hands. The light of their torch on my face was like a blow.

"Lomba!"

"Come here! Move!"

"Oya, out. Now!"

I moved, stepping high over the stirring bodies on the floor. A light fell on my rucksack.

"What's that in your hand, eh? Where you think say you dey carry am go? Bring am. Come here! Move!"

Outside. The cell door clanked shut behind us. All the compounds were in darkness. Only security lights from poles shone at the sentry posts. In the distance the prison wall loomed huge and merciless, like a mountain. Broken bottles. Barbed wire. Then they threw the blindfold over my head. My hands instinctively started to rise, but they were held and forced behind me and cuffed.

"Follow me."

One was before me, the other was behind, prodding me with his baton. I followed the footsteps, stumbling.

At first it was easy to say where we were. There were eight compounds within the prison yard; ours was the only one reserved for political detainees. There were four other Awaiting Trial Men's compounds surrounding ours. Of the three compounds for convicted criminals, one was for lifers and one, situated far away from the other compounds, was for condemned criminals. Now we had passed the central lawn where the warders conduct their morning parade. We turned left towards the convicted prisoners' compound, then right towards... we turned right again, then straight... I followed the boots, now totally disoriented. I realised that the forced march had no purpose to it, or rather its purpose was not to reach anywhere immediately. It was part of the torture. I walked. On and on. I bumped into the front warder whenever he stopped abruptly.

"What? You no de see? Idiot!"

Sometimes I heard their voices exchanging pleasantries and amused chuckles with other warders. We marched for over 30 minutes; my slippered feet were chipped and bloody from hitting into stones. My arms locked behind me robbed me of balance and often I fell down, then I'd be prodded and kicked. At some places – near the light poles – I was able to see brief shimmers of light. At other places the darkness was thick as walls, and eerie. I recalled the shuffling, chain-clanging steps we heard late at nights through our cell window. Reluctant, sad steps. Hanging victims going to the hanging room; or their ghosts returning. We'd lie in the dark, stricken by immobility as the shuffling grew distant and finally faded away. Now we were on concrete, like a corridor. The steps in front halted. I waited. I heard metal knock against metal, then the creaking of hinges. A hand took my wrist, cold metal touched me as the handcuffs were unlocked. My hands felt light with relief. I must have been standing right before the cell door because when a hand on my back pushed me forward I stumbled inside. I was still blindfolded, but I felt the consistency of the darkness change: it grew thicker, I had to wade through it to feel the walls, the bunk, the walls and walls. That was all: walls so close together that I felt like a man in a hole. I reached down and touched the bunk. I sat down. I heard the door close. I heard footsteps retreating. When I removed the blindfold the darkness remained the same, only now a little air touched my face. I closed my eyes. I don't know how long I remained like that, hunched forward on the bunk, my sore, throbbing feet on the floor, my elbows on my knees, my eyes closed. As if realising how close I was to tears, the smells got up from their corners, shook the dust off their buttocks and lined up to make my acquaintance – to distract me from my sad thoughts. I shook their hands one by one: Loneliness Smell, Anger Smell, Waiting Smell, Masturbation Smell, Fear Smell. The most noticeable was Fear Smell, it filled the tiny room from floor to ceiling, edging out the others. I did not cry. I opened my lips and slowly, like a Buddhist chanting his mantra, I prayed:

Let this one also pass over me, lightly,
Like a smooth rock rolling down the hill
Down my back, my skin, like soothing water.

*   *   *

He was in solitary for three days. This is how he described the cell in his diary: *The floor was about six feet by ten, and the ceiling was about seven feet from the floor. There were exactly two pieces of furniture: the iron bunk with its tattered, lice-ridden mat, and the slop bucket in the corner.*

His only contacts with the outside were in the nights when his mess of beans, once daily, at six p.m., was pushed into the cell through a tiny flap at the bottom of the wrought iron door, and at precisely eight p.m. when the cell door was opened for him to take out the slop bucket and take in a fresh one. He wrote that the only way he distinguished night from day was by the movement of his bowels – in hunger or in purgation. Once a day.

Then on the third day, late in the evening, things began to happen. Like Nichodemus, the superintendent came to him, covertly, seeking knowledge.

Third Day. Solitary Cell
When I heard metal touch the lock on the door I sat down from my blind pacing. I composed my countenance. The door opened, bringing in unaccustomed rays of light. I blinked. *"Oh, sweet light. May your face meeting mine bring me good fortune."* When my eyes adjusted to the light, the superintendent was standing on the

threshold – the cell entrance was a tight, lighted frame around his looming form. He advanced into the cell and stood in the centre, before my disadvantaged position on the bunk. His legs were planted apart, like an A. He looked like a cartoon figure: his jodhpurs-like uniform trousers emphasised the skinniness of his calves, where they disappeared into the glass glossy boots. His stomach bulged and hung like a belted sack. He cleared his voice. When I looked at his face I saw his blubber lips twitching with the effort of attempted smile. But he couldn't quite carry it off. He started to speak, then stopped abruptly and began to pace the tiny space before the bunk. When he returned to his original position he stopped. Now I noticed the sheaf of papers in his hands.

He gestured in my face with it.

"These. Are the. Your papers." His English was more disfigured than usual: soaking wet with the effort of saying whatever it was he wanted to say. "I read. All. I read your file again. Also. You are journalist. This is your second year. Here. Awaiting trial. For organising violence. Demonstration against. Anti-government demonstration against the military legal government."

He did not thunder as usual.

"It is not true."

"Eh?" The surprise on his face was comical. "You deny?"

"I did not organise a demonstration. I went there as a reporter."

"Well..." He shrugged. "That is not my business. The truth. Will come out at your. Trial."

"But when will that be? I have been forgotten. I am not allowed a lawyer, or visitors. I have been awaiting trial for two years now..."

"Do you complain? Look. Twenty years I've worked in prisons all over this country. Nigeria. North. South. East. West. Twenty years. Don't be stupid. Sometimes it is better this way. How. Can you win a case against government? Wait. Hope."

Now he lowered his voice, like a conspirator, "Maybe there'll be another coup, eh? Maybe the leader will collapse and die; he is mortal after all. Maybe a civilian government will come. Then. There will be amnesty for all political prisoners. Amnesty. Don't worry. Enjoy yourself."

I looked at him planted before me like a tree, his hands clasped behind him, the papier-mâché smile on his lips. *Enjoy yourself.* I turned the phrase over and over in my mind.

When I lay to sleep rats kept me awake, and mosquitoes, and lice, and hunger, and loneliness. The rats bit at my toes and scuttled around in the low ceiling, sometimes falling onto my face from the holes in the ceiling. *Enjoy yourself.*

"Your papers," he said, thrusting them at me once more. I was not sure if he was offering them to me. "I read them. All. Poems. Letters. Poems, no problem. The letters, illegal. I burned them. Prisoners sometimes smuggle out letters to the press to make us look foolish. Embarrass the government. But the poems are harmless. Love Poems. And diaries. You wrote the poems for your girl, isn't it?" He bent forward; he clapped a hand on my shoulder. I realised with wonder that the man, in his awkward, flatfooted way, was making overtures of friendship to me. My eyes fell on the boot that had stepped on my neck just five days ago. What did he want?

"Perhaps because I work in Prison. I wear uniform. You think I don't know poetry, eh? Soyinka, Okigbo, Shakespeare."

It was apparent that he wanted to talk about poems, but he was finding it hard to begin.

"What do you want?" I asked.

He drew back to his full height. "I write poems too. Sometimes," he added quickly when the wonder grew and grew on my face. He dipped his hand into his jacket pocket and came out with a foolscap paper. He unfolded it and handed it to me.

"Read."

It was a poem; handwritten. The title was written in capital letters: "MY LOVE FOR YOU". Like a man in a dream I ran my eyes over the bold squiggles. After the first stanza I saw that it was a thinly veiled imitation of one of my poems. I sensed his waiting. He was hardly breathing. I let him wait. Lord, I can't remember another time when I had felt so good. So powerful. I was Samuel Johnson and he was an aspiring poet waiting anxiously for my verdict, asking tremulously: "Sir, is it poetry, is it Pindar?"

I wanted to say, with as much sarcasm as I could put into my voice: "Sir, your poem is both original and interesting, but the part that is interesting is not original, and the part that is original is not interesting."

But all I said was, "Not bad, you need to work on it some more."

The eagerness went out of his face and for a fleeting moment the scowl returned. "I promised my lady a poem. She is educated, you know. A teacher. You will write a poem for me. For my lady."

"You want me to write a poem for you?" I tried to mask the surprise, the confusion, and yes, the eagerness in my voice. He was offering me a chance to write.

"I am glad you understand. Her name is Janice. She has been to a university. She has class. Not like other girls. She teaches in my son's school. That is how we met."

Even jailors fall in love, I thought inanely.

"At first she didn't take me seriously. She thought I only wanted to use her and dump her. And. Also. We are of different religion. She is Christian, I am Muslim. But no problem. I love her. But she still doubted. I did not know what to do. Then I saw one of your poems... yes, this one."

He handed me the poem. "It said everything I wanted to tell her."

It was one of my earliest poems, rewritten from memory.

" 'Three Words'. I gave it to her yesterday when I took her out."

"You gave her my poem?"

"Yes."

"You... you told her you wrote it?"

"Yes, yes, of course. I wrote it again in my own hand," he said, unabashed. He had been speaking in a rush; now he drew himself together and, as though to reassert his authority, began to pace the room, speaking in a subdued, measured tone.

"I can make life easy for you here. I am the prison superintendent. There is nothing I cannot do, if I want. So write. The poem. For me."

There is nothing I cannot do: You can get me cigarettes, I am sure, and food. You can remove me from solitary. But can you stand me outside these walls free under the stars? Can you connect the tips of my upraised arms to the stars so that the surge of liberty passes down my body to the soft downy grass beneath my feet?

I asked for paper and pencil. And a book to read.

* * *

He was removed from the solitary section that day. The pencil and papers came, the book too. But not the one he had asked for. He wanted Wole Soyinka's prison notes, *The Man Died*; but when it came it was *A Brief History of West Africa*. While writing the poems in the cell Lomba would sometimes let his mind wander; he'd picture the superintendent and his lady out on a date, how he'd bring out the poem and unfold it and hand it to her and say boldly, "I wrote it for you. Myself."

They sit outside on the verandah at her suggestion. The light from the hanging, wind-swayed Chinese lanterns falls softly on them. The breeze blowing from the lagoon below smells fresh to her nostrils; she loves its dampness on her bare arms and face. She looks across the circular table, with its vase holding a single rose petal, at him. He appears nervous. A thin film of sweat covers his forehead. He removes his cap and dabs at his forehead with a white handkerchief.

"Do you like it, a Chinese restaurant?" he asks, like a father anxious to please his favourite child. It is their first outing together. He pestered her until she gave in. Sometimes she is at a loss what to make of his attentions. She sighs. She turns her plump face to the deep blue lagoon. A white boat with dark stripes on its sides speeds past; a figure is crouched inside, almost invisible. Her light, flower-patterned gown shivers in the light breeze. She watches him covertly. He handles his chopsticks awkwardly, but determinedly.

"Waiter!" he barks, his mouth full of fish, startling her. "Bring another bottle of wine!"

"No. I am all right, really," she says firmly, putting down her chopsticks.

After the meal, which has been quite delicious, he lifts the tiny, wine-filled porcelain cup before him and says: "To you. And me."

She sips her drink, avoiding his eyes.

"I love you, Janice. Very much. I know you think I am not serious. That I only want to suck. The juice and throw away the peel. No." He suddenly dips his hand into the pocket of his well-ironed white kaftan and brings out a yellow paper.

"Read and see." He pushes the paper across the table to her. "I wrote it. For you. A poem."

She opens the paper. It smells faintly of sandalwood. She looks at the title: "Three Words." She reaches past the vase with its single, white rose petal, past the wine bottle, the wine glasses, and covers his hairy hand with hers briefly. "Thank you."

She reads the poem, shifting in her seat towards the swaying light of the lantern:

Three Words

When I hear the waterfall clarity of your laughter,
When I see the twilight softness of your eyes,

I feel like draping you all over myself, like a cloak,
To be warmed by your warmth.

Your flower petal innocence, your perennial
Sapling resilience – your endless charms
All these set my mind on wild flights of fancy:
I add word unto word,
I compare adjectives and coin exotic phrases
But they all seem jaded, corny, unworthy
Of saying all I want to say to you.

So I take refuge in these simple words
Trusting my tone, my hand in yours, when I
Whisper them, to add depth and new
Twists of meaning to them. Three words:
I love you.

With his third or fourth poem for the superintendent, Lomba began to send Janice cryptic messages. She seemed to possess an insatiable appetite for love poems. Every day a warder came to the cell, in the evening, with the same request from the superintendent: "The poem." When he finally ran out of original poems, Lomba began to plagiarise the masters from memory. Here are the opening lines of one:

Janice, your beauty is to me
Like those treasures of gold...

Another one starts:

I wonder, my heart, what you and I
Did till we loved…

But it was Lomba's bowdlerization of Sappho's "Ode" that brought the superintendent to the cell door:

A peer of goddesses she seems to me
The lady who sits over against me
Face to face,
Listening to the sweet tones of my voice,
And the loveliness of my laughing.
It is this that sets my heart fluttering
In my chest,
For if I gaze on you but for a little while
I am no longer master of my voice,
And my tongue lies useless
And a delicate flame runs over my skin
No more do I see with my eyes;
The sweat pours down me
I am all seized with trembling
And I grow paler than the grass
My strength fails me
And I seem little short of dying.

He came to the cell door less than 20 minutes after the poem had reached him, waving the paper in the air, a real smile splitting his granite face.

"Lomba, come out!" he hollered through the iron bars. Lomba was lying on his wafer-thin mattress, on his back, trying to imagine figures out of the rain designs on the ceiling. The door officer hastily threw open the door.

The superintendent threw a friendly arm over Lomba's shoulders. He was unable to stand still. He walked Lomba up and down the grassy courtyard.

"This poem. Excellent. With this poem. After. I'll ask her for marriage." He was incoherent in his excitement. He raised the paper and read aloud the first line, straining his eyes in the dying light: "'A peer of goddesses she seems to me'. Yes. Excellent. She will be happy. Do you think I should ask her for. Marriage. Today?"

He stood before Lomba, bent forward expectantly, his legs planted in their characteristic A-formation.

"Why not?" Lomba answered. A passing warder stared at the superintendent and the prisoner curiously. The twilight fell dully on the broken bottles studded in the concrete of the prison wall.

"Yes. Why not. Good." The superintendent walked up and down, his hands clasped behind him, his head bowed in thought. Finally he stopped before Lomba and declared gravely: "Tonight. I'll ask her."

Lomba smiled at him, sadly. The superintendent saw the smile; he did not see the sadness.

"Good. You are happy. I am happy too. I'll send you a packet of cigarette. Two packets. Today. Enjoy. Now go back inside."

He turned abruptly on his heels and marched away.

July

Janice came to see me two days after I wrote her the Sappho. I thought, she has discovered my secret messages, my scriptive Morse tucked innocently in the lines of the poems I've written her.

Two o'clock is compulsory siesta time. The opening of the cell door brought me awake. My limbs felt heavy and lifeless. I feared I might have an infection. The warder came directly to me. "Oya, get up. The superintendent wan see you." His skin was coarse, coal black. He was fat and his speech came out in laboured gasps.

"Oya, get up. Get up," he repeated impatiently.

I was in that lethargic, somnambulistic state condemned people surely fall into when, in total inanition and despair, they await their fate – without fear or hope, because nothing could be changed. No dew-wet finger of light would come poking into the parched gloom of the abyss they tenanted. I did not want to write any more poems for the superintendent's lover. I did not want any more of his cigarettes. I was tired of being pointed at behind my back, of being whispered about by the other inmates as the superintendent's informer, his fetch-water. I wanted to recover my lost dignity. Now I realise that I really had no 'self' to express; that self had flown away from me the day the chains touched my hands; what is left here is nothing but a mass of protruding bones and unkempt hair and tearful eyes; an asshole for shitting and farting; and a penis that in the mornings grows turgid in vain. This left-over self,

71

this sea-bleached wreck panting on the iron-filing sands of the shores of this penal island is nothing but hot air, and hair, and ears cocked, hopeful...

So I said to the warder: "I don't want to see him today. Tell him I'm sick."

The fat face contorted. He raised his baton in Pavlovian response. "What!" But our eyes met. He was smart enough to decipher the bold "No Trespassing" sign written in mine. Smart enough to obey. He moved back, shrugging. "Na you go suffer!" he blustered, and left.

I was aware of the curious eyes staring at me. I closed mine. I willed my mind over the prison walls to other places. Free. I dreamt of standing under the stars, my hands raised, their tips touching the blinking, pulsating electricity of the stars. My naked body surging with the surge. The rain would be falling. There'd be nothing else: just me and rain and stars and my feet on the wet downy grass earthing the electricity of freedom.

He returned almost immediately. There was a smirk on his fat face as he handed me a note. I recognised the superintendent's clumsy scrawl. It was brief, a one-liner: *Janice is here. Come. Now.* Truncated, even in writing. I got up and pulled on my sweat-grimed shirt. I slipped my feet into my old, worn-out slippers. I followed the warder. We passed the parade ground, and the convicted men's compound. An iron gate, far to our right, locked permanently, led to the women's wing of the prison. We passed the old laundry, which now served as a barbershop on Saturdays – the prison's sanitation day. A gun-carrying warder opened a tiny door in the huge gate that led into a foreyard where the prison officials had their offices. I had been here before, once, on my first day in prison. There were cars parked before the offices, cadets in their well-starched uniforms came and went, their young faces looking comically stern. Female secretaries with time on their hands stood in the corridors gossiping. The superintendent's office was not far from the gate; a flight of three concrete steps led up to a thick wooden door, which bore the single word: SUPERINTENDENT.

My guide knocked on it timidly before turning the handle.

"The superintendent wan see am," he informed the secretary. She barely looked up from her typewriter; she nodded. Her eyes were bored, uncurious.

"Enter," the warder said to me, pointing to a curtained doorway beside the secretary's table. I entered. A lady sat in one of the two visitors' armchairs. Her back to the door; her elbows rested on the huge Formica topped table before her. Janice. She was alone. When she turned I noted that my mental image of her was almost accurate. She was plump. Her face was warm and homely. She came half way out of her chair, turning it slightly so that it faced the other chair. There was a tentative smile on her face as she asked: "Mr Lomba?"

I almost said no, surprised by the 'mister'. I nodded. She pointed at the empty chair. "Please sit down."

She extended a soft, pudgy hand to me. I took it and marvelled at its softness. She was a teacher; the hardness would be in the fingers: the tips of the thumb and the middle finger, and the side of the index finger.

"Muftau... the superintendent, will be here soon. He just stepped out," she said. Her voice was clear, a little high-pitched. Her English was correct, each word carefully pronounced and projected. Like in a classroom. I was struck by how clean she looked, squeaky-clean; her skin glowed like a child's after a bath. She had obviously taken a lot of trouble with her appearance: her blue evening dress looked almost new, a slash of red lipstick extended to the left cheek after missing the curve of the lip. She crossed and uncrossed her legs, tapping the left foot on the floor. She was nervous. That was when I realised I had not said a word since I entered.

"Welcome to the prison," I said, unable to think of anything else.

She nodded. "Thank you. I told Muftau I wanted to see you. The poems, I just knew it wasn't him writing them. I went along with it for a while, but later I told him."

She opened the tiny handbag in her lap and took out some papers. The poems. She put them on the table and unfolded them, smoothing out the creases, uncurling the edges. "After the Sappho I decided I must see you. It was my favourite poem in school, and I like your version of it."

"Thank you," I said. I liked her directness, her sense of humour.

"So I told him – look, I know who the writer is, he is one of the prisoners, isn't he? That surprised him. He couldn't figure out how I knew. But I was glad he didn't deny it. I told him that. And if we are getting married, there shouldn't be secrets between us, should there?"

Ah, I thought, so my Sappho has worked the magic. Aloud, I said, "Congratulations."

She nodded. "Thanks. Muftau is a nice person, really, when you get to know him. His son, Farouk, was in my class – he's finished now – really, you should see them together. So touching. I know he has his awkward side, and that he was once married – but I don't care. After all, I have a little past too. Who doesn't?" She added the last quickly, as if scared she was revealing too much to a stranger. Her left hand went up and down as she spoke, like a hypnotist, like a conductor. After a brief pause, she continued:

"After all the pain he's been through with his other wife, he deserves some happiness. She was in the hospital a whole year before she died."

Muftau. The superintendent had a name, and a history, maybe even a soul. I looked at his portrait hanging on the wall, he looked young in it, serious-faced and smart, like the cadet warders outside. I turned to her and said suddenly and sincerely: "I am glad you came. Thanks."

Her face broke into a wide, dimpled smile. She was actually pretty. A little past her prime, past her sell-by date, but still nice, still viable. "Oh, no. I am the one that should be glad. I love meeting poets. I love your poems. Really I do."

"Not all of them are mine."

"I know – but you give them a different feel, a different tone. And also, I discovered your S.O.S. I had to come..." She picked the poems off the table and handed them to me. There were 13 of them. Seven were my originals, six were purloined. She had carefully underlined in red ink certain lines in some of them – the same line, actually, recurring.

There was a waiting-to-be-congratulated smile on her face as she awaited my comment.

"You noticed," I said.

"Of course I did. S.O.S. It wasn't apparent at first. I began to notice the repetition with the fifth poem. 'Save my soul, a prisoner'."

Save my soul, a prisoner... The first time I put down the words, in the third poem, it had been non-deliberate, I was just making alliteration. Then I began to repeat it in the subsequent poems. But how could I tell her that the message wasn't really for her, or for anyone else? It was for myself, perhaps, written by me to my own soul, to every other soul, the collective soul of the universe.

I said to her: "The first time I wrote it an inmate had died. His name was Thomas. No, he wasn't sick. He just started vomiting after the afternoon meal, and before the warders came to take him to the clinic, he died. Just like that. He died. Watching his stiffening face, with the mouth open and the eyes staring, as the inmates took him out of the cell, an irrational fear had gripped me. I saw myself being taken out like that, my lifeless arms dangling, brushing the ground. The fear made me sit down, shaking uncontrollably amidst the flurry of movements and voices excited by the tragedy. I was scared. I felt certain I was going to end up like that. Have you ever felt like that, certain that you were going to die? No? I did. I was going to die. My body would end up in some anonymous mortuary, and later in an unmarked grave, and no one would know. No one would care. It happens every day here. I am a political detainee, if I die I am just one antagonist less. That was when I wrote the S.O.S. It was just a message in a bottle, thrown without much hope into the sea..." I stopped speaking when my hands started to shake. I wanted to put them in my pocket to hide them from her. But she had seen it. She left her seat and came to me. She took both my hands in hers.

"You'll not die. You'll get out alive. One day it will all be over," she said. Her perfume, mixed with her female smell, rose into my nostrils; flowery, musky. I had forgotten the last time a woman had stood so close to me. Sometimes, in our cell, when the wind blows from the female prison, we'll catch distant sounds of female screams and shouts and even laughter. That is the closest we ever come to women. Only when the wind blows, at the right time, in the right direction. Her hands on mine, her smell, her presence, acted like fire on some huge, prehistoric glacier locked deep in my chest. And when her hand touched my head and the back of my neck, I wept.

When the superintendent returned my sobbing face was

buried in Janice's ample bosom, her hands were on my head, patting, consoling, like a mother, all the while cooing softly, "One day it will finish."

I pulled away from her. She gave me her handkerchief.

"What is going on? Why is he crying?"

He was standing just within the door – his voice was curious, with a hint of jealousy. I wiped my eyes; I subdued my body's spasms. He advanced slowly into the room and went round to his seat. He remained standing, his hairy hands resting on the table.

"Why is he crying?" he repeated to Janice.

"Because he is a prisoner," Janice replied simply. She was still standing beside me, facing the superintendent.

"Well. So. Is he realising that just now?"

"Don't be so unkind, Muftau."

I returned the handkerchief to her.

"Muftau, you must help him."

"Help. How?"

"You are the prison superintendent. There's a lot you can do."

"But I can't help him. He is a political detainee. He has not even been tried."

"And you know that he is never going to be tried. He will be kept here forever, forgotten." Her voice became sharp and indignant. The superintendent drew back his seat and sat down. His eyes were lowered. When he looked up, he said earnestly, "Janice. There's nothing anyone can do for him. I'll be implicating myself. Besides, his lot is far easier than that of other inmates. I give him things. Cigarettes. Soap. Books. And I let him. Write."

"How can you be so unfeeling! Put yourself in his shoes – two years away from friends, from family, without the power to do anything you wish to do. Two years in CHAINS! How can you talk of cigarettes and soap, as if that were substitute enough for all that he has lost?" She was like a teacher confronting an erring student. Her left hand tapped the table for emphasis as she spoke.

"Well." He looked cowed. His scowl alternated rapidly with a smile. He stared at his portrait on the wall behind her. He spoke in a rush, "Well. I could have done something. Two weeks ago. The Amnesty International. People came. You know, white men. They wanted names of. Political detainees held. Without trial. To

76

pressure the government to release them."

"Well?"

"Well." He still avoided her stare. His eyes touched mine and hastily passed. He picked a pen and twirled it between his fingers, the pen slipped out of his fingers and fell to the floor.

"I didn't. Couldn't. You know... I thought he was comfortable. And, he was writing the poems, for you..." His voice was almost pleading. Surprisingly, I felt no anger at him. He was just Man. Man in his basic, rudimentary state, easily moved by the powerful emotions, like love, lust, anger, greed, fear; but totally dumb to the finer, acquired emotions like pity and mercy and humour, and justice.

Janice slowly picked up her bag from the table. There was enormous dignity to her movements. She clasped the bag under her left arm. Her words were slow, almost sad, "I see now that I've made a mistake. You are not really the man I thought you were..."

"Janice." He stood up and started coming round to her, but a gesture stopped him.

"No. Let me finish. I want you to contact these people. Give them his name. If you can't do that, then forget you ever knew me."

Her hand brushed my arm as she passed me to the door. He started after her, then stopped halfway across the room. We stared in silence at the curtained doorway, listening to the sound of her heels on the bare floor till it finally died away. He returned slowly to his seat and slumped into it. The wood creaked audibly in the quiet office.

"Go," he said, not looking at me.

The above is the last entry in Lomba's diary. There's no record of how far the superintendent went to help him regain his freedom, but like he told Janice, there was very little he could have done for a political detainee – especially since about a week after that meeting a coup was attempted against the military leader, General Sani Abacha, by some officers close to him. There was an immediate crackdown on all pro-democracy activists, and the prisons all over the country swelled with political detainees. A lot of those already in detention were transferred randomly to other prisons around the country –

for security reasons. Lomba was among them. He was transferred to Agodi Prison in Ibadan. From there he was moved to the far north, a small desert town called Gashuwa. There was no record of him after that.

A lot of these political prisoners died in detention, although only the prominent ones made the headlines – people like Moshood Abiola and General Yar Adua.

But somehow it is hard to imagine that Lomba died, a lot seems to point to the contrary. His diary, his economical expressions, show a very sedulous character at work. A survivor. The years in prison must have taught him not to hope too much, not to despair too much, that for the prisoner nothing kills as surely as too much hope or too much despair. He had learned to survive in tiny atoms, piecemeal, a day at a time. It is probable that in 1998, when the military dictator, Abacha, died, and his successor, General Abdulsalam Abubakar, dared to open the gates to democracy, and to liberty for the political detainees, Lomba was in the ranks of those released.

This is how it might have happened: Lomba was perhaps seated in a dingy cell in Gashuwa, his eyes closed, his mind soaring above the glass-studded prison walls, mingling with the stars and the rain in elemental union of freedom; then the door clanked open, and when he opened his eyes, it was Liberty standing over him, smiling kindly, extending an arm.

And Liberty said softly, "Come. It is time to go."

And they left, arm in arm.

Helon Habila is a Nigerian who currently teaches creative writing at George Mason University, Virginia, US. 'Love Poems' appeared first in his anthology *Prison Stories*, Epik Books, Lagos 2000. He won the Commonwealth Writers Prize in 2003 and his novel *Measuring Time* was published by Hamish Hamilton/Penguin and WW Norton in 2007. His second novel *The River* will be published in June 2010 by Hamish Hamilton.

Discovering Home

Binyavanga Wainaina – winner of the 2002 Caine Prize

Cape Town, June 1995 – There is a problem.

Somebody has locked themselves in the toilet. The upstairs bathroom is locked and Frank has disappeared with the keys. There is a small riot at the door, as drunk women with smudged lipstick and crooked wigs bang on the door.

There is always that point at a party when people are too drunk to be having fun; when strange smelly people are asleep on your bed; when the good booze runs out and there is only Sedgwick's Brown Sherry and a carton of sweet white wine; when you realise that all your flat-mates have gone and all this is your responsibility; when the DJ is slumped over the stereo and some strange person is playing "I'm a Barbie girl, in a Barbie Wo-o-orld" over and over again.

I have been working here, in Observatory, Cape Town, for two years and rarely breached the boundary of my clique. Fear, I suppose, and a feeling that I am not quite ready to leave a place that has let me be anything I want to be – and provided not a single predator. That is what this party is all about:

I am going home for a year.

So maybe this feeling that my movements are being guided is explicable. This time tomorrow I will be sitting next to my mother. We shall soak each other up. Flights to distant places always arouse in me a peculiar awareness: that what we refer to as reality – not the substance, but the organisation of reality – is really a strand as thin as the puffy white lines that planes leave behind as they fly.

It will be so easy – I will wonder why I don't do this every day. I hope to be in Kenya for 13 months. I intend to travel as much as possible and finally to attend my grandparents' 60th wedding anniversary in Uganda in December.

There are so many possibilities that could overturn this journey, yet I will get there. **If there is a miracle in the idea of life it is this: that**

we are able to exist for a time – in defiance of chaos.

Later, we often forget how dicey everything was: how the tickets almost didn't materialise; how the event almost got postponed. Phrases swell, becoming bigger than their context and speak to us with TRUTH. We wield this series of events as our due, the standard for gifts of the future. We live the rest of our lives with the utter knowledge that there is something deliberate, a vein in us that transports everything into place – *if* we follow the stepping stones of certainty.

After the soft light and mellow manners of Cape Town, Nairobi is a shot of whisky. We drive from the airport into the City Centre; around us, Matatus: those brash, garish Minibus-Taxis, so irritating to every Kenyan except those who own one, or work for one. I can see them as the best example of contemporary Kenyan Art. The best of them get new paint jobs every few months. Oprah seems popular right now, and Gidi Gidi Maji Maji, one of the hottest bands in Kenya, and the inevitable Tupak. The coloured lights, and fancy horn and the purple interior lighting; the Hip Hop blaring out of speakers I will never afford.

This is Nairobi! This is what you do to get ahead: make yourself boneless, and treat your straitjacket as if it is a game, a challenge. The city is now all on the streets, sweet-talk and hustle. Our worst recession ever has just produced brighter, more creative Matatus.

It is good to be home.

In the afternoon, I take a walk down River Road, all the way to Nyamakima. This is the main artery of movement to and from Public Transport Vehicles. It is ruled by Manambas (taxi touts) and their image: a cynical, hard demeanour – every laugh is a sneer, the city is a war or a game. It is a useful face to carry, here where humanity invades all the space you do not claim with conviction.

The desperation that is for me the most touching is the expressions of the people who come from the rural areas into the City Centre to sell their produce: thin-faced, with the massive cheekbones common amongst Kikuyus – so dominating they seem like an appendage to be embarrassed about – something that draws attention to their faces, when attention is the last thing they want. Anywhere else those faces are beauty. Their eyes dart about in a permanent fear, unable to train themselves to a background of so much chaos. They do not know how to put on a glassy expression.

Those who have been in the fresh produce business for long

are immediately visible: mostly old women in khanga sarongs with weary take-it-or-leave-it voices. They hang out in groups, chattering away constantly, as if they want no quiet where the fragility of their community will reveal itself.

*   *   *

I am at home. The past eight hours is already receding into the forgotten; I was in Cape Town this morning, I am in Nakuru, Kenya now.

Blink.

Mum looks tired and her eyes are sleepier than usual. She has never seemed frail, but does so now. I decide that it is I who is growing, changing, and my attempts at maturity make her seem more human.

I make my way to the kitchen: the Nandi woman still rules the corridor.

After 10 years, I can still move about with ease in the dark. I stop at that hollow place, the bit of wall on the other side of the fireplace. My mother's voice, talking to my Dad, echoes in the corridor. None of us has her voice: if crystal was water solidified, her voice would be the last splash of water before it solidifies.

Light from the kitchen brings the Nandi woman to life. A painting.

I was terrified of her when I was a kid. Her eyes seemed so alive and the red bits growled at me menacingly. Her broad face announced an immobility that really scared me; I was stuck there, fenced into a tribal reserve by her features. *Rings on her ankles and bells on her nose, she will make music wherever she goes.*

Why? Did I sense, so young, that her face could never translate to acceptability? That, however guised, it could not align itself to the programme I aspired to ? In Kenya there are two sorts of people:

Those on one side of the line will wear third-hand clothing till it rots, they will eat dirt, but school fees will be paid.

On the other side of the line live people you may see in coffee-table books. Impossibly exotic and much fewer in number than the coffee table books suggest. They are like an old and lush jungle that continues to flourish its leaves and unfurl extravagant blooms, refusing to realise that somebody cut off the water, somebody from the other side of the line.

These two groups of people are fascinated by one another. We, the modern ones, are fascinated by the completeness of the old ones. To us it seems that everything is mapped out and defined for them – and everybody is fluent in those definitions. The old ones are not much impressed with our society, or manners – what catches their attention is our tools, the cars and medicines and telephones and wind-up dolls and guns.

In my teens, I was set alight by the poems of Senghor and Okot P'Bitek; the Nandi woman became my Negritude. I pronounced her beautiful, marvelled at her cheekbones and mourned the lost wisdom in her eyes, but I still would have preferred to sleep with Pam Ewing or Iman.

It was a source of terrible fear for me that I could never love her. I covered that betrayal with a complicated imagery that had no connection to my gut: O Nubian Princess, and other bad poetry. She moved to my bedroom for a while, next to the kente wall-hanging, but my mother took her back to her pulpit.

Over the years, I learned to look at her amiably. She filled me with a lukewarm nostalgia for things lost. I never again attempted to look beyond her costume.

She is younger than me now; I can see that she has a girlishness about her. Her eyes are the artist's only real success – they suggest mischief, serenity, vulnerability and a weary wisdom. Today, I don't need to bludgeon my brain with her beauty, it just sinks in, and I am floored by lust: It makes me feel like I have desecrated something.

Then I see it.

Have I been such a bigot? Everything. The slight smile, the angle of her head and shoulders, the mild flirtation with the artist: *I know you want me, I know something you don't.*

Mona Lisa: not a single thing says otherwise. The truth: the truth is that I never saw the smile; her thick lips were such a war between my intellect and emotion, I never noticed the smile.

The artist is probably not African, not only because of the obvious Mona Lisa business but also because, for the first time, I realise that the woman's expression is *inaccurate*. In Kenya, you will only see such an expression in girls who went to private schools, or who are brought up in the richer surburbs of the larger towns.

That look, that toying slight smile could not have happened with an actual Nandi woman. In the portrait, she has covered her vast sexuality with a shawl of ice, letting only the hint of smile reveal that she has a body that can quicken: a flag on the moon. The artist has got the dignity right but the sexuality is European: it would be difficult for an African artist to get that wrong.

The lips too seem wrong. There's an awkwardness about them, as if a shift of aesthetics has taken place on the plain of muscles between her nose and her mouth. Also, the mouth strives too hard for symmetry, as if to apologise for its thickness. That mouth is meant to break open like the flesh of a ripe mango; restraint of expression is not common in Kenya and certainly not among the Nandi.

I turn, and head for the kitchen. I cherish the kitchen at night. It is cavernous, chilly and echoing with night noises that are muffled by the vast spongy silence outside. After so many years in cupboard-sized South African kitchens, I feel more thrilled than I should.

On my way back to my room, I turn and face the Nandi woman thinking of the full-circles since I left. When I left, White people ruled South Africa. When I left, Kenya was a one-party dictatorship. When I left, I was relieved that I had escaped the burdens and guilts of being in Kenya, of facing my roots, and repudiating them. Here I am, looking for them again.

I know, her red-rimmed eyes say. *I know.*

A Fluid Disposition: Masailand

August 1995 – A few minutes ago, I was sleeping comfortably in the front of a Landrover Discovery. Now I have been unceremoniously dumped by the side of the road as the extension officer makes a mad dash for the night comforts of Narok town. Driving at night hereabouts is not a bright idea.

The first few minutes out of the car are disturbing – it is an interesting aspect of travelling to a new place that your eyes cannot concentrate on the particular. I am swamped by the glare of dusk, by the shiver of wind on undulating acres of wheat and barley, by the vision of mile upon mile of space free from our wirings. So much is my focus derailed that when I return unto myself I find, to my surprise, that my feet are not off the ground – that the landscape had grabbed me with such force it sucked up the awareness of myself for a moment.

There are rotor-blades of cold chopping away in my nostrils: the silence, after the non-stop drone of the car, is as persistent as cobwebs, as intrusive as the loudest of noises. I have an urge to claw it away.

It occurs to me that there is no clearer proof of the subjectivity (or selectivity) of our senses than at moments like this. Seeing is always only noticing. We pass our eyes upon the landscapes of our familiars and choose what to acknowledge.

The cold air is really irritating. I want to breathe in – suck up the moist mountain-ness of the air, the smell of fever tree and dung – but the process is just too painful. What do people do in wintry places? Do they have some sort of nasal sensodyne?

I am in Masailand.

Not Television Masailand – rolling grasslands, lions, and acacia trees.

We are high up in the Mau Hills. Here there aren't vast fields of grain – there are forests. Here impenetrable weaves of highland forest, dominated by bamboo cover the landscape. Inside them, there are many elephants, which come out at night and leave enormous pancakes of shit on the road. When I was a kid, I used to think that elephants use dusty roads as toilet paper like cats – sitting on the sand with their haunches and levering themselves forward with their forelegs.

Back on the *choosing to see* business: I know, chances are I will see no elephants for the weeks I am here. I will see people. It occurs to me that if I was White, chances are I would choose to see elephants – and this would be a very different story. That story would be about the wide, empty spaces people from Europe yearn to get lost in, rather than the cosy surround of kin we Africans generally seek.

Whenever I read something by some White writer who stopped by Kenya, I am astounded by the amount of game that appears for breakfast at their patios and the snakes that drop into the baths and the lions that terrorise their calves. I have seen one snake in my life. I don't know anybody who has ever been bitten by one.

I can see our ancient Massey Ferguson wheezing up a distant hill. They are headed this way. Relief!

*   *   *

I am on a tractor, freezing my butt off, as we make our way from the wheat fields and back to camp. We've been supervising the spraying of wheat and barley in the fields my father leases here.

There isn't much to look forward to at night here, no pubs hidden in the bamboo jungle. You can't even walk about freely at night because the areas outside are full of stinging nettles. We will be in bed by seven to beat the cold. I will hear stories about frogs that sneak under one's bed and turn into beautiful women who entrap you. I will hear stories about legendary tractor drivers – people who could turn the jagged roof of Mt Kilimanjaro into a neat afro. I will hear about Masai people – about so-and-so, who got 14,000 rand for barley grown on his land, and how he took off to the Majengo Slums in Nairobi, leaving his wife and children behind, to live with a prostitute for a year.

When the money ran out, he discarded his suit, pots and pans, and furniture. He wrapped a blanket around himself and walked home, whistling happily all the way.

Most of all, I will hear stories about Ole Kamaro, our landlord, and his wife Eddah (names changed).

My dad has been growing wheat and barley in this area since I was a child. All this time, we have been leasing a portion of Ole Kamaro's land to keep our tractors and things and to make Camp. I met Eddah when she had just married Ole Kamaro. She was his fifth wife, 13 years old. He was very proud of her. She was the daughter of some big time chief near Mau Narok *and she could read and write!* Ole Kamaro bought her a pocket radio and made her follow him about with a pen and pencil everywhere he went, taking notes.

I remember being horrified by the marriage – she was so young! My sister Ciru was eight and they played together one day. That night, my sister had a terrible nightmare that my dad had sold her to Ole Kamaro in exchange for 50 acres.

Those few years of schooling were enough to give Eddah a clear idea of the basic tenets of Empowerment. By the time she was 18, Ole Kamaro had dumped the rest of his wives.

Eddah leased out his land to Kenya Breweries and opened a bank account where all the money went.

Occasionally, she gave her husband pocket money.

Whenever he was away, she took up with her lover, a wealthy young Kikuyu shopkeeper from the other side of the hill who kept her supplied with essentials like soap, matches and paraffin.

Eddah was the local chairwoman of KANU (Kenya's Ruling Party) Women's League and so remained invulnerable to censure from the conservative elements around. She also had a thriving business, curing hides and beading them elaborately for the tourist market at the Mara. Unlike most Masai women, who disdain growing of crops, she had a thriving market garden with maize, beans, and various vegetables. She did not lift a finger to take care of this garden. Part of the co-operation we expected from her as landlady meant that our staff had to take care of that garden. Her reasoning was that Kikuyu men are cowardly women anyway and they do farming so-oo well.

Something interesting is going on today. There is a tradition amongst Masai, that women are released from all domestic duties a few months after giving birth. The women are allowed to take over the land and claim any lovers that they choose. For some reason I don't quite understand, this all happens at a particular season – and this season begins **today**. I have been warned to keep away from any bands of women wandering about.

We are on some enormous hill and I can feel the old Massey Ferguson tractor wheezing. We get to the top, turn to make our way down, and there they are: led by Eddah, a troop of about 40 women marching towards us dressed in their best traditional clothing.

Eddah looks imperious and beautiful in her beaded leather cloak, red khanga wraps, rings, necklaces and earrings. There is an old woman amongst them, she must be 70 and she is cackling in toothless glee. She takes off her wrap and displays her breasts – they resemble old gym socks.

Mwangi, who is driving, stops, and tries to turn back, but the road is too narrow: on one side there is the mountain, and on the other, a yawning valley. Kipsang, who is sitting in the trailer with me, shouts for Karanja to drive right through them: *"DO NOT STOP!"*

It seems that the modernised version of this tradition involves men making donations to the KANU Women's Group. Innocent enough, you'd think – but the amount of these donations must satisfy them or they will strip you naked and do unspeakable things to your body.

So we take off at full speed. The women stand firm in the middle of the road. We can't swerve. We stop.

Then Kipsang saves our skins by throwing a bunch of coins onto the road. I throw down some notes and Mwangi (renowned across Masailand for his stinginess) empties his pockets, throws down notes and coins. The women start to gather the money, the tractor roars back into action and we drive right through them.

I am left with the picture of the toothless old lady diving to avoid the tractor. Then standing, looking at us and laughing, her breasts flapping about like a Flag of Victory.

*   *   *

I am in bed, still in Masailand.

I pick up my father's *World Almanac and Book of Facts 1992*. The language section has new words, confirmed from sources as impeccable as the *Columbia Encyclopedia* and the *Oxford English Dictionary*. The list reads like an American Infomercial: Jazzercise, Assertiveness-Training, Bulimarexic, Microwavable, Fast-tracker.

There is a word there – *skanking*: a style of West Indian dancing to reggae music, in which the body bends forward at the waist and the knees are raised and the hands claw the air in time to the beat; dancing in this style.

I have some brief flash of ourselves in 40 years' time, in some generic Dance Studio. We are practising for the Senior Dance Championships, plastic smiles on our faces as we skank across the room.

The tutor checks the movement: shoulder up, arms down, move this-way, move-that: Claw, baby. Claw!

In time to the beat, dancing in this style.

Langat and Kariuki have lost their self-consciousness around me, and are chatting away about Eddah Ole Kamaro, our landlady.

"Eh! She had ten thousand shillings and they went and stayed in a Hotel in Narok for a week. Ole Kamaro had to bring in another woman to look after the children!"

"He! But she sits on him!"

Their talk meanders slowly, with no direction – just talk, just connecting, and I feel that tight wrap of time loosen, the anxiety of losing time fades and I am a glorious vacuum for a while just letting what strikes my mind strike my mind, then sleep strikes my mind.

*   *   *

Ole Kamaro is slaughtering a goat today! For me!

We all settle on the patch of grass between the two compounds. Ole Kamaro makes quick work of the sheep and I am offered the fresh kidney to eat. It tastes surprisingly good. It tastes of a slippery warmth, an organic cleanliness.

Ole Kamaro introduces me to his sister-in-law, tells me proudly that she is in form-four. Eddah's sister – I spotted her this morning staring at me from the tiny window in their Manyatta. It was disconcerting at first – a typically Masai stare – unembarrassed, not afraid to be vulnerable. Then she noticed that I had seen her, and her eyes narrowed and became sassy – street-sassy, like a girl from Eastlands in Nairobi.

So I am now confused how to approach her. Should my approach be one of exaggerated politeness, as is traditional, or with a casual cool, as her second demeanour requested? I would have opted for the latter but her uncle is standing eagerly next to us.

She responds by lowering her head and looking away. I am painfully embarrassed. I ask her to show me where they tan their hides.

We escape with some relief.

"So where do you go to school?"

"Oh! At St Teresa's Girls in Nairobi."

"Eddah is your sister?"

"Yes."

We are quiet for a while. English was a mistake. Where I am fluent, she is stilted. I switch to Swahili and she pours herself into another person: talkative, aggressive, a person who must have a Tupac t-shirt stashed away somewhere.

"Arhh! It's so boring here! Nobody to talk to! I hope Eddah comes home early."

I am still stunned. How bold and animated she is, speaking *sheng*, a very hip street language that mixes Swahili and English.

"Why didn't you go with the women today?"

She laughs, "I am not married. Ho! I'm sure they had fun! They are drinking Muratina somewhere here I am sure. I can't wait to get married."

"Kwani? You don't want to go to University and all that?"

"Maybe, but if I'm married to the right guy, life is good. Look at Eddah – she is free – she does anything she wants. Old men are good. If you feed them, and give them a son, they leave you alone."

"Won't it be difficult to do this if you are not circumcised?"

"Kwani, who told you I'm not circumcised? I went last year."

I am shocked, and it shows. She laughs.

"He! I nearly shat myself! But I didn't cry!"

"Why? Si, you could have refused."

"Ai! If I would have refused, it would mean that my life here was finished. There is no place here for someone like that."

"But..."

I cut myself short. I am sensing this is her compromise – to live two lives fluently. As it is with people's reasons for their faiths and choices – trying to disprove her is silly. As a Masai she will see my statement as ridiculous.

In sheng, there is no way for me to bring it up that would be diplomatic, in sheng she can only present this with a hard-edged bravado, it is humiliating. I do not know of any way we can discuss this successfully in English. If there is a courtesy every Kenyan practises, it is that none of us ever questions each other's contradictions – we all have them, and destroying someone's face is sacrilege.

There is nothing wrong with being what you are not in Kenya – just be it successfully. Every Kenyan joke is about somebody who thought they had mastered a new persona and failed. For us, life is about having a fluid disposition.

You can have as many as you want.

Christmas in Bufumbira

Dec 20, 1995 – The drive through the Mau Hills, past the Rift Valley and onwards to Kisumu is a drag. I haven't been this way for ten years, but my aim is to be in Uganda. We arrive in Kampala at ten in the evening. We have been on the road for over eight hours.

This is my first visit to Uganda, a land of incredible mystery for me. I grew up with her myths and legends and her horrors – narrated with the intensity that only exiles can muster. It is my first visit to my mother's ancestral home, the occasion is her parents' 60th wedding anniversary.

It will be the first time that she and her ten surviving brothers and sisters have been together since the early '60s. The first time that my grandparents will have all their children and most of their grandchildren at home together – more than a hundred people are expected.

My mother, and the many visitors who came to visit, always filled my imagination with incredible tales of Uganda. I heard how you had to wriggle on your stomach to see the Kabaka; how the Tutsi king in Rwanda (who was seven feet tall) was once given a bicycle as a present. Because he couldn't walk on the ground (being a king and all), he was carried everywhere, on his bicycle, by his bearers.

Apparently, in the old kingdom in Rwanda, Tutsi women were not supposed to exert themselves or mar their beauty in any way. Some women had to be spoon-fed by their Hutu servants and wouldn't leave their huts for fear of sunburn.

I was told about a trip my grandfather took when he was young, with an uncle, where he was mistaken for a Hutu servant and taken away to stay with the goats. A few days later his uncle asked about him and his hosts were embarrassed to confess that they didn't know he was 'one of us'.

This must really irritate people here – that we seem to be interested only in the schism between the Tutsi and the Hutu.

It has been a year of mixed blessings for Africa. This is the year that I sat at Newlands Stadium during the Rugby World Cup in the Cape and watched South Africans reach out to each other before giving New Zealand a hiding. Mandela, wearing the Number Six rugby jersey, managed to melt away for one incredible night all the hostility that had gripped the country since he was released from jail. Black people, for long supporters of the All Blacks, embraced the Springboks with enthusiasm. For just one night most South Africans felt a common Nationhood.

It is the year that I returned to my home, Kenya, to find people so way beyond cynicism that they looked back on their cynical days with fondness.

Uganda is different: this is a country that has not only reached the bottom of the hole countries sometimes fall into, it has scratched through that bottom and free-fallen again and again, and now it has rebuilt itself and swept away the hate. This country gives me hope that this continent is not incontinent.

This is the country I used to associate with banana trees, old and elegant kingdoms, rot, Idi Amin, and hopelessness. It was an association I had made as a child, when the walls of our house would ooze and leak whispers of horror whenever a relative or friends of the family came home, fleeing from Amin's literal and metaphoric crocodiles.

I am rather annoyed that the famous Seven Hills of Kampala are not as clearly defined as I had imagined they would be. I have always had a childish vision of a stately city filled with royal paraphernalia. I had expected to see elegant people dressed in flowing robes, carrying baskets on their heads and walking arrogantly down streets filled with the smell of roasting bananas; and Intellectuals from a '60s dream, burning the streets with their Afrocentric rhetoric.

Images formed in childhood can be more than a little bit stubborn.

Reality is a better aesthetic. Kampala seems disorganised, full of potholes, bad management, and haphazardness. The African city that so horrifies the West. The truth is that it is a city being overwhelmed by enterprise. I see smiles, the shine of healthy skin, and teeth; no layabouts lounging and plotting at every street corner. People do not walk about with walls around themselves as they do in Nairobbery.

All over, there is a frenzy of building: a blanket of paint is slowly spreading over the city, so it looks rather like one of those Smirnoff adverts where inanimate things get breathed to Technicolor by the sacred burp of 30 per cent or so of clear alcohol.

It is humid, and hot, and the banana trees flirt with you, swaying gently like fans offering a coolness that never materialises.

Everything smells musky, as if a thick, soft steam has risen like a Broth of Life: if the air was any thicker, it would be a gel. The plants are enormous. They flutter arrogantly about, like traditional dancers. Mum once told me that when travelling in Uganda in the '40s and the '50s, if you were hungry you could simply enter a banana plantation and eat as much as you wished – you didn't have to ask anybody, but you were not allowed to carry so much as a single deformed banana out of the plantation.

*   *   *

We are booked in at the Catholic Guesthouse. As soon as I have dumped my stuff on the bed, I call up an old school friend, who promises to pick me up.

Musoke comes at six and we go to find food. We drive past the famous Mulago Hospital and into town. He picks up a couple of friends and we go to a place called Yakubu's.

We order a couple of beers, lots of roast pork brochettes and sit in the car. The brochettes are delicious. I like them so much, I order more. Nile beer is okay, but nowhere near Kenya's Tusker.

The sun is drowned suddenly and it is dark.

We get onto the highway to Entebbe. On both sides of the road, people have built flimsy houses: bars, shops, and cafes line the road the whole way. What surprises me is how many people are out. Especially teenagers, flouncing about, weighed down by hormones. It is still hot outside and the fronts of all these premises are lit by paraffin lamps. It is just too tempting.

I turn to Musoke and ask, "Can we stop at one of those pubs and have a beer?"

"Ah! Wait till we get to where we are going, it's much nicer than this dump!"

"I'm sure it is; but you know, I might never get a chance to drink in a real Entebbe pub, not those bourgeois places. Come on, I'll buy a round."

Magic words.

The place is charming. Ugandans seem to me to have a knack for making things elegant and comfortable, regardless of income. In Kenya, or South Africa, a place like this would be dirty, and buildings would be put together with a sort of haphazard self-loathing; sort of like saying "I won't be here long, why bother?"

The inside of the place is decorated simply, mostly with reed mats. The walls are well finished, and the floor, simple cement, has no cracks or signs of misuse. We are served by women in the traditional Baganda getup. I find Baganda women much sexier than the Shay women. They carry about with them a look of knowledge, a proud and naked sensuality – daring you to satisfy.

Also, they don't seem to have that generic cuteness many city women have, that I have already begun to find irritating. Their features are strong; their skin is a deep, gleaming copper and their eyes have that oil-film-over-black pupils look common in the tropics (often referred to as sultry).

Baganda women traditionally wear a long, loose Victorian-style dress. It fulfils every literal aspect the Victorians desired, but manages despite itself to suggest sex. The dresses are usually in bold colours. To emphasize their size, many women tie a band just below their buttocks (which are often padded).

What makes the difference is the walk.

Many women visualise their hips as an unnecessary evil, an irritating accessory that needs to be whittled down. I guess, a while back, women looked upon their hips as a cradle for the depositing of desire, for the nurturing of childlings. Baganda women see their hips as great ball bearings, rolling, supple things moving in lubricated circles – so they make the best Tombolo dancers in the world. In those loose dresses, their hips brushing the sides of the dress as they move, they are a marvel to watch.

Most appealing about them is the sense of stature they carry about them. Baganda women seem to have found a way to be traditional and powerful at the same time – most I know grow more beautiful with age and many compete with men in industry, without seeming to compromise themselves as women.

*   *   *

I sleep on the drive from Kampala to Kisoro.

We leave Kisoro and begin the drive to St Paul's Mission, Kigezi, Uganda. My sister Ciru is sitting next to me. She is a year younger than me. Chiqy, my youngest sister, has been to Uganda before and is taking full advantage of her vast experience to play the adult tour guide. At her age, cool is a god.

I have the odd feeling we are puppets in some Christmas story. It is as if a basket weaver were writing this story in a language of weave; tightening the tension on the papyrus strings every few minutes, and superstitiously refusing to reveal the ending (even to herself) until she has tied the very last knot.

We are now in the mountains. The winding road and the dense papyrus in the valleys seem to entwine me, ever tighter, into my fictional weaver's basket. Every so often, she jerks her weave to tighten it.

I look up to see the last half-hour of road winding along the mountain above us. We are in the Bufumbira range now, driving through Kigaland on our way to Kisoro, the nearest town to my mother's home.

There is an alien quality to this place. It does not conform to any African topography that I am familiar with. The mountains are incredibly steep and resemble inverted ice-cream cones: a hoe has tamed every inch of them.

It is *incredibly green*.

In Kenya, 'green' is the ultimate accolade a person can give land: green is scarce, green is wealth, fertility.

Bufumbira green is not a tropical green, no warm musk, like in Buganda; it is not the harsh green of the Kenyan savannah, either: that two-month-long green that compresses all the elements of life – millions of wildebeest and zebra, great carnivores feasting during the rains, frenzied ploughing and planting, and dry riverbeds overwhelmed by soil and bloodstained water; and Nairobi underwater.

It is not the green of grand waste and grand bounty that my country knows.

This is a mountain green, cool and enduring. Rivers and lakes occupy the cleavage of the many mountains that surround us.

Mum looks almost foreign now; her Kinyarwanda accent is more pronounced, and her face is not as reserved as usual. Her beauty, so exotic and head-turning in Kenya, seems at home here. She does not stand out here, she belongs; the rest of us seem like tourists.

As the drive continues, I become imbued with the sense of where we are. We are no longer in the history of Buganda, of Idi Amin, of the Kabakas, or civil war, Museveni, and Hope.

We are now on the outskirts of the theatre where the Hutus and the Tutsis have been performing for the world's media. My mother has always described herself as a *Mufumbira*, one who speaks Kinyarwanda. She has always said that too much is made of the differences between Tutsi and Hutu; and that they are really more alike than anything. She insists that she is Bufumbira – a MnyaRwanda. Forget the rest, she says.

I am glad she hasn't, because it saves me from trying to understand. I am not here about genocide or hate. Enough people have been here for that (try typing 'Tutsi' on any search engine).

I am here to be with family.

I ask my mother where the border with Rwanda is. She points it out, and points out Zaire as well. They are both nearer than I thought. Maybe this is what makes this coming together so urgent. How amazing life seems when it stands around death. There is no grass as beautiful as the blades that stick out after the first rain.

As we move into the forested area I am enthralled by the smell and by the canopy of mountain vegetation. I join the conversation in the car. I have become self-conscious about displaying my dreaminess and absent-mindedness these days.

I used to spend hours gazing out of car windows, creating grand battles between battalions of clouds. I am aware of a conspiracy to get me back to Earth, to get me to be more practical. My parents are pursuing this cause with little subtlety, aware that my time with them is limited. It is necessary for me to believe that I am putting myself on a gritty road to personal success when I leave home. Cloud travel is well and good when you have mastered the landings. I never have. I must live, not dream about living.

We are in Kisoro, the main town of the district, weaving through roads between people's houses. We are heading towards Uncle Kagame's house.

The image of a dictatorial movie director manipulating our movements replaces that of the basket-weaver in my mind. I have a dizzy vision of a supernatural moviemaker slowing down the action before the climax by examining tiny details instead of grand scenes.

I see a Continuity Presenter in the fifth dimension saying: "And now our Christmas movie: a touching story about the reunion of a family torn apart by civil war and the genocide in Rwanda. This movie is sponsored by Sobbex, hankies for every occasion (repeated in Zulu, then a giggle and a description of the soapie that will follow).

My fantasy escalates and there is a motivational speaker/aerobics instructor shouting at Christmas TV viewers: "Jerk those tear glands, baby!"

I am still dreaming when we get to my uncle's place.

I am at my worst, half in dream, clumsy, tripping and unable to focus. I have learnt to move my body resolutely at such times, but it generally makes things worse. Tea and every possible thing we could want will be available to us on demand (and so we must not demand).

My uncle Gerald Kagame and his wife both work at the mission hospital. I discover it is their formidable organisational skills that have made this celebration possible. There are already around 100 visitors speaking five or six languages.

Basically, the Binyavangas have taken over the Kisoro town and business is booming. During such an event, hotels are not an option. The church at St Paul's is booked, the dorms are booked, homes have been hijacked, and so on.

We are soon driving through my grandfather's land. In front of us is a saddle-shaped hill with a large, old, imposing church ruling the view. My mother tells us that my grandfather donated this land for the building of the church. The car squishes and slides up the muddy hills, progress impeded by a thick mat of grass.

I see Ankole cattle grazing, their enormous horns like regal crowns.

"Look, that's the homestead. I know this place."

It is a small brick house. I can see the surge of family coming towards the car. After the kissing and hugging, the crowd parts for my grandparents. They seem tall but aren't, just lean and fit. Age and time has made them start to look alike.

My grandmother stretches a long-fingered hand to Ciru's cheek and exclaims: "She still has a big forehead!"

How do you keep track of 60 grandchildren?

She embraces me. She is very slender and I feel she will break. Her elegance surrounds me and I can feel a strong pull to dig into her, burrow in her secrets, see with her eyes. She is a quiet woman, and unbending, even taciturn – and this gives her a powerful charisma. Things not said. Her resemblance to my mother astounds me.

My grandfather is crying and laughing, exclaiming when he hears that Chiqy and I are named after him and his wife (Kamanzi and Binyavanga). We drink rgwagwa (banana wine) laced with honey. It is delicious, smoky and sweet.

Ciru and Chiqy are sitting next to my grandmother. I see why my grandfather was such a legendary schoolteacher: his gentleness and love of life are palpable.

At night, we split into our various age groups and start to bond with one another. Of the cousins, Manwelli, the eldest, is our unofficial leader. He works for the World Bank.

Aunt Rosaria and her family are the coup of the ceremony. They were feared dead during the war in Rwanda and hid for months in their basement, helped by a friend who provided food. They all survived; they walk around carrying expressions that are more common in children – delight, sheer delight at life.

Her three sons spend every minute bouncing about with the high of being alive. They dance at all hours, sometimes even when there is no music. In the evenings, we squash into the veranda, looking out as far as the Congo, and they entertain us with their stand-up routines in French and Kinyarwanda; the force of their humour carries us all to laughter. Manwelli translates one skit for me: they imitate a vain Tutsi woman who is pregnant and is kneeling to make a confession to the shocked priest:

"Oh please God, let my child have long fingers, and a gap between the teeth; let her have a straight nose and be ta-a-all. Oh lord, let her not have (gesticulations of a gorilla prowling) a mashed banana nose like a Hutu. Oh please, I shall be your grateful servant!"

The biggest disappointment so far is that my Aunt Christine has not yet arrived. She has lived with her family in New York since the early '70s. We all feel her loss keenly as it was she who urged us all years ago to gather for this occasion at any cost.

She and my Aunt Rosaria are the senior aunts, and they were very close when they were younger. They speak frequently on the phone and did so especially during the many months that Aunt Rosaria and her family were living in fear in their basement. They are, for me, the summary of the pain the family has been through over the years. Although they are very close, they haven't met since 1961. Visas, wars, closed borders and a thousand triumphs of chaos have kept them apart. We are all looking forward to their reunion.

As is normal on traditional occasions, people stick with their peers; so I have hardly spoken to my mother the past few days. I find her in my grandmother's room, trying, without much success, to get my grandmother to relax and let her many daughters and granddaughters do the work.

I have been watching Mum from a distance for the past few days. At first, she seemed a bit aloof from it all; but now she's found fluency with everything and she seems far away from the Kenyan Mother we know. I can't get over the sight of her cringing and blushing as my grandmother machine-guns instructions to her. How alike they are. I want to talk with her more, but decide not to be selfish, that I am trying to establish possession of her. We'll have enough time on the way back.

I've been trying to pin down my grandfather, to ask him about our family's history. He keeps giving me this bewildered look when I corner him, as if he is asking, *Can't you just relax and party?*

Last night, he toasted us all and cried again before dancing to some very hip gospel rap music from Kampala. He tried to get Grandmother to join him but she beat a hasty retreat.

Gerald is getting quite concerned that when we are all gone, they will find it too quiet.

We hurtle on towards Christmas. Booze flows, we pray, chat and bond under the night rustle of banana leaves. I feel as if I am filled with magic and I succumb to the masses. In two days, we feel a family. In French, Swahili, English, Kikuyu, Kinyarwanda, Kiganda and Ndebele we sing one song, a multitude of passports in our luggage.

At dawn on December 24 I stand smoking in the banana plantation at the edge of my grandfather's hill and watch the mists disappear. Uncle Chris saunters up to join me. I ask: "Any news about Aunt Christine?"

"It looks like she might not make it. Manwelli has tried to get in contact with her and failed. Maybe she couldn't get a flight out of New York. Apparently the weather is terrible there."

The day is filled with hard work. My uncles have convinced my grandfather that we need to slaughter another bull as meat is running out. The old man adores his cattle but reluctantly agrees. He cries when the bull is killed.

There is to be a church service in the sitting room of my grandfather's house later in the day.

The service begins and I bolt from the living room, volunteering to peel potatoes outside.

About halfway through the service, I see somebody staggering up the hill, suitcase in hand and muddied up to her ankles. It takes me an instant to guess. I run to her and mumble something. We hug. Aunt Christine is here.

The plot has taken me over now. Resolution is upon me. The poor woman is given no time to freshen up or collect her bearings. In a minute we have ushered her into the living room. She sits by the door, facing everybody's back. Only my grandparents are facing her. My grandmother starts to cry.

Nothing is said, the service motors on. Everybody stands up to sing. Somebody whispers to my Aunt Rosaria. She turns and gasps soundlessly. Others turn. We all sit down. Aunt Rosaria and Aunt Christine start to cry. Aunt Rosaria's mouth opens and closes in disbelief. My mother joins them, and soon everybody is crying.

The Priest motors on, fluently. Unaware.

Binyavanga Wainaina is a Kenyan writer who founded the influential Kenyan literary magazine *Kwani?*. 'Discovering Home' was first published in the internet journal G21Net in 2001. He has been working on his first novel, due to be published by Granta in 2010.

Weight of Whispers

Yvonne Adhiambo Owuor – winner of the 2003 Caine Prize

The collection of teeth on the man's face is a splendid brown. I have never seen such teeth before. Refusing all instruction, my eyes focus on dental contours and craters. Denuded of any superficial pretence – no braces, no fillings, no toothbrush – it is a place where small scavengers thrive.

"Evidence!" The man giggles.

A flash of green and my US$50 disappears into his pocket. His fingers prod: shirt, coat, trousers. He finds the worked snake-skin wallet. No money in it, just a picture of Agnethe-mama, Lune and Chi-Chi, elegant and unsmiling, diamonds in their ears, on their necks and wrists. The man tilts the picture this way and that, returns the picture into the wallet. The wallet disappears into another of his pockets. The man's teeth gleam.

"Souvenir." Afterwards, a hiccupping *"Greeeheeereeehee"* not unlike a National Geographic hyena, complete with a chorus from the pack.

"Please... it's... my mother... all I have."

His eyes become thin slits, head tilts and the veins on his right eye pulse. His nostrils flare, an indignant goat.

A thin sweat-trail runs down my spine, the backs of my knees tingle. I look around at the faceless others in the dank room. His hand grabs my goatee and twists. My eyes smart. I lift up my hand to wipe them. The man sees the gold insignia ring, glinting on my index finger.

The ring of the royal household. One of only three. The second belonged to my father. Agnethe-mama told me that when father appeared to her in a dream to tell her he was dead, he was still wearing it. The third... no one has ever spoken about.

The policeman's grin broadens. He pounces. Long fingers. A girl would cut her hair for fingers like his. He spits on my finger, and draws out the ring with his teeth; the ring I have worn for 18 years – from the day I was recognised by the priests as a man and a prince. It was supposed to have been passed on to the son I do not have. The policeman twists my hand this way and that, his tongue caught between his teeth; a study of concentrated avarice.

"Evidence!"

Gargoyles are petrified life-mockers, sentries at entry points, sentinels of sorrow, spitting at fate. I will try to protest.

"It is sacred ring... Please... please." To my shame, my voice breaks.

"Evidence!"

Cheek: nerve, gall, impertinence, brashness.

Cheek: the part of my face he chose to brand.

Later on, much later on, I will wonder what makes it possible for one man to hit another for no reason other than the fact that he can. But now, I lower my head. The sum total of what resides in a very tall man who used to be a prince in a land eviscerated.

* * *

Two presidents died when a missile launched from land forced their plane down. A man of note, a prince, had said, on the first day, that the perpetrators must be hunted down. That evil must be purged from lives. That is all the prince had meant. It seems someone heard something else. It emerges later on, when it is too late, that an old servant took his obligation too far, in the name of his prince.

We had heard rumour of a holocaust, of a land haemorrhaging to death. Everywhere, hoarse murmurs, eyes white and wide with an arcane fear. Is it possible that brothers would machete sisters-in-law to stew-meat-size chunks in front of nephews and nieces?

It was on the fifth day after the presidents had disintegrated with their plane, that I saw that the zenith of existence cannot be human.

In the seasons of my European sojourn, Brussels, Paris, Rome, Amsterdam, rarely London, a city I could accommodate a loathing for, I wondered about the unsaid; hesitant signals and interminable reminders of 'What *They* Did'. Like a mnemonic device, the swastika would grace pages and/or screens, at least once a week, unto perpetuity. I wondered.

I remembered a conversation in Krakow with an academician, a man with primeval eyes. A pepper-coloured, quill-beard obscured the man's mouth, and seemed to speak in its place. I was, suddenly, in the thrall of an irrational fear; that the mobile barbs would shoot off his face and stab me.

I could not escape.

I had agreed to offer perspectives on his seminal work, a work in progress he called, 'A Mystagogy of Human Evil'. I had asked, meaning nothing, a prelude to commentary:

"Are you a Jew?"

So silently, the top of his face fell, flowed towards his jaw, his formidable moustache-beard lank, his shoulders shaking, his eyes flooded with tears. But not a sound emerged from his throat. Unable to tolerate the tears of another man, I walked away.

Another gathering, another conversation, with another man. Mellowed by the well-being engendered by a goblet of Rémy Martin, I ventured an opinion about the sacrificial predilection of being; the necessity of oblation of men by men to men.

"War is the excuse," I said. I was playing with words, true, but, oddly the exchange petered into mumbles of 'Never Again'.

A year later, at a balcony party, when I asked the American Consul in Luxembourg to suggest a book which probed the slaughter of Germans during World War II, she said:

"By whom?"

Before I could answer, she had spun away, turning her back on me as if I had asked "Cain, where is your brother?"

What had been Cain's response?

To my amusement, I was, of course, never invited to another informal diplomatic gathering. Though I would eventually relinquish my European postings – in order to harness, to my advantage, European predilection for African gems – over *après-diner* Drambuie, now and again, I pondered over what lay beneath the unstated.

Now, my world has tilted into a realm where other loaded silences lurk. And I can sense why some things must remain buried in silence, even if they resuscitate themselves at night in dreams where blood pours out of phantom mouths. In the empire of silence, the 'turning away' act is a vain exorcism of a familiar daemon which invades the citadels we ever change, we constantly fortify. Dragging us back through old routes of anguish, it suggests: "Alas, human, your nature relishes fratricidal blood."

But to be human is to be intrinsically, totally, resolutely good. Is it not?

Nothing entertains the devil as much as this protestation.

* * *

Roger, the major-domo, had served in our home since before my birth 37 years ago. He re-appeared at our door on the evening of the fifth day after the death of the two presidents. He had disappeared on the first day of the plane deaths. The day he resurfaced, we were celebrating the third anniversary of my engagement to Lune. I had thought a pungent whiff which entered the room with his presence was merely the Gorgonzola cheese Lune had been unwrapping.

Roger says:

"*J'ai terminé. Tout a été nettoyé.*" It is done. All has been cleaned.

"What Roger?"

"The dirt." He smiles.

The bottle of Dom Pérignon Millésimé in my hand, wavers. I observe that Roger is shirtless, his hair stands in nascent, accidental dreadlocks. The bottom half of his trousers are torn, and his shoeless left foot, swollen. His fist is black and caked with what I think is tar. And in his wake, the smell of smouldering matter. Roger searches the ground, hangs his head, his mouth tremulous:

"They are coming... Sir."

Then Roger stoops. He picks up the crumbs of *petits fours* from the carpet; he is fastidious about cleanliness. The Dom Pérignon Millésimé drops from my hand, it does not break, though its precious contents soak into the carpet. Roger frowns, his mouth pursed. He also disapproves of waste.

* * *

In our party clothes and jewellery, with what we had in our wallets, and two packed medium-size Chanel cases, we abandoned our life at home. We counted the money we had between us: US$3,723. In the bank account, of course, there was more. There was always more. As President of the Banque Locale, I was one of three who held keys to the vault, so to say. Two weeks before the presidents died, I sold my Paris apartment. The money was to be used to expand our bank into Zaire. We got the last four of the last eight seats on the last flight out of our city. We assumed then, it was only right that it be so. We landed at the Jomo Kenyatta International Airport in Nairobi, Kenya at ten p.m.

I wondered about Kenya. I knew the country as a transit lounge and a stop over base on my way to and out of Europe. It was only after we got a three-month visitor's pass that I realised that Kenya was an Anglophone country. Fortunately, we were in transit. Soon, we would be in Europe, among friends.

I am Boniface Louis R Kuseremane. It has been long since anyone called me by my full name. The 'R' name cannot be spoken aloud. In the bustle and noises of the airport, I glance at Agnethe-mama, regal, greying, her diamond earrings dance, her nose is slightly raised, her forehead unlined. My mother, Agnethe, is a princess in transit. She leans lightly against Lune, who stands, one foot's heel touching the toes of the other, one arm raised and then drooping over her shoulder.

I met Lune on the funeral day of both her parents, royal diplomats who had died in an unfortunate road crash. She was then, as she is now, not of Earth. Then, she seemed to be hovering atop her parents' grave, deciding whether to join them, fly away or stay. I asked her to leave the *corps ballet* in France where she was studying – to stay with me, forever. She agreed and I gained a sibylline fiancée.

"*Chéri, que faisons-nous maintenant?*" What do we do now? Lune asks, clinging to my mother's hand. Her other arm curved into mine. Chi-Chi, my sister, looks up at me, expecting the right answer, her hand at her favourite spot, my waist band – a childhood affectation that has lingered into her twentieth year. Chi-Chi, in thought, still sucks on her two fingers.

"*Bu-bu*," Chi-Chi always calls me Bu-Bu. "*Bu-Bu, dans quel pays sommes-nous?*"

"Kenya," I tell her.

Chi-Chi is an instinctive contemplative. I once found her weeping and laughing, awed, as it turns out, by the wings of a monarch butterfly.

Low voiced, almost a whisper, the hint of a melody, my mother's voice. "*Bonbon, je me sens très fatiguée, où dormons-nous cette nuit?*"

Agnethe-mama was used to things falling into place before her feet touched the ground. Now she was tired. Now she wanted her bed immediately. Without thinking about it, we checked into a suite of the Nairobi Hilton. We were, after all going to be in this country for just a few days.

*   *   *

"Mama, such ugliness of style!" Lune's summation of Kenyan fashion, of Kenyan hotel architecture. Mama smiles and says nothing. She twists her sapphire bracelet, the signal that she agrees.

"Why do I see not see the soul of these people? Bonbon... are you sleeping?" Chi-Chi asks.

"Shh", I say.

Two days later, Agnethe-mama visited the jewellery shop downstairs. Not finding anything to suit her tastes, she concluded: "Their language and manner are not as sweet and gentle as ours."

She straightens her robes, eyes wide with the innocence of an unsubtle put-down.

"Mama!' I scold. The women giggle as do females who have received affirmation of their particular and unassailable advantage over other women.

*   *   *

A week has passed already. In the beginning of the second one, I am awakened by the feeling I had when I found my country embassy gates here locked and blocked. The feeling of a floor shifting beneath one's feet. There is no one in authority. The ambassador is in exile. Only a guard. Who should I speak to? A blank stare. I need to arrange our papers to go to Europe. A blank stare. A flag flutters in the courtyard. I do not recognise it. Then I do. It is my country's flag, someone installed it upside down. It flies at half-mast. An inadvertent act, I believe. Shifting sands: I am lost in this sea of English and I suspect that at 5,000 Kenyan shillings I have spent too much for a 30-kilometre taxi ride. Old friends have not returned phone calls.

The lines here are not reliable.

*   *   *

Lune is watching me, her long neck propped up by her hands. Her hair covers half her face. It is always a temptation to sweep it away from her eyes, a warm silk. When the tips of my fingers stroke her hair, the palms of my hand skim her face. Lune becomes still, drinking, feeling and tasting the stroking.

Soon, we will leave.

But now, I need to borrow a little money: US$5,000. It will be returned to the lender, of course, after things settle down. Agnethe, being a princess, knows that time solves all problems. Nevertheless she has ordered me to dispatch a telegram to sovereigns in exile, those who would be familiar with our quandary and could be depended on for empathy, cash assistance and even accommodation. The gratitude felt would extend generation unto generation.

Eight days later, Agnethe-mama sighs; a hiss through the gap of her front teeth. She asks, her French rolling off her tongue like an old scroll: "When are we leaving, Bonbon?"

A mother's ambush. I know what she really wants to know.

"Soon," I reply.

"Incidentally," she adds, folding Lune's lace scarf, "What of the response of our friends in exile… ah! Not yet… a matter of time," she says, answering herself.

"Agnethe-mama," I should have said, "We must leave this hotel… to save money."

It is simpler to be silent.

*　*　*

A guard with red-rimmed eyes in a dark blue uniform watches me counting out fifteen 1,000 Kenyan shilling notes. The eyes of the president on the notes blink with every sweep of my finger. The Indian lady in a pink sari with gold trim, the paint flaking off, leans over the counter, her eyes empty. My gold bracelet has already disappeared. Two days from this moment, while standing with Celeste on Kenyatta Avenue, where many of my people stand and seek news of home, or just stand and talk the language of home or hope that soon we will return home, I discover that 15,000 Kenya shillings is insufficient compensation for a 24-carat, customised gold and sapphire bracelet. Celeste knew of another jeweller who would pay me a hundred thousand for the bracelet.

I return to confront the Indian lady, she tells me to leave before I can speak. She dials a number and shouts, high-voiced, clear: "Police". I do not want trouble so I leave the jewellery shop, unable to speak, but not before I see her smile. Not before I hear her scold the guard with the red-rimmed eyes.

"Why you let *takataka* to come in, *nee*?"

Outside the shop, my hands are shaking. I have to remind myself to take the next step and the next step and the next step. My knees are light. I am unable to look into the eyes of those on the streets. What is my mind doing getting around the intricacies of a foreign currency? I have to get out with my family. Soon.

The newspaper on the streets, a vendor flywhisks dust fragments away. A small headline reads: "Refugees: Registration commences at the UNHCR."

The Kuseremanes are not refugees. They are visitors, tourists, people in transit, universal citizens with an affinity... well... to Europe.

"Kuseremane, Kuseremane, Kuseremane..." Unbeknown to me, one whisper had started gathering other whispers around it.

* * *

The Netherlands, the Belgians, the French, the British are processing visa applications. They have been processing them for three, four, five... nine days. At least they smile with their teeth as they process the visa applications. They process them until I see that they will be processed unto eternity, if only Agnethe, Chi-Chi, Lune and I could wait that long. There are other countries in the world.

Chi-Chi's ramblings yield an array of useless trivia:

In Nairobi, a woman can be called *Aunti* or *chilé*, a president called *Moi*, pronounced Moyi, a national anthem that is a prayer and 20 shillings is a *pao*.

"But Bu-Bu... So many faces... So many spirits gather here..."

We must leave soon.

* * *

The American embassy visa section woman has purple hair. Her voice evokes the grumbling of a he-toad which once lived in the marsh behind our family house in the country. One night, in the middle of its anthem, I had said; *"Ça suffit !"* Enough!

Roger led the gardeners in the hunt which choked the croak out of the toad. At dawn, Roger brought the severed head to me, encased in an old cigar case which he had wiped clean.

I cannot believe what this purple hair woman has asked of me.

"What?"

"Bank details... bank statement... how much money."

My eyes blink, lashes entangle. Could it be possible another human being can simply ask over the counter, casually and with certainty of response, for intimate details of another person's life?

I look around the room. Is it to someone else she addresses this question?

"And title deed. Proof of domicile in country of origin... And letter from employer."

Has she not looked at my passport in her hands?

"I'm not Kenyan."

She folds her papers, bangs them on the table and frowns as if I have wasted her time. She tosses my passport out of her little window into my hands that are outstretched, a supplication on an altar of disbelief.

"All applications made at source country... next!"

"Madame... my country... is..."

"Next!"

Woven in the seams of my exit are the faces in the line winding from the woman's desk, into the street. Children, women and men, faces lined with... hope? I must look at that woman again, that purveyor of hope. So I turn. I see a stately man, his beard grey. His face as dark as mine. He stoops over the desk – a posture of abnegation. So that is what I looked like to the people in the line. I want to shout to the woman; I am Boniface Kuseremane, a prince, a diplomat.

I stumble because it is here, in this embassy, that the fire-streaking spectre of the guns which brought down two presidents find their mark in my soul. Like the eminent-looking man in a pin-striped suit, I am now a beggar.

*   *   *

We have US$520 left. My head hurts. When night falls, my mind rolls and rings. I cannot sleep.

The pharmacist is appealing in her way, but wears an unfortunate weave that sits on her head like a mature thorn bush. Eeeh! The women of this land! I frown. The frown makes the girl jump when she sees me. She covers her mouth with both her hands and gasps. I smile. She recovers:

"Sema!"

"Yes, sank you. I not sleep for sree nights and I feel…" I plane my hands, rocking them against my head. She says nothing, turns around, counts out ten Piritons and seals the envelope: "Three, twice a day, 200 shillings."

These Kenyans and their shillings!

It is possible that tonight I will sleep. The thought makes me laugh. A thin woman wearing a red and black choker glances up at me, half-smiling. I smile back.

I cannot sleep. I have taken five of the white pills. Lune, beside me, in the large bed is also awake.

"*Qu'est-ce que c'est?* " What is it?

"*Rien.*" Nothing.

Silence. Her voice, tiny. "I am afraid."

I turn away from her, to my side. I raise my feet, curling them beneath my body. I too am afraid. In the morning, the white Hilton pillow beneath my head is wet with tears. They cannot be mine.

* * *

The sun in Nairobi in May is brutal in its rising. A rude glory. My heart longs to be eased into life with the clarion call of an African rooster. Our gentle sunrises, rolling hills. Two months have passed. A month ago, we left the hotel. I am ashamed to say we did not pay our bill. All we had with us was transferred into and carried out in laundry bags. We left the hotel at intervals of three hours. We also packed the hotel towels and sheets. It was Lune's idea. We had not brought our own. We left our suitcases behind. They are good for at least US$1,500. Agnethe-mama is sure the hotel will understand.

We moved into a single-roomed place with an outside toilet in River Road. I have told Agnethe-mama, Lune and Chi-Chi not to leave the room unless I am with them. Especially Chi-Chi.

"Bu-Bu, when are we leaving?"

Soon Agnethe-mama. Soon Lune. Soon Chi-Chi.

Chi-Chi has learned to say "*Tafadhali, naomba maji.*" She asks for water this way, there are shortages.

We must leave soon.

Every afternoon, a sudden wind runs up this street, lifting dust, and garbage and plastic bags and whispers.

Kuseremane, Kuseremane, Kuseremane.

I turn to see if anyone else hears my name.

Sometimes, I leave the room to walk the streets, for the sake of having a destination. I walk, therefore I am. I walk therefore I cannot see six expectant eyes waiting for me to pull out an aeroplane from my pocket.

Ah! But tonight! Tonight, Club Balafon. I am meeting a compatriot and friend, René Katilibana. We met as I stood on the edge of Kenyatta Avenue, reading a newspaper I had rented from the vendor for five Kenya shillings. Four years ago, René needed help with a sugar deal. I facilitated a meeting which proved lucrative for him. René made a million francs. He offered me 50,000 in gratitude. I declined. I had enjoyed humouring a friend. I am wearing the Hugo Boss mauves and the Hervé handkerchief. I am hopeful, a good feeling to invoke.

"*Où vas-tu, chéri ?*" Where are you going ? A ubiquitous question I live with.

I stretch out my arms, Lune flies into them as she always does. She wraps her arms around me. Her arms barely span my waist.

I tell her; "I am hopeful today. Very hopeful."

I still have not heard from the friends I have called. Every night, their silence whispers something my ears cannot take hold of. Deceptive murmurings. This country of leering masses – all eyes, hands and mouths, grasping and feeding off graciousness – invokes paranoia.

My friends will call as soon as they are able to. They will.

I realise this must be one of those places I have heard about; where international phone calls are intercepted and deals struck before the intended, initial recipient is reached.

* * *

A contact, Félicien, who always knows even what he does not know, tells me that a list of *génocidaires* has been compiled and it is possible a name has been included. *Kuseremane.* Spelled out by a demure man, an aide he had said he was.

Soon we will be gone. To Europe, where the wind's weight of whispers do not matter; where wind, and all its suggestions have been obliterated.

Even as she stays in the room, Chi-Chi leaves us more often than ever, a forefinger in her mouth. She has no filters. I worry that the soul of this place is soaking into her.

The city clock clicks above my head into the two a.m. position. Rain has seeped into my bones and become ice. My knees burn. The rainwater squelches in my feet. My Hugo Boss suit is ruined now, but I squeeze the water from the edges.

Club Balafon was a microcosm of home and the Zaïroise band was nostalgic and superior. The band slipped into a song called '*Chez Mama*'. The hearth of home. The women were beautiful and our laughter loud. It was good to taste good French cognac served in proper glasses. We lamented the fact that Kenyans are on the whole, so unchic.

And then René asked me where I was and what I was doing. I told him I needed his help, a loan. US$5,000, to be returned when things settle down back home. He listened and nodded and ordered for me a Kenyan beer named after an elephant. He turned to speak to Pierre who introduced him to Jean-Luc. I touched his shoulder to remind him of my request. He said in French: I will call you. He forgot to introduce me to Pierre and Jean-Luc. Two hours later, he said, in front of Pierre, Jean-Luc and Michel: "Refresh my memory, who are you?"

My heart threatens to pound a way out of my chest. Then the band dredges up an old anthem of anguish, which, once upon a time, had encapsulated all our desires. *Ingénues Francophones* in Paris, giddy with hope. This unexpected evocation of fragile, fleeting, longings, drives me into an abyss of remembering.

'*L'indépendance, ils l'ont obtenue/La table ronde, ils l'ont gagnée...*'

Indépendance Cha-cha, the voice of Joseph Kabasellé.

Then, we were, vicariously, members of Kabasellé 's '*Le Grand Kalle*'. All of us, for we were bursting with dreams encapsulated in a song.

Now, at Balafon, the exiles were silent, to accommodate the ghosts of saints:

Bolikango... Kasavubu... Lumumba... Kalondji... Tshombe...

I remember heady days in Paris; hair parted, like the statement we had become, horn-rimmed glasses worn solely for aesthetic purposes, dark-suited, black-tied, dark-skinned radicals moving in a cloud of enigmatic French colognes. In our minds and footsteps, always, the slow, slow, quick, quick slow, mambo to rumba, of Kabasellé's *Indépendance Cha-cha.*

"*L'indépendance, ils l'ont obtenue...*
La table ronde, ils l'ont gagnée..."

I dance at Club Balafon, my arms around a short girl who wears yellow braids. She is from Kenya and is of the opinion that 'Centro African' men are *soooo* good. And then the music stops. There can be no other footnote, so the band packs their musical tools, as quietly as we leave the small dance floor.

When I looked, René, Pierre, Jean-Luc, Michel and Emanuel were gone. Perhaps this was not their song.

"Which way did they go?" I ask the guard in black with red stripes on his shoulder. He shrugs. He says they entered into a blue Mercedes. Their driver had been waiting for them. He thinks they went to the Carnivore. It is raining as I walk back to River Road. Three fledglings are waiting for me, trusting that I shall return with regurgitated good news.

I am Boniface Kuseremane. Refresh my memory, who are you? There are places within, where a sigh can hide. It is cold and hard and smells of fear. In my throat something cries, "*hrgghghg*". I cannot breathe. And then I can. So I hum:

"Mhhhh... *L'indépendance, ils l'ont obtenue...*"

It is odd, the sounds that make a grown man weep.

*   *   *

I sleep and dream of whispers. They have crossed the borders and arrived in Nairobi. Like many passing snakes. *Kuseremane. Kuseremane. Kuseremane. Kuseremane. Kuseremane.*

But we left on the fifth day!

Now whenever I approach Kenyatta Avenue, they, my people, disperse. Or disappear into shops. Or avert their eyes. If I open a conversation, there is always a meeting that one is late for. Once on the street a woman started wailing like an old and tired train when she saw me. Her fingers extended, like the tip of a sure spear, finding its mark.

Kuseremane. Kuseremane. Kuseremane . Kuseremane. Kuseremane.
The whispers have found a human voice.

I can tell neither Agnethe-mama nor Chi-Chi nor Lune. I tell them to stay where they are; that the city is not safe.

Agnethe wants to know if the brother-monarchs-in-exile have sent their reply.

"Soon," I say.

One morning, in which the sun shone pink, I found that a certain sorrow had become a tenant of my body and weighed it down on the small blue safari bed, at the end of which my feet hang. The sun has come into the room but it hovers above my body and cannot pierce the shadow covering my life. A loud knock on the door, so loud the door shakes. I do not move so Lune glides to the door.

"*Reo ni Reo, ni siku ya maripo.* Sixi hundred ant sevente shirrings." Kenyans and their shillings! The proprietor scratches his distended belly. His fly is undone and the net briefs he wears peek through. I want to smile.

Lune floats to my side, looks down at me. I shut my eyes. From the door a strangely gentle, "I donti af all dey."

I open my eyes.

Lune slips her hand into my coat pocket. How did she know where to look? She gives him the money, smiling as only she can. The proprietor thaws. He counts shillings. Then he smiles, a beatific grin.

I have shut my eyes again.

And then a hand – large, soft, warm – strokes my face, my forehead. Silence, except for the buzzing of a blue fly. Agnethe-Mama is humming '*Sur le Pont d'Avignon*'. I used to fall asleep wondering how it was possible to dance on the Avignon bridge. Soon, we will know. When we leave.

I slept so deeply that when I woke up I thought I was at home in my bed and for a full minute I wondered why Roger had not come in with fresh orange juice, eggs and bacon, croissants and coffee. I wondered why mama was staring down at me, hands folded. Lune looks as if she has been crying. Her eyes are red-rimmed. She has become thin, the bones of her neck jut out. Her fingers are no longer manicured. There! Chi-Chi. Her face has disappeared into her eyes which are large and black and deep. I look back at Agnethe-mama and see then that her entire hair front is grey. When did this happen?

"We must register. As refugees. Tell UNHCR we are here."

Now I remember that we are in Kenya; we are leaving Kenya soon. Am I a refugee?

"You slept the sleep of the dead, *mon fils*." Agnethe said, lowering the veil from her head. If only she knew how prophetic her words were. Being a princess once married to her prince, she would have been more circumspect. I have woken up to find the world has shifted, moved, aged and I with it. Today I will try to obtain work. There cannot be too many here who have a PhD in Diplomacy or a Masters in Geophysics. The immigration offices will advise me. In four days we will have been here three and a half months.

The sun is gentle and warm. The rain has washed the ground. Kenyans are rushing in all directions. A street child accosts me. I frown. He runs away and pounces on an Indian lady. Everybody avoids the child and the lady, rushing to secret fates. Destiny. Who should I meet at the immigration office but Yves Fontaine, a former college mate. We had been at the Sorbonne together. He was studying art but dropped out in the third year. We were drawn together by one of life's ironies. He was so white, so short, and so high voiced. I was so tall, so black and deep voiced. We became acquainted rather than friendly because it was a popular event to have the two of us pose for photographs together. It did not bother me. It did not bother him.

"Yves!"

"Boni-papa". His name for me. Boni-papa. We kiss each other three times on either cheek.

"It is inevitable we meet again?"

"It is inevitable."

"What are you doing here?"

"A visa renewal... I am chief technician for the dam in the valley."

"Ah, you did engineering?"

Yves shrugs " Pfff. *Non*. It is not necessary here." The sound of a stamp hitting the desk unnecessarily hard. A voice.

"Whyves Fontana."

Yves changes his posture, his nose rises, he whose nose was always in the ground avoiding eyes so he would not be carried off by campus clowns.

"*Ouais?*" It is an arrogant *oui*. The type of *oui* Yves would never have tried at the Sorbonne

"Your resident visa."

Yves grabs his passport, swivels on his feet and exits. But first he winks at me.

"Next!" The voice shouts. I am next.

* * *

From outside the window of a travel agency, on Kaunda Street, a poster proclaims:

'Welcome to your own private wilderness'. At the bottom of the poster: 'Nature close at hand: Walking safaris available'. The picture in the foreground is that of a horse, a mountain and a tall, slender man wrapped in a red blanket, beads in his ears. It is all set within a watermark of the map of Kenya. I keep walking.

Beneath the steeple where the midday Angelus bells clang, I sit and watch the lunchtime prayer crowds dribble into the Minor Basilica. The crowds shimmer and weave behind my eyelids.

The immigration officer demanded papers. He would not listen to me. I told him about my PhD and he laughed out loud. He said:

"*Ati PhD. PhD gani? Wewe refugee, bwana!*"

He whispers that he is compelled by Section 3(f) of the immigration charter to report my illegal presence. He cracks his knuckles. 'Creak Crack.' He smiles quickly. Fortunately, all things are possible. The cost of silence is US$500. I have 3,000 shillings.

He took it all. But he returned 50 shillings for 'bus fare'.

"Eh, your family... where are they?"

"Gone," I say.

"*Si* I'll see you next week? Bring all your documents... eh. Write your address here." A black book. Under 'name' I write René Katilibana. Address, Club Balafon. He watches every stroke of my pen.

A resumption of knuckle cracking. His eyes deaden into a slant.

"To not return... is to ask for the police to find you." He turns his head away. He calls: "Next!"

I have used five shillings to buy small round green sweets from a mute street vendor. Good green sweets which calm hunger grumbles. A few more days and we will be leaving. I have resolved not to bother compiling a curriculum vitae.

I join the flow into the church, sitting at the back. Rhythm of prayer, intonation of priests; I sleep sitting before the altar of a God whose name I do not know.

Chi-Chi says: "They laugh at themselves... They are shy... they

hide in noise... but they are shy."
Who?
"Kenya people."
We must leave soon.

* * *

We woke up early, Agnethe, Chi-Chi, Lune and I, and walked to
Westlands, 45 minutes' walk away from our room just before River
Road. We reached the gates of the UNHCR bureau at ten a.m. We were
much too late because the lists of those who would be allowed entry
that day had been compiled. The rest of us would have to return the
next day. We did, at seven a.m. We were still too late because the lists
of those who would be allowed entry had already been compiled. We
returned at four a.m. But at two p.m. we discovered we were too late
because the lists of those who would be allowed in had already been
compiled. I decided to ask the guard at the gate, with long, black hair
and an earring, a genuine sapphire.
"How can list be compiled? We are here for sree days."
"New arrivals?" he asks.
"Yes?"
"A facilitation fee is needed to help those who are compiling
the list."
"Facilitation fee?"
"Yes. That's all."
"And what is zis facilitation fee?"
"US$200 per person."
"And if one... he does not have US$200?"
"Then unfortunately, the list is full."
"But the UN... Sir?"
He raises his brow.
I told Lune and Chi-Chi. They told Agnethe. Agnethe covered her
face and wailed. It is fortunate she wailed when a television crew
arrived. The guard saw the television crew and realised that the list
was not full. Five UN staffers wearing large blue badges appeared
from behind the gate and arranged us into orderly lines, shouting
commands here and commands there. Three desks materialised at the
head of the queue as did three people who transferred our names and
addresses into a large black book. After stamping our wrists we were

sent to another table to collect our Refugee Registration Numbers. Chi-Chi returned briefly from her spirit realm to say: "Is it not magical how so full a list becomes so empty in so short a time?"

*   *   *

"*Toa Kitambulisho!*" I know this to be a request for identification. A policeman, one of three, grunted to me. I shivered. I was standing outside the hotel building watching street vendors fight over plastic casings left behind by an inebriated hawker. I was smoking my fifth Sportsman cigarette in two hours.

"*Sina.*" I don't have an identity card.

"*Aya! Toa kitu kidogo*". I did not understand the code. Something small, what could it be? A cigarette. One each. It was a chilly evening. The cigarettes were slapped out of my hand. I placed my hand up and the second policeman said:

"Resisting arrest."

A fourth one appeared and the second policeman said:

"Illegal alien... resisting arrest."

They twisted my arm behind my back and, holding me by my waistband, the trouser crotch cutting into me, I was frog-marched across town. Some people on the street laughed loudly, pointing at the tall man with his trouser lines stuck between the cracks of his bottom.

"Please... please chef... I'll walk quietly." My hand is raised, palm up. "Please."

Someone, the third one I think, swipes my head with a club. In a sibilant growl.

"Attempted escape."

A litany of crimes.

"What's your name?"

"I... I..." Silence. Again, I try. "I... I... I..."

"Aaaaaaa... aaaaii... eee." It amuses them.

What is my name? I frown. What is my name?

I was once drinking a good espresso in a café in Breda, in the Netherlands, with three European business contacts. Gem dealers. We were sipping coffee at the end of a well-concluded deal. A squat African man wearing spectacles danced into the café. He wore a black suit, around his neck a grey scarf, in his hand a colourful and large bag, like a carpet bag. Outside it was cold. So easy to recall the feeling of well-being a hot espresso evokes in a small café where the light is muted and the music a gentle jazz and there is a knowing that outside it is cold and grey and windy.

The squat African man grinned like an ingratiating hound, twisting and distorting his face, raising his lips and from his throat a thin high sound would emerge: "Heee heee heee, heh heh heh."

Most of the café turned back to their coffees and conversations. One man in a group of three put out his foot. The squat African man stumbled, grabbed his back to him. Rearranged himself and said to the man: "Heee heee heee, heh heh heh."

He flapped his arm up and down. I wondered why, and then it dawned on me. He was simulating a monkey. He flapped his way to where I was, my acquaintances and I.

Sweat trickled down my spine. I think it was the heat in the café.

"What is your country of origin?" I ask him. Actually, I snarl the question at him and I am surprised by the rage in my voice.

He mumbles, his face staring at the floor. He lowers his bag, unzips it and pulls out ladies' intimate apparel designed and coloured in the manner of various African animals. Zebra, leopard, giraffe and colobus. There is a crocodile skin belt designed for the pleasure of particular sado-masochists. At the bottom of the bag a stack of posters and sealed magazines. Nature magazines? I think I see a mountain on one. I put out my free hand for one. It is not a mountain, it is an impressive arrangement of an equally impressive array of Black male genitalia. I let the magazine slide from my hand and he stoops to pick it up, wiping it against the sleeve of his black coat.

"Where are you from?" I ask in Dutch.

"Rotterdam."

"No, man... your origin?"

"Sierra Leone."

"Have you no shame?"

His head jerks up, his mouth opens and closes, his eyes meet mine for the first time. His eyes are wet. It is grating that a man should cry.

"Broda." he savours the word. "Broda... it's fine to see de eyes of anoda man... it is fine to see de eyes."

Though his Dutch is crude, he read sociology in Leeds and mastered it. He is quick to tell me this. He has six children. His wife Gemma is a beautiful woman. On a good day he makes 200 guilders, it is enough to supplement the Dutch state income and it helps sustain the illusions of good living for remnants of his family back home. He refuses to be a janitor, he tells me. To wear a uniform to clean a European toilet? No way. This is why he is running his own enterprise.

"I be a Business Mon."

"Have you no shame?"

"Wha do ma childs go?"

"You have a master's degree from a good University. Use it!"

Business man picks up his bags. He is laughing, so deeply, so low, a different voice. He laughs until he cries. He wipes his eyes.

"Oh mah broda... tank you for de laughing... tank you... you know... Africans we be overeducated fools. Dem papers are for to wipe our bottom. No one sees your knowing when you has no feets to stand in."

He laughs again, patting his bag, smiling in reminiscence.

"My broda for real him also in Italy. Bone doctor. Specialist. Best in class. Wha he do now? Him bring Nigeria woman for de prostitute." Business man chortles.

"Maybe he fix de bone when dem break."

I gave him 20 guilders. "For the children."

It was when Joop van Vuuren, the gem dealer, idly, conversationally asked me what the business man's name was that I remembered I had not asked and he had not told me.

In exile we lower our heads so that we do not see in the mirror of another's eyes, what we suspect: that our precarious existence rests entirely on the whim of another's tolerance of our presence. A phrase crawls into my mind; 'Psychic Oblation'. But what does it mean?

*   *   *

"What is your name?"

I can smell my name. It is the smell of salt and the musk of sweat. It is... surprise... surprise... remembered laughter and a woman calling me "*Chéri...*"

I want to say... I want to say Yves Fontaine. As Yves Fontaine I would not be a vagrant immigrant, a pariah. As Yves Fontaine I would be 'expatriate' and therefore desirable. As Yves Fontaine I do not need an identity card.

"I… I… My… I…" Silence.

The sibilant hoarseness of the Superintendent: "Unco-oparatif. Prejudising infestigesons."

* * *

Agnethe-mama saw it happen. She had just raised her shawl to uncover her face so that she could shout at me to bring her some paracetamol for her headache. At first she thought she was reliving an old tale. Three men had arrived for her husband. She crawled up the stairs, lying low lest she be seen. Lune told me mama had sat on the bed rocking to and fro and moaning a song and whispering incantations she alone knew words to. In the four days I was away, making an unscheduled call on the Kenyan Government, my mother's hair deepened from grey to white. We did not know that her blood pressure began its ascent that first day. Time, as she had always believed, would accomplish the rest.

It was at their station that the policemen found all manner of evidence in my pocket. All of which they liked and kept. After three days I was charged with 'loitering with intent'. At the crucial moment the proprietor turned up with my refugee registration card. My case was dismissed and I was charged to keep the peace.

Lune paid the proprietor with her engagement ring. Whatever he had obtained from the sale of the ring caused him to put an arm around me, call me brother and drag me into a bar where he bought me three beers. He said: "*Pole.*" Sorry.

He said we did not need to pay rent for three months. He wanted to know if we had any more jewellery to sell. I said no. He bought me another beer. He slides a note into my pocket before he leaves. A thousand shillings.

The UNCHR are shifting people out of Kenya, resettlement in third countries. Soon, it will be us. Agnethe-mama now wakes up in the night, tiptoes to my bed. When she sees it is me, she whispers: "*Mwami*", My Lord.

Sunday is a day in which we breathe a little easier in this place. There are fewer policemen and diffident laughter hiding in hearts' surfaces. It is simpler on Sunday to find our kind, my people in an African exile. We visit churches. Agnethe, Chi-Chi always go in. Lune sometimes joins them and sometimes joins me. I am usually sitting beneath a tree, on a stone bench, walking the perimeter wall and, if it is raining, sitting at the back of the church watching people struggling for words and rituals indicating allegiance to a God whose face they do not know. The hope peddlers become rich in a short while, singing, "Cheeeeessus!". Even the devastated destitute will tithe to commodified gods, sure that in the theatrics of frothing messengers, hope is being doled out. Investing in an eternal future? I do not have a coin to spare. Not now, maybe later, when all is quiet and normal, I will evaluate the idea of a Banker God created in the fearful image of man.

After church, to Agnethe's delight she found Maria. Maria and Agnethe used to shop in Paris together. Once they by-passed France and landed in Haiti. Maria's brother was an associate of Baby Doc's wife. They returned home unrepentant to their husbands and children; they treated their daring with the insouciance it deserved. It was fortunate Agnethe met Maria here because it was from Maria we learned that the Canadian government had opened its doors to those of us in Kenya.

Chi-Chi emerged from her sanctuary to say "Bu-Bu… patterns of life… somewhere lines meet, *non*?"

A statement of fact. I am hopeful.

Maria was living well. Her brother had settled in Kenya years ago. His wife was from Kenya. Maria was with them.

"Is Alphonse with you?"

Agnethe, being a princess, had been unaware that after the two presidents had died, one never asked one's compatriots where so and so was. If one did not see so and so, one did not ask until the party spoken to volunteered the information of whereabouts. Alphonse was not with Maria. That was all Maria said. Even if Agnethe was a princess, because she was a princess in exile, she read nuances. She kept her mouth shut, and looked to the ground.

Maria's brother, Professor George, and his wife and his two children were going to the Nairobi Animal Orphanage. Did we want to visit animals with them?

"Oh yes. Unfortunately… as you imagine… money is…"

"Don't worry, it is my pleasure," Professor George said.

So we went to meet animals. We met Langata the leopard who did not want people staring at him while he slept. Langata felt the intimacy of sleep is sacred and should be recognised as such.

Apparently, he told Chi-Chi this. So Chi-Chi told us. Professor George glared at her. Chi-Chi refused to look at the animals. Lune said animals lived behind fences to protect them from humans. Agnethe-mama was surprised to find that her dead prince did indeed look like a lion. She and Maria stared at Simba who stared back at them as if he knew he was being compared to a prince and the prince was increasingly found to be lacking.

"Why the name 'Professor George'?" I said to Professor George.

"They find it hard to say Georges Nsibiriwa."

'They' were his wife's people. I sensed the 'and' so I said: "And?"

Professor George walked quietly, he pointed out the difference between a Thomson's gazelle and a Grant's gazelle. Something about white posteriors. At a putrid pool, in which sluggish algae brewed a gross green soup, in between withered reeds and a hapless hyacinth, Professor George sighed and smiled. A dead branch, half-submerged, floated on the surface of the pool.

"Ah. Here we are... look... in the place you find yourself... in the time... camouflage!" A glorious pronouncement.

Surreptitious glance. Professor George then picks up a twig and throws it into the pond. From within the depths, what had been the dead branch twisted up a surge of power. Its jaws snapped the twig in two; a white underbelly displayed before transforming itself once again into a dead branch, half-submerged, floating on the surface of the pool.

"Ah! See! Camouflage... place dictates form, *mon ami*. Always."

I start to tell him about the police.

Professor George nods. "Yes... yes... it is the time." And he asks if I have heard word from Augustine, a mutual friend who lives in Copenhagen.

"Augustine has changed address, it seems."

Professor George says: "Yes... it is the time."

I need to ask something. "You have heard about the list?"

He looks up at me, his face a question. "*Les génocidaires?* Ah yes... but I pay no attention."

The relief of affirmation. A name's good can be invoked again. So I tell him, "Ah! It's difficult, *mon ami*, and... Agnethe-mama doesn't know."

"Know what?"

"Our name is on the list."

With the same agility that the crocodile used to become a log again, Professor George pulls away from the fence. He wipes his hand, the one I had shaken, against his shirt. He steps away, one step at a time, then he turns around and trots, like a donkey, shouting, looking over his shoulder at me:

"Maria! We leave... now!"

The first lesson of exile – camouflage. When is a log... not a log? When a name is not a name.

* * *

On Monday we were outside the UNHCR at four-thirty a.m. We hope that the list is not full. It is not. Instead there is a handwritten sign leading to an office of many windows which says 'Relocations, Resettlement'. At the front, behind the glass, are three men and two women with blue badges that say UNHCR. They have papers in front of them. Behind them, four men, a distance away. They watch us all, their bodies still. I straighten my coat and stand a little taller.

We are divided into two groups, men and women: the women are at the front. The women are divided into three groups: Young Girls, Young Women, Old Women.

At the desks, where there is a desk sign which says 'Records Clerk', they write out names and ages, previous occupation and country of origin and of course, the RRN – refugee registration number. Those who do not have an RRN must leave, obtain one in room 2004 and return after two weeks.

Later, flash! And a little pop. Our faces are engraved on a piece of paper. Passport photograph. Movement signified, we are leaving.

"Next," the photographer says. Defiance of absence. Photographer, do you see us at all? Inarticulation as defence. Let it pass. Soon, we will be gone from this place.

The Young Women are commanded to hand over babies to the Old Women. Young Girls and Young Women are taken into another room. A medical examination, we are informed. We are told to wait outside the office block, the gate. Perhaps we will be examined another day.

* * *

Agnethe-mama and I are sitting on a grassy patch opposite a petrol station. Agnethe bites at her lips. Then she tugs my sleeve.

"Bonbon... do other monarchs-in-exile live in Canada?

"Perhaps."

Chi-Chi and Lune emerge, holding hands. It is two hours later and the sun hovers, ready to sink into darkness. They do not look at either of us. We walk back, silently. Chi-hi has hooked her hand into my waistband. Lune glides ahead of us all, her stride is high, the balance of her body undisturbed. A purple *matatu*, its music 'thump thumping', slows down and a tout points north with a hand gesture. I decline. It speeds off in a series of 'thump thumps'. Agnethe frowns. We walk in silence. Long after the *matatu* has gone, Agnethe says, her face serene again:

"The reason they are like that... these Kenyans... is because they do not know the cow dance."

*   *   *

When Lune dipped her hand into my coat pocket while I slept and took out 800 shillings, returning in an hour with a long mirror, I should have listened to the signal from the landscape.

Chi-Chi used Lune's mirror to cut her hair. She cut it as if she were hacking a dress. She stepped on and kicked her shorn locks. Agnethe-mama covered her mouth, she said nothing as if she understood something. For Lune, the mirror evokes memories of ballet technique. She executes all her movements with her legs rotated outward. Agnethe-mama looks to the mirror so she can turn away and not look.

Two weeks later, I kick the mirror down. I smash it with my fists. They bleed. Agnethe screamed once, covering her mouth. Silence enters our room. Silence smells of the Jevanjee Garden roasted Kenchic chicken; one pack feeds a frugal family of four for three days.

On the third day, I find Lune looking down at me.

"It was mine. It was mine." She smiles suddenly and I am afraid.

From across the room, Agnethe-mama; "Ah Bonbon... still... no word from the kings in exile?"

The anger with which the rain launches itself upon this land, the thunder which causes floors to creak sparks a strange foreboding in me. That night, while we were eating cold beans and maize dinner, Lune pushed her plate aside, looked at me, a gentle, graceful crane, her hands fluttering closed, a smile in her eyes.

"*Chéri*, we can leave soon, but it depends on a certain... co-operation."

"Co-operation?"

"A condition from the medical examination."

Agnethe looks away. Chi-Chi clutches her body, staving off in her way something she is afraid of.

"How do we co-operate?" I am afraid to know.

"By agreeing to be examined," she laughs, high, dry, cough-laugh. "...examined by the officials at their homes for a night."

"I see." I don't. Silence. Agnethe is rocking herself to and fro. She is moaning a song. I know the tune. It is from the song new widows sing when the body of their dead spouse is laid on a bier.

Annals of war decree that conquest of landscapes is incomplete unless the vanquished's women are 'taken'. Where war is crudest, the women are discarded afterwards for their men to find. Living etchings of emasculation. Lune has not finished yet. I sense I am being taunted for my ineffectuality by this woman who would be my wife.

"Now... it has been discussed with family, it is not a question of being forced."

A recitation. I lower my head. The incongruity of tears. A persistent mosquito buzzes near my ear. The food on my plate is old. Lune leaves the table, pushing back her chair, she places her feet in a parallel arrangement, one in front of the other, the heel of a foot in line with the toes of the other. Her right arm extends in front of her body, and the left is slightly bent and raised. She moves the weight of her body over the left foot and bends the left knee. She raises her right heel, pointing the toe. Her body is bent toward the extended knee. She holds the pose and says; "*Pointe tendue!*"

Conscious now, I read the gesture. She will perform as she must, on this stage. I can only watch.

"No."

Now Chi-Chi raises her head, like a beautiful cat. I know the look; tentative hope, tendrils reaching out and into life. Lune closes her feet, the heel of one now touching the toes of the other; she pushes up from the floor and jumps, her legs straight, feet together and pointed. She lands and bows before me. Then she cracks and cries, crumbling on the floor.

Outside, the window, the drone of traffic which never stops and the cackle of drunkards. Creeping up the window a man's voice singing:

"*Chupa na debe. Mbili kwa shilling tano. Chupa na debe.*"
Bottle and tin, two for five shillings, bottle and tin, Kenyans and their shillings.

*   *   *

I stood on the balcony staring at the traffic, counting every red car I could see. Nine so far. Behind me, Agnethe approached. In front of my face she dangled her wedding ring.
"Sell it."
"No."
She let it fall at my feet.
We used the money to leave the room on River Road. We went to a one-roomed cottage with a separate kitchen and an outside toilet. It was in Hurlingham, the property of a former government secretary, Mr Wamathi, a drinking acquaintance of the proprietor. I observed that his gardening manners were undeveloped; he had subdivided his quarter-acre plot, cutting down old African olive trees and uprooting the largest bougainvillea I had ever seen, on the day we arrived. He was going to put up a block of flats. Mr Wamathi was delirious with glee about selling the trees to the 'City Canjo' for 15,000 shillings. His laughter was deep, rounded and certain with happiness.
He laughed and I felt hope joining us.
Agnethe started tending a small vegetable patch. Her eyes gleamed when the carrot tops showed. Lune made forays into a nearby mall, an eye-fest of possibilities satiating her heart, extending her wants. Chi-Chi, over the fence, befriended an Ethiopian resident who introduced her to his handsome brother, Matteo.
The day Chi-Chi met Matteo she slipped her hand into my waistband, looking up at me she said: "He... can... see..."
Every day I tried to contact home, seeking cash for four air tickets on a refugee pass. Word appeared in dribs and drabs. Detail gleaned from conversations heard, strangers approached and newspapers slyly read.
The bank? Burned down. The money? Missing from the safes. And once, the sound of a name accused, accursed: *Kuseremane.*
But hadn't we left on the fifth day?
The day flows on. I sit in different cafés, telling the waiters that I am waiting for a friend. Thirty minutes in some cafes. In the more

confident ones, the ones which are sure of their identity, I can wait for a full hour before I make a face, glance at my non-existent watch, frown as if tardy friends are a source of annoyance and I exit.

Whispers had floated over the land of hills and nestled in valleys and refused to leave, had in fact given birth to volleys of sound. Now tales had been added of a most zealous servant instructed by an heir to sluice stains.

"Ah! Roger. *Mon oncle…*"

Excoriating women's wombs, crushing foetal skulls, following the instructions of a prince.

They said.

Today I woke up as early as the ones who walk to work manoeuvring the shadows of dawn, crochet-covered radios against ears, in pockets, or tied to bicycle saddles. Sometimes music, rumba. And in the dawn dark I can forget where I am and let others' footsteps show me the way. I hear Franklin Bukaka's plea, pouring out of so many radios, tenderly carried in so many ways. *'Aye! Afrika, O! Afrika…'*

I return from so many journeys like this and one day, I find Agnethe-mama lying on her back in her vegetable patch. At first I think she is soaking up the sun. Then I remember Agnethe-mama never let the sun touch her skin. An African princess, melanin management was an important event of toilette. I lean over her body. Then, head against her chest, I cannot hear a heartbeat.

I carry my mother and run along the road. The evening traffic courses past. Nairobi accommodates. Room for idiosyncrasies. So to those who pass by, it is not strange that a tall, tall man should carry a slender woman in his arms.

At the first hospital. "My mother… she is not heart beating… help."

"Kshs 12,000 deposit, Sir."

"But my mother…"

"Try Kenyatta."

At Kenyatta, they want a 4,000-shilling deposit and I will still have to wait, one of about 300 people waiting for two doctors to see them. I do not have 4,000 shillings.

"Where can I go?"

"*Enda* Coptic." Go to the Copts.

"*Tafadhali…* please, where are they?"

"Ngong Rd."
'How far....?"
"Next!"

*   *   *

Agnethe sighs, opens her eyes and asks:
"Have the monarchs-in-exile sent our reply yet, Bonbon?"
"Soon... mama."
She had suffered a mild stroke.
I return to the cottage to pack a bag for mama. Exile blurs lines.
So a son, such as I, can handle a mother's underwear. Agnethe-mama
told Chi-Chi once, in my hearing, that all in a woman may fall apart,
may become unmatched, but never her underwear. I place sets of
underwear for Agnethe; black, brown and lacy purple.

*   *   *

Kuseremane, Kuseremane, Kuseremane.
It seems that the whispers have infringed upon the place where
my tears hide. I cannot stop bawling, snivelling like a lost ghoul. My
shoulders bounce with a life of their own. Lune watches me, her eyes
veiled in a red, feral glow.
At six p.m. I rejoin a river of workers returning to so many homes.
To be one of many, is to be, anyway, if only for a moment. The sun
is setting and has seared into the sky a golden trail; it has the look of
a machete wound bleeding yellow light. It is an incongruous time to
remember Roger's blackened hands.
Agnethe has taken to sitting in the garden rocking her body, to
and fro, to and fro. She does not hum. But sometimes, in between the
fro and to, she asks:
"Have the brother sovereigns sent a letter?"
"Soon."
At night, Chi-Chi shakes me awake, again. My pillow is soaked,
my face wet. Not my tears.
The next morning, I left the cottage before sunrise. I have learned
of hidden places; covered spaces which the invisible inhabit. The
Nairobi Arboretum. The monkeys claim my attention as do the
frenzied moaning of emptied people calling out to frightened gods

for succour. Now, it starts to rain. I walk rapidly, then start to jog, the mud splattering my already stained coat. The other hidden place is through the open doors of a Catholic Church. Hard wooden benches, pews upon which a man may kneel, cover his eyes and sleep or cry unheeded before the presence that is also an absence.

*   *   *

My return coincides with Mr Wamathi's winding his way into the house. He rocks on his feet:

"Habe new yearghh." 'Year' ends with a burp and belch.

"Happy New Year." It is July and cold and time is relative.

Agnethe outside, uncovered. Rocking to and fro. She clutches thin arms about herself, shivering.

"Aiiee, mama!" I lean down to lift her up.

"Bonbon, il fait froid, oui?' It is cold.

"Lune? Chi-Chi? Lune?" Why is mama sitting out in the night alone?

"Où est Lune... Chi-Chi, mama?"

Agnethe stares up at the sky, from my arms.

"Bonbon... il fait froid." Two anorexic streams glide down, past high cheekbones and nestle at the corner of her mouth. She looks up and into my eyes. The resolute eyes of an ancient crone. Now... now the cold's tendrils insinuate themselves, searing horror in my heart.

Chi-Chi returned first. She stumbled through the door, her body shuddering. She is wiping her hand up and down her body, ferociously, as if wiping away something foul only she can sense.

"Everything has a pattern... Bu-Bu, *non*?" She gives me the folded papers.

Three *laisses-passer*. Tickets to rapture. Let them pass. It favours Agnethe, Boniface and Chi-Chi Kuseremane.

I am not there.

I watch from afar, the ceiling I think, as the tall man tears the papers to shreds. I am curious about the weeping woman with shorn hair crawling on the ground gathering the fragments to her chest. I frown when I see the tall, dark man lift his hand up, right up and bring it crashing into the back of the girl who falls to the floor, lies flat on her belly and stops crying. She is staring into herself where no one else can reach her. A sound at the door. The tall, tall man walks up to his fiancée. Who bows low, the end of a performance. She too has a clutch of papers in her hand. The tall man sniffs the girl as if he were a dog and he bites her on the cheek, the one upon which another man's cologne lingers. Where the teeth marks are, the skin has broken. Drops of blood. Lune laughs.

"We can leave any time now."

"*Putaine!*"

She giggles. "But I shall live, *chéri*... we shall live... we shall live well."

Agnethe-mama heaves herself up from the bed and brushes her long white hair. I return to the body of the tall, black man whose arms are hanging against his side, his head bowed. He sees that Lune's feet are close, the heel of one touching the toes of the other. She slowly raises hands over her head, paper clutched in the right, she rounds her arms slightly, *en couronne* – in a crown.

Paper fragments, a mosaic on the floor. I stoop, the better to stare at them. I pick up my sister. She is so still. But then she asks, eyes wide with wanting to know: "Bu-Bu... there's a pattern in everything. *Oui?*"

"*Oui*, Ché-Ché." A childhood name, slips easily out of my mouth. Now when she smiles, it reaches her eyes. She touches my face with her hand.

* * *

That night, or more accurately, the next morning, it was three a.m., Agnethe went to the bathroom outside. Returning to the room she had stepped into and slid in a puddle. She stepped out again to clean her feet and then she screamed and screamed and screamed.

"Ahh! Ahh! Ahhhee!"

She points at the rag upon which she has wiped her feet. It is covered in fresh blood. She points into the room, at the floor. I return to look. Lune is now awake. Lights in the main house are switched on and Mr Wamathi appears on the doorway, a knobkerrie in his hand.

"Where, where?" he shouts.

The neighbourhood dogs have started to howl. The sky is clear and lit up by a crescent moon. I remember all this because I looked up as I carried my bleeding sister, my Chi-Chi-Ché-Ché into Mr Wamathi's car, cushioned by towels and blankets while her blood poured out.

At the hospital emergency wing where we had been admitted

quickly, a tribute to Mr Wamathi's threats, I watched the splayed legs of my sister, raised and stirruped. My sister, led to and stripped bare in the wilderness of lives altered when two presidents were shot to the ground from the sky. I remember a blow bestowed on a back by a defenceless brother-prince.

How can a blow be unswung?

A doctor and a nurse struggle to bring to premature birth a child we did not know existed. Chi-Chi's eyes are closed. Her face still. When she left us I felt a tug on my waistband as in days of life and her body lost its shimmer, as if a light within had gone off for good. She left with her baby.

The child's head was between her legs. A boy or girl, only the head was visible and one arm, small fists slightly open as if beckoning. Skin like cream coffee. The offspring of African exiles. An enigma solved. The Ethiopians had abruptly disappeared from the radar of our lives and Chi-Chi had said nothing. The dying child of African exiles in an African land. I stroked the baby's wet head. Did baby come to lure Chi-Chi away? A word shimmers into my heart: fratricide. I douse it with the coldness of my blood. I am shivering. A distant voice... mine.

"Leave them... leave the children." Keep them together... the way they are.

Landscape speaks. The gesture of an incomplete birth. Of what have we to be afraid? Metamorphoses of being. There must be another way to live.

"Is there a priest?" Even the faithless need a ritual to purge them of the unassailable scent of mystery.

'What shall we do with the body?"

A body... my sister. When did a pool of blood become this... absence? They let me cover her face after I have kissed her eyes shut.

Vain gesture.

Agnethe and Lune are outside, waiting. Islands in their hope. I open the door to let them in, gesturing with my hand. They step into the room and I step out. I let the door close behind me and try to block out the screams emanating from within. Staccato screams. Screams in a crescendo and then a crushing moan.

A nurse offers forms to be filled in.

"Nairobi City Mortuary"

It will cost 8,000 Kenyan shillings to rent space for Chi-Chi. I do not have 8,000 shillings. It's okay, the nurse says. I can pay it tomorrow at the mortuary.

Eeeh! Kenyans and their shillings.

Nurse turns: "*Pole.*" Sorry.

But Mr Wamathi makes an arrangement with his wives, and they find 35,000 shillings for Agnethe.

Is this it?

Later. After all the bluster of being... this? A body in a box, commended to the soil.

A brother's gesture: 12 torches alight in a sister's cheap coffin. Chi-Chi and her Nameless One will see in the dark.

* * *

It is a challenge to match paper fragments so that they match just right. It is fortunate there are words on the paper, it makes it easier. Three *laisses-passer*. Chi-Chi's is complete, almost new.

Lune has returned to my bed. Agnethe's resumed her rocking, which has accelerated in both speed and volume. Her eyes are brown and a ceaseless rivulet of tears drips onto her open palm. But she smiles at us, Lune and I, and does not utter a word. Sometimes her eyes have a film of white over them as if she had become a medium, in constant communion with the dead. Sometimes I imagine that they look at me with reproach. I look to the ground; the quest for patterns.

I have lost the feeling of sleep. I will not touch Lune nor can I let her touch me. It is the ghost of another man's cologne which lingers in my dreams and haunts my heart. I am bleeding in new places. But we are leaving.

"Bu-Bu, everything has a pattern, *non*?"

We will be leaving for Canada on Saturday night.

* * *

Agnethe shocked us by dying on Friday morning in my arms as I entered the gates of the Coptic hospital. On the streets, as before, no one found it strange, the idea of a tall, tall man carrying a slender woman in his arms. A pattern had been established, a specific madness accommodated.

When Agnethe-mama left, the energy of her exit made me

stumble.

"Ah! Bonbon! Ah!" she says.

At the Coptic gate, "*Mwami!*"

She leaves with such force, her head is thrown back against my arms.

Agnethe-mama.

The Copts cannot wrench her from my arms. They let me sit in their office and rock my mother to and fro, to and fro. I am humming a song. It is the melody of '*Sur le pont d'Avignon*" where we shall dance.

At the cottage, old bags with few belongings are packed. On the bed, a manila bag with Agnethe's clothes, the bag she was packing when her body crumbled to the ground.

"*Où est maman?*" Lune asks. Where is mama?

I stretch out my arms and she lifts her hand to her long silk hair and draws it away from her face. She rushes into my arms and burrows her face into my shoulder.

"Forgive me."

We do what we can to live. Even the man whose cologne stayed on her face. I have no absolution to give. So I tell her instead that Agnethe has just died. And when Lune drops to the ground like a shattered rock, I slap her awake, harder than necessary on the cheek upon which another man's cologne had strayed and stayed. She does not move, but her eyes are open. Arms above her head, hair over her face.

She smirks. "I'm leaving. I am living."

She grabs my arm, a woman haunted by the desire for tomorrow where all good is possible. "I am leaving."

"*Ma mère... Lune-chérie.*"

Lune covers her ears, shuts her eyes.

For the most fleeting of moments, I enter into her choice. To slough the skin of the past off. To become another life form. I look around the room. Agnethe-mama's slippers by the bed. What traces have they left on the surface of the earth? The gossip of landscape. It is getting clear. I stoop low and kiss Lune on her forehead. In the pattern of things, there is a place in which the body of a princess may rest. Isn't there?

A Coptic priest, a Coptic doctor, Lune and I, Mr and Mrs Wamathi – the sum total of those gathered around Agnethe-mama. Lune's airplane bags are over her shoulders, her plane ticket in her purse. In four hours' time she will be in a plane taking her to the Canada of her dreams. We forgot grave-diggers must be paid, their spades attached to Kenya shillings. So I will cover my mother's grave myself, when the others are gone.

*　*　*

A plane departs from Nairobi. Kenya Airways to London. From London, Air Canada to Ottawa.

I have been laughing for an hour now. True, the laughter is interspersed with hot, sour, incessant streams of tears. Squatting on my mother's grave. The unseen now obvious.

Life peering out of lives. Life calling life to dance. Life, the voyeur.

I will start dancing now.

"L'indépendance, ils l'ont obtenue/ La table ronde, ils l'ont gagnée..."

"Mhhhh...Mhhhh...Mhh...Mhh...Mhhhh"

"L'indépendance, ils l'ont obtenue..."

Kabasellé laughs.

Who can allay the summon of life to life? The inexorable attraction for fire. The soul knows its keeper. Inexorable place, space and pace. I see. I see.

There!

Life aflame in a fire-gold sun. And dust restoring matter to ash. The ceaseless ardour for life now requited:

"Mhhhh... Mhhhh... Mhh... Mhh... Mhhhh."

"L'indépendance, ils l'ont obtenue/ La table ronde, ils l'ont gagnée..."

"Cha-cha-cha!"

Thus began the first day of my second life.

*　*　*

One day, a letter trudged to Kenya from Canada. Its first line is:

"Chéri, please, let me know the date of your arrival."

A tall, tall man straightens the lapels of a fading Hugo Boss coat. He cradles a shovel, listening to the sighing sentences of dust fragments filling a new grave. In his heart, an old phrase bubbles to the fore:

Soon.

Another week, another letter: "...when is your flight arriving?"

And another the week after that, and the next, until a year has gone and then six months more.

I have joined the sentinels of the cemetery; an assorted collection of life's creatures, through which life gazes at life. Devoted dogs, gypsy cats, two birds which perch over certain graves, a hundred unobtrusive trees and of course, spirits caught between worlds. Living gargoyles guarding entry points through which humans pass, dreaming in the day about shy, wise, night shadows with which conversations broken off at dawn can resume.

The discovery of listening...

Catching landscape in its surreptitious gestures – patterns which point to meaning...

Waiting for the return of a name set ablaze when fire made dust out of two presidents' bodies...

I live in the silence-scope and perform the rituals of return, for life. Where I am, the bereaved know they will find, if they visit, that the reminder of their beloved's existence – the grave – is safe, that life watches and leaves signs on tombs; mostly flowers, sometimes trees.

I prefer trees.

Soon now, the wind-borne whispers will fall silent.

Yvonne Adhiambo Owuor is a Kenyan writer. She has recently been working on a novel, provisionally titled *A Season of Dust and Memory*. 'Weight of Whispers' was first published in *Kwani?* in 2003.

Seventh Street Alchemy

Brian Chikwava – winner of the 2004 Caine Prize

B y five am most of Harare's struggling inhabitants are out of their hovels. They are on their way to innumerable places to waylay the dollars they so desperately need to stave hunger off their doorsteps. Trains and commuter omnibuses burst with exploitable human material. Its excess finds its way onto bicycles, or simply self-propels, tilling earth with bare frost-bitten feet all the way to the city centre or industrial areas.

The modes of transport are diverse, poverty the trendsetter. Like a colony of hungry ants, it crawls over the multitudes scattered along the city roads, ravaging all etches of dignity that only a few years back stood resilient. Threadbare resignation is concealed underneath threadbare shirts, together with socks and underpants that resemble a ruthless termite job. In spite of poverty's glorious march into every household, the will to be dignified by underpants and socks remains intact.

Activities in the city centre tend towards the paranormal. A voodoo economy flourishes as daylight dwindles: fruit and vegetable vendors slash their prices by half and still fail to sell. The following morning the same material is carted back onto the streets, selling at higher than the previous day's peak rates. In some undertakings the enthusiasm to participate is expressed in wads of notes; in some, simple primitive violence – or the threat of its use – is common currency. As the idea of ensuring that your demands are backed up by violence is fast gaining hold among the city's prowlers, business carried out in pin-striped suits is fleeing the city centre, ill-equipped to deal with the proliferation of scavenger tactics. Pigeons too have joined the new street entrepreneurs: they relieve themselves on pedestrians when least expected and never alight on the same street corner for more than two days in a row.

Even the supposedly civilised well-to-do section of the population, a pitiful lot typified by their indefatigable amiability, now finds itself anchored down by a State whose methods of governance involve incessant roguery. Instead of facing up to their circumstances with a modicum of honour, they weekly hurl themselves into churches to petition a disinterested God to subvert the laws of the universe in their favour.

At the corner of Samora Machel Avenue and Seventh Street, in a flat whose bedroom is adorned with two newspaper cuttings of the President, lives a 52-year-old quasi-prostitute with 37 teeth and a pair of six-inch heeled perspex platform shoes. It has been decades since she realised that, armed with a vagina and a will to survive, destitution could never lay claim to her. With these weapons of destruction she has continued to fortify her liberty against poverty and society. Fiso is her name and like a lot of the city's inhabitants she has conjured that death is mere spin, nobody ever really dies.

On the night a street kid got knocked down by a car it was a tranquil hour. A discerning ear would have been able to hear two flies fornicating several metres away. But to Anna Shava, a civil servant, soaked to the bone with matrimonial distress, the flies would have had to be inside her nose to get her attention. Her tearful departure from home after another scuffle with her husband set in motion a violent symphony of events. Security guards who scurried off the streets for safety could not have imagined that an exasperated spouse in a car vibrating to the frenzied rhythms of her anguished footwork could beget such upheaval.

Right in the middle of the lane, at the corner of Samora Machel Avenue and Seventh Street, a street kid staggers from left to right, struggling to tear himself out of a stupor acquired by sniffing glue all day. The car devours the tarmac, and in a screech of tyres the corner is gobbled up together with the small figure endeavouring to grasp reality. Sheet metal grudgingly gives in to a dent, bones snap, glass shatters. The kid never had a chance. His soul's departure is punctuated by one final baritone fart relinquishing life. Protruding out of the kid's back pocket is a tube of Z68 glue.

A couple of blocks from the scene, blue lights flashed from a police car while two officers shared the delicate task of trying to convince a grouchy young musician to part with some of his dollars for having gone though red traffic lights.

"You've been having a good time. That's no problem. But you

must understand we also need something to keep us happy while doing our rounds," one of the officers said with a well-drilled, venal smile before continuing. "Since you are a musician we know you can't afford much, Stix, but if you could just make us happy with a couple of Nando's takeaways..."

Anna, realising that they were not going to pay her any attention without some effort on her part, marched over to the officers. "Will you please come to my help, haven't you seen what happened?" she said, donning that look of nefarious servitude that she often inspired on the faces of applicants at the immigration office. She knew better than anybody that being nice to people in authority could render purchasable otherwise priceless rights, and simplify one's life.

"We are off duty now. Madam, call Central Police Station," one of the officers yodelled over. Returning to her car and periodically glancing over her shoulder in disbelief, she saw the offending driver stick out of his window a clenched handful of notes to pacify the vultures that had taken positions around his throttled freedom. His liberties resuscitated, he sped off in his scarlet ramshackle car.

Two days before, Anna, no less fed up with her errant husband, had followed him to the city's most popular rhumba club. She had found him leaning against the bar, with men she did not recognise. They talked at the top of their voices in the dim smudged lighting. Her husband, who had been tapping his foot to the sound of loud Congolese music, recoiled at the sight of her. Befuddled, he grappled with the embarrassment of having been tracked down to a night-club crawling with prostitutes. And then there was the thought of his mates saying that his balls had long been liberated from him and safely deposited in his wife's bra. His impulse was to thump her thoroughly, but lacking essential practice, he could not lift a finger.

"What do you want?" he asked, icily.

"Buy me a drink too," she brushed the question aside.

He stared at Anna as she grinned. Outrage lay not far beneath such grins – experience had schooled him. Reluctantly he turned to the bar to order her a Coke, struggling to affect an air of ascendancy in the eyes of his peers. He tossed a 500-dollar note at the bartender, as if oblivious to his wife's presence.

Half an hour later when Anna visited the ladies' toilet, transgression would catch up with her husband. There a lady with greying hair, standing with what looked like a couple of prostitutes, cut short her conversation to remark innocently, "Be careful with that man. He's a problem when it comes to paying up. Ask these girls. Make sure he pays you before you do anything or he will make excuses like, 'I didn't think you were that kind of girl'."

Anna was transfixed, hoping – pretending – that the words were directed at someone else.

"You could always grab his cellphone, you know," the woman added kindly.

That woman was Fiso who, at the time Anna ran into a street kid, was engrossed in the common ritual of massaging her dementia. Having spent a whole day struggling to sell vegetables – a relatively new engagement imposed on her by the autumn of her street life – she was exhausted and was not bothered by the screeching tyres down the road. It did not occur to her that what had registered in her ears was an incident precipitated by her well-meaning advice.

Beside her, sharing her bed, lay her daughter Sue, a 26-year-old flea-market vendor. In the midst of her mother's furious campaign against a pair of rogue mosquitoes, which relentlessly circled their heads before attacking, Sue came to the tired realisation that in spite of all the years on the streets, her mother still had undepleted stocks of a compulsive disorder from her youthful days.

In the sooty darkness her mother blindly clapped, hoping to deal one or both of them a fatal blow. Precision however remained in inverse proportion to determination. The mosquitoes circled, mother waited, her desire to snuff out a life inflated. They would dive, she would clap. Sound and futility reigned supreme. At last, jumping off the bed, Fiso switched on the light. A minute later one of the mosquitoes, squashed by a sandal, was a smudge of blood on the President's face, but Fiso could not be bothered to make good the insignia of her patriotism. A few months before, she would have wiped the blood away. But the novelty of affecting patriotic sentiment in the hope of dreaming herself out of prostitution to the level of First Lady had long worn off.

The following morning Sue switched on her miniature radio, to be confronted by the continuously recycled maxims of State propaganda, which ranged from the importance of being a sovereign nation to defending the gains of independence in the face of a 'neo-colonialist onslaught'. Leaning against the sink, she failed to grasp the value of the messages to her life. She gulped her tea and went to the Union Avenue flea-market. There, among other vendors slugging it out for survival, she could at least learn where to get the next bag of sugar or cooking oil.

On the same Saturday afternoon that marked the climax to Anna's marital woes, Stix, a struggling, young jazz pianist, had a call from his friend, Shamiso, inviting him to an impromptu dinner at Mvura Restaurant. Her friends and elements of her 'tribe', as she liked to refer to her cousins, were to be part of the company. With only the prospect of being part of a nondescript crowd at a glum, low-key music festival in the Harare Gardens, Stix committed himself to Shamiso's plans. At 7.30 p.m. he made his way to the restaurant. By midnight he had made a pathetic retreat to his flat, having shared part of his meagre income with two police officers fortunate enough to witness him driving through red lights. From his flat he had called Shamiso, and threatened to cremate her for inviting him to a restaurant where they would be saddled with a bill of over $15,000 each. That it was a restaurant with 'melted mars bar' on its dessert menu wickedly swelled his appetite for arson.

"So don't say you have not been warned about Mvura Restaurant," Stix said to Fiso the day after the incident. "If, however, out of curiosity you decide to go there, your experience will approximate to something like this; you get there, the car park is full of cars with diplomatic registration plates and there is not even space to open the car doors. At this point a security guard..." Stix pauses to light his cigarette, "...will run like a demon to find your parking space – but since you don't own a car, Fiso, you won't experience that bit."

"So you're not going to take me there?" Fiso asks, but Stix ignores her and continues.

"You may be at a table where you sit back to back with the Japanese ambassador, and you will be confronted by a waiter wielding a menu without prices. By the end of the evening you will be sorry. Never assume that such restaurants price their food reasonably!"

Fiso listened, thinking what a curious person Stix was, and well aware that save for living in the same dilapidated block of flats, they did not have much in common. The nice restaurants, elitist concerts and well-dressed friends existed only in the stories that Stix told her on their doorsteps on sluggish afternoons. They were just another spectral reality that Stix was fond of invoking. And after an hour or two of reciprocal balderdash, one of them would just stand up and walk into his or her flat, leaving the other to wean themselves from that hallucinogenic indulgence.

Defining one's relationship with the world demands daily renegotiating one's existence. So far-reaching are the consequences of neglecting exigencies imposed by this, that those unwilling or unable to participate eventually find themselves trapped in a parallel universe, the existence of which is not officially recognised. These are the people who never die, Sue and her mother being a quintessential sample. Sue has no birth certificate because her mother does not have one. Officially they were never born and so will never die. For how do authorities issue a death certificate when there is no birth certificate?

Several other official declarations only perfect the parallel existence of most of Harare's residents. Officially basic food commodities are affordable because prices are State-controlled. Officially no one starves because there is plenty of food on supermarket shelves. And if it is not there, it is officially somewhere, being hoarded by Enemies of the State. With all its innumerable benefits who would not want to exist in this other world spawned by the authorities – where your situation does not daily remind you what a liability your mouth and stomach are. It was therefore towards this official existence that Sue and her mother strove. Fed up with galloping food prices in their parallel universe, they took a chance and tried to take the leap into official existence.

It was an ordinary Monday morning when mother and daughter walked to the Central Registry offices hoping to get birth certificates, metal IDs and, eventually, passports. Sue had been told she could make a good income buying things from South Africa and selling them at the flea markets. But because the benefit of her deathless existence did not also confer upon her freedom of movement across national boundaries, she needed a passport. Fiso had decided to assist her daughter and get herself a passport too. Little did they know that they would find the door out of their parallel existence shut, and bolted.

By mid-afternoon Fiso was on her doorstep relating the events of the morning to Stix. Back in her humble flat, she felt better having spent half a day surrounded by the smell of dust, apathy and defeat.

Such were the Central Registry offices: an assemblage of Portakabins that had outlived its lifespan a dozen times over. With people enduring never-ending queues, just to have their dignity thrown out of rickety windows by sadistic officials, inevitably a refugee camp ambience prevailed.

"If your mother and father are dead and you do not have their birth certificates, then there is nothing that I can do," the man in office number 28 had said, his fat fist thumping the desk. He wore a blue and yellow striped tie that dug painfully into his fat neck, accentuating the degradation of his torn collar.

"But what am I supposed to do?" Fiso asked, exasperated.

"Woman, just do as I say. I need one of your parents' birth or death certificates to process your application. You are wasting my time. You never listen. What's wrong with you people?"

"Aaaah you are useless! Every morning you tell your wife that you are going to work when all you do is frustrate people!" Fiso stormed out of the office. Having learnt the false nature of authority and law from the streets, she was certain that he was her only obstacle. Men, she knew, could have the most perverse idiosyncrasies and at least one vice. In her experience, doctors, lawyers and the most genteel of politicians could gleefully discard their masks to become the most brutal perverts. It was a male trait, an official trait, and it accounted for her failure to acquire the papers she and her daughter needed.

Fiso's parents had died long back in deep rural Zhombe where peasant life had confined them to a radius of less than a hundred kilometres, and where an innate suspicion of anything involving paperwork was nurtured. Back in the Forties, stories of people having their names changed by authorities horrified semi-literate peasants such as Fiso's parents, who swore they would never have anything to do with the wicked authorities of that era.

"We were told to go to office number 28, but there was no one there. After about 40 minutes, we went back to the office that had referred us, but there was no one there either. Returning to office number 28, and seeking help from an official who was strolling past we were told, 'Look? Can't you see that jacket? It means he is not far away. Wait for him.' So we waited – for three hours – only to be told to bring one of my parents' death or birth certificates."

"Civil servants are like that, Fiso. They all have two jobs you know," Stix said, mildly. Fiso was being too naive for a seasoned sex purveyor, he thought.

"Look: a Japanese firm is making big money generating electricity out of sewage waste. All you have to do to bring your electricity bill down is shit a lot!" Stix, his eyes on the newspaper, was trying to steer the conversation in another direction.

That afternoon, it was Fiso who disappeared into her flat first, inexplicably regretting that she had let Stix have sex with her a couple of months before. They had been drunk, and she had found herself naked and collapsing onto Stix's bed, his fiendish shaft plumbing her hard-wearing orifice.

"Ey, you! That's not a good starting point!" was her only protest, and she cursed the alcohol that still swirled inside her head.

"If you'd been a virgin, Fiso, I would have washed my penis with milk, just for you," Stix said after contenting himself. Fiso ignored the remark. More incensed with herself than with Stix, she simply decided to sleep over the anger in the hope that it would go.

In Harare, vegetable vendors can yield useful connections. After Fiso and Sue had failed to get their papers, a woman at the Central Registry was brought to the attention of Fiso by a fellow vendor. This woman, a relative, could assist her to get any form of ID for a fee. Because the vendor and her relative went to the same church, she suggested that this would be the ideal place to introduce Fiso.

Less than a hundred metres from the church building, a man of Fiso's age stood by a corner selling single cigarettes and bananas. Fiso, sensing her increasingly disagreeable nerves, sought to calm them down with a cigarette.

"Sekuru," she addressed the man. "How much are your cigarettes?"

"I'm not your Sekuru. Harare does not have any Sekurus. They are all in the rural areas. If you desire a Sekuru then make one for yourself out of cardboard."

"How much are your cigarettes?" she asked again, avoiding the contentious term.

"Fifteen dollars."

She quietly retrieved three brand new five-dollar coins from her purse, handed them over and picked a Madison Red from among the many on display. Contentedly lighting the cigarette and avoiding eye contact, she heard the man ask, "What time is it?"

"If you need a watch why don't you make yourself one out of cardboard?" she retorted, and walked away, victorious.

With what panache does fate deliver the person of a harlot into a church building? Cockroaches appear through the cracks in the walls and wave their antennae in response to an almost primeval call. The priest, beneath his holy regalia, shudders, aware of the relative paleness of his cloistered virtues in the face of a salvation cobbled together on street corners. Against the tide of attrition of the human condition, what man of cloth can offer a soul a better salvation than the sheer dogged will to live? In the priest's mind, however, such sentiments only manifested themselves in vague notions of jealousy and contempt.

As Fiso strolled in carefree, the holy man recoiled, the congregation's heads turned, and the devil chuckled. A Dynamos Football Club T-shirt, fluorescent green mini-skirt and six-inch-high perspex platform shoes upstaged the holy word.

Destructive distillation is a process by which a substance is subjected to a high temperature with the absence of oxygen so that it simply degenerates into its several constituent substances without burning. After her silent confessions and having received the body and blood of Christ, Mrs Shava found herself subjected to destructive distillation by an ogling congregation. Like anyone being introduced to a person of dubious appearance on sanctified premises, she degenerated into her constituent attributes of self-righteousness and caution.

"The church services are short here – or was I late?" Fiso remarked after being introduced to Mrs Shava by her vending friend.

"No, we're not like those Pentecostal churches, we're less fanatical," Mrs Shava said, unable to look Fiso straight in the eyes and bewildered, her mind whirling with an elliptical sense of déjà vu as she wondered where they had met before. She could also feel the stares of the congregation pecking at her back from several metres away. She resented them but neither did she like talking to Fiso.

However, having listened to her plight, she agreed to help her out. Everyone had to live, after all.

"Eeeek, ahh, it's complicated," Mrs Shava moaned, a technique that she had perfected after helping several people. "It's no easy task," she continued, wanting to justify her fee.

"I understand, but I must have a birth certificate. And my daughter cannot get one if I don't have one – and she needs a passport."

"I can try, but it is a risk, I could lose my job." Mrs Shava assumed a pious expression. Fiso knew that it was time to tie up her end of the deal. She understood what Mrs Shava meant when she said that success depended on a number of factors; Fiso knew it meant one thing only.

"I understand it's a big risk, but I intend to reward you for your efforts." Fiso glanced at her friend for clues but the vendor's face was as blank as a hospital wall. "I don't know what you would like, but I'll leave you to decide, my sister."

Mrs Shava's lips parted dispassionately to reveal her white teeth. "Okay, call me on Wednesday and I will see if it's all right for you to come to my office. People at my workplace will be on strike but I can't risk my job. If it's okay, I'll give you the forms, you fill them in and I'll take them back. And don't forget my fee: $15,000!" She smiled for the first time and turned to walk away.

"Uhh, huh, your phone number at work?" Fiso stammered.

"Nyasha will give it to you, I have to see someone else," came the reply.

Fiso turned to Nyasha, and they smiled at each other.

Contentedly walking off, Mrs Shava could not have guessed that in less than a minute she would be caressed by more poltergeistic echoes of a recent past. She was walking out of the church premises when Stix stopped by to pick up Fiso in his scarlet car. A shiver descended Mrs Anna Shava's spine as she recalled the night she killed the street kid. Fiso's face, though, defiantly refused to fit into the jigsaw puzzle, and Mrs Shava could only watch in bewilderment as the old harlot jumped into the car, which rattled away, accelerating sideways like a crab.

In a mortuary at the central hospital, clad in a blue suit, white shirt, and seemingly asphyxiated by the tie around its neck, lies a slightly overweight corpse. A cellphone is still stuck in one of the pockets and when it rings for the third time, it is answered by a being who, after years as a mortuary cleaner, picking his wages from its floor, has become indifferent to death.

"Hullo, Central Hospital," he answers.

"Hullo, I'm looking for my husband, is that his phone you are using? Who are you? Is he there?"

"Aah, I don't know, but unless this is the body of a thief who stole the phone from your husband, your husband is dead. The police shot him in the head. They said he was rioting in the city centre."

The previous night Anna's husband had not returned from work. That he would have come to such a rough end, no one could have guessed. But being in the insurance industry he would have appreciated it, if he'd been told that the value of his life was equivalent to twenty condoms, and in all likelihood would not have contested such a settlement being awarded to Anna. His death, though, had consequences that reverberated through to Fiso, because on the day she was supposed to call Mrs Shava, grief and its attendant ceremonies had already claimed her. Then on Monday, having spent all night at Piri-Piri, the city's sleaziest night-club, Fiso decided to take the Central Registry juggernaut head-on. Suffering from a hangover, and caring not about consequences, she went straight to the Registrar General's office.

"I've been trying to get a birth certificate and can't, because your staff members only care about getting bribes!" The Registrar General's secretary remained calm, picked up the phone and dialled, but before she had uttered a word, the RG had emerged from his office. Being a constant target of ridicule by the press as the man heading one of the most inefficient and corrupt government departments, he was very sensitive to criticism.

"How can I help you, lady?" he demanded impatiently.

"I only need a birth certificate, but your staff is only interested in frustrating people into paying bribes!"

"Those are serious allegations." The RG's interest lay only in smothering public objections.

"All I want is a birth certificate, Sir. My womanhood is an old rag. I've paid the price of living. Please do not waste my time, I'm too old for that."

The Registrar nearly had convulsions. "Sandra, call security!" he ordered.

The secretary fumbled, dropped her pen and spilt her coffee.

"Your staff members all want bribes. I come to you and all you do is get rid of me! I suppose you want a bribe too? What else can you do apart from sitting on your empty scrotum all day?"

In a little less than half an hour Fiso was behind police bars facing a charge of public disorder. The police, however, soon found their case stalling. There was no way of establishing her identity because she did not have an ID. After she told the investigating officer that she was trying to get just such an ID when she was arrested, the officer called the Registrar General who offered to quickly process an ID, if it was in the interest of facilitating the course of justice. That afternoon

Fiso was bundled into the back of a Landrover Defender in handcuffs and taken to the Central Registry to make an application for an ID. Predictably she refused to co-operate, so she was later thrown back into the vehicle and taken to the police cells.

Two days went by, each bringing a new face into the cell she shared with six other women. On the third day two cellmates went for trial and never returned – either freed or sent to Chikurubi Maximum. Then a new inmate arrived. From her appearance one would have surmised that she was a teenager picked up from the vicinity of a village while herding goats. It was her carefree disposition that won her the attention of the other cellmates.

"What are those for?" she asked, looking up at the left corner of the cell. The officer who had brought her had hardly locked up.

No immediate answer came until the officer had disappeared.

"Those are CCTV cameras," someone finally answered her.

"What is CCTV?" the girl asked again.

"Closed Circuit Television. It enables them to watch us from their offices all the time on one of their televisions."

Later in the evening when another new face was brought in, the goat-herd girl asked the officer: "Is it true that you have a TV and that you are watching us?"

The officer just continued with his duty of locking up the gate as if nothing had been said. Goat-girl was, however, unfazed.

"I think you people are going to be in trouble when the President finds out that you are wasting TVs on criminals. I'm sure he would like to be watched on TVs too. Or watch himself so that he's safe from assassins and perverts?"

After five days in the cell Fiso was cautioned and released without charge – not even that of failing to produce an ID. The investigating officer, seeing that the case was going nowhere, had managed to convince his superior to release her with just one statement: "It's only an ageing whore."

Brian Chikwava is a Zimbabwean writer whose first novel *Harare North* has just been published by Jonathan Cape, to widespread acclaim. He currently lives in England. 'Seventh Street Alchemy' appeared first in *Writing Still*, Weaver Press, Harare 2003.

Monday Morning

Segun Afolabi – winner of the 2005 Caine Prize

"I want to piss," the boy said in their language. He held his mother's hand as they walked, but his feet skipped to and fro.

The mother scanned the area, but she could not find a place for her son; there were too many people beside the trees, talking, laughing. "Take the boy to the edge of the water so he can piss," she said to her husband.

The boy and his father hurried towards the lake. The father was glad to see that his son could find relief. They did not notice how people looked at them with their mouths turned down. Sour. The eyes narrowed to slits.

The breeze blew and the ducks and swans floated past. The boy was afraid of them, but his need to evacuate was urgent. Steam rose from the stream that emerged from him as it fell into the water, and he marvelled at this. There was so much that was new to understand here. He had seen on the television at the hostel how water could become hard like glass, but the lake was not like that. The swans pushed their powerful legs and the ducks dipped their heads beneath the surface. The father held on to his son's jacket so he would not fall in. There were bits of flotsam at the bank where the water rippled. The boy looked away, a little disgusted, and gazed into the clean centre of the lake.

They came away from the water's edge and joined the mother and the boy's brother, and the boy from the hostel whose name was Emmanuel. The father looked at his wife and the children. He wondered at how beautiful everything was in this place with the whispering leaves and the green grass like a perfect carpet and the people so fine in their Sunday clothes. He thought, With God's help it can surely happen. You are distraught, time passes and you are away from it. You can begin to reflect and observe. It was difficult now, to think of artillery and soldiers and flies feeding on abandoned corpses.

The little one laughed and said, "My piss made fire in the water," but the mother slapped his shoulder. "It's enough," she said.

They joined the people on the path as they strolled through Regent's Park. Only Emmanuel wanted to walk on the grass, but he did not dare because the father had forbidden it. He was a feeble man, Emmanuel thought, so timid in this new place, but his sons were different. Bolder. They had already grasped some of the new language.

A breeze gathered up leaves and pushed the crowds along. A clump of clouds dragged across the sun. People pulled their clothes tight around themselves. The mother adjusted her scarf so there were no spaces for the wind to enter. She reached across with her good hand to secure her husband's baseball cap. The area in the centre of his scalp was smooth as marble and he felt the cold easily. She shoved her mittened hand back into her coat pocket and watched the children as they drifted further away. After a moment she called, "Ernesto, come away from there," to her eldest boy. They had wandered towards an area where people were playing a game with a ball and a piece of wood, and she did not want there to be any trouble. Not today, not on Sunday. She knew his friend was leading him to places he would not have ventured on his own and she feared there would be difficulties ahead. The youngest boy skipped between them: the mother and father, his brother, the brother's best friend. He was her little one and she would hold on to him for as long as she was able.

The father sighed and called out to his children. The cold was setting in again and their walk was too leisurely. They would have to return to the hostel before the sun disappeared. He called to Ernesto, "Come, it is time for us to go. Tell your brother." It would take at least half an hour for them to walk back.

Ernesto turned to Alfredo, the little one, who giggled as they played a game among themselves – *Kill the Baron*. The friend, Emmanuel, ran about them, laughing, until the father called again. "We are going back, you hear me? Ernesto, hold your brother! We go!"

Emmanuel looked at him. He did not speak their language, but regardless, he thought the father was a stupid man – too fat, too quiet. The boy had lost his own father in his own country in his own village home. Now he could only see the faults in them, the other fathers, their weaknesses, what they did not understand. He had thought his father remarkable at one time, but with his own eyes, he had seen him cut down, destroyed. They were all foolish and clumsy, despite their arrogance. He would never become such a man himself.

The children trailed behind the mother and father as they navigated paths that took them to the edge of the park. As they came to the road, Alfredo raced to walk beside his mother, and a passing car screeched to a halt.

"Keep 'em off the road, for fuck's sake!" the driver shouted.

The mother held her son, and the father looked at the driver without expression. The boy had not run across the road, but the driver had made an assumption, and now he did not want to lose face.

"Keep the buggers off the road!" he shouted again and shook his head when there was no response.

The father glanced at the mother who only shrugged and held her boy. Emmanuel turned to the driver and waved an apology on behalf of the father, grinning to indicate he understood. But he did not know the appropriate words, and the driver failed to notice or did not care for the gesture. He sped away, complaining bitterly to his passenger. There were people on the pavement who had seen the incident, who now stood watching. The mother and father did not understand the signs and gestures the people used. They did not feel the indignation. They knew only that they were scrutinized and they were sometimes puzzled by this, but they were not overwhelmed.

They trudged along the main road near the building where the books lived. The huge railway stations teemed with people. In the mornings sometimes, the father walked in the vicinity of the stations. At night the area was forsaken, but during the day, workers emerged in their thousands. Often he looked at them and it seemed impossible that he could ever be a part of this. The people moved as if they were all one river, and they flowed and they did not stop.

"Here is the one!" Alfredo squealed to Emmanuel when they came to the glass hotel. "I will live here!"

"You're crazy," Emmanuel said to the boy. But he could not fail to notice the guests in the lobby, the people sipping tea in the café, the lights warm, the atmosphere congenial.

The sign at the building read Hotel Excelsior, but this was not a hotel. The orange carpet was threadbare, the linen was stained with the memory of previous guests, the rooms sang with the clamour of too many people. When they had arrived, the mother knew it was not a place to become used to. They had their room, the four of them, and it was enough: the bed, the two narrow cots. There was warmth even though the smell of the damp walls never left them. They could not block out the chatter and groans of other occupants. In the mornings the boys feasted on hot breakfasts in the basement dining room where there was a strange hum of silence as people ate. They were gathering strength after years of turmoil in other places. This was the best part of the day.

As they approached the hostel the sky was already turning even though it was still afternoon. Men and women walked up and down the road, but they did not have a destination. They glanced at the family with eyes like angry wounds. A woman knelt on the pavement with her head upturned, swaying, and when the family passed, Alfredo could see that she was dazed. The mother cupped her hand against his face so he could no longer look at her. Another man guided a woman in a miniskirt hurriedly by the elbow. He was shouting at her. He crossed the road so he would not have to meet the family and then re-crossed it after they had passed. Every day they saw these people, the lost ones, who seemed to hurt for the things they were looking for but could not find. The mother wondered sometimes, Have they never been young like my boys? Where does innocence flee? She wanted to be away from this place, away from the Excelsior. She wanted her family's new life to begin.

The father had begun to work. He could not wait for any bureaucratic decision when there were people who relied on him for food and shelter, for simple things: his mother, his sister and her family, his wife's people. It had begun easily enough. A man at the hostel had told him there was work on a construction site in the south of the city. They did not ask for your papers there, he said. It was a way to help yourself, and if it ended, well, there were other places to work. It was important not to be defeated, he warned, even though you were disregarding the rules. The man had been an architect in his own country, but now he did the slightest thing in order to help himself. He was ebullient, and when the father looked at him and listened, he was filled with hope.

Four of them journeyed from the Excelsior to the building site in the south. Every day they took their breakfast early and joined the people who became a river on their way to work. The job was not complex, but one could easily become disheartened by the cold and the routine. The father dreamed of the day when he could return to his own occupation, to the kitchen where he handled meat and

150

vegetables and the spices he loved so much. He had not touched any ingredients for many months now and sometimes he was afraid he would forget what he had learned. But already it was ingrained in him and he could not lose it, this knowledge, but he did not realise it yet.

He moved building materials from one place to another, and when they needed a group of men to complete a task, he became essential. But he did not know the English words. Most of the others did, but there was no one from his country here. Sometimes they would slowly explain to him the more difficult tasks, and every day, it seemed, the work became more intricate. The father moved his head so they would think he had understood, but he did not understand one word. He began to sense that words were not necessary; he could learn by observation and then repeat what he saw. In his own country he had not been an expressive man. Even as a child he had only used words when absolutely necessary. People often thought he was mute or he was from another country or his mind was dull. But all of that did not matter; he had learned to cook and he had discovered the love of a woman who did not need him to be someone he was not.

The woman touched the man at the meat of his shoulder and when he felt her, his body relaxed. It was not like coming home when they returned to the Excelsior; the strangeness of the place and the noise of the people there discomfited them. A woman was crying behind the door of the room opposite theirs and they wondered, Has she received some terrible news? Will she be returning to the place she has run away from? The hostel was a sanctuary, but it was also a place of sadness for many, and often it was only the children who gave it life.

"Tomorrow," Emmanuel said to Ernesto, and he touched him lightly on the back and then ran to another floor of the building where he and his mother lived. He did not acknowledge the father and the mother. Alfredo turned so he could say goodbye to his brother's friend, but the boy was already gone. He could not understand how Emmanuel had spent the day with them and could then disappear without a word to him. He too wanted a friend, like the children he had played with in his own country.

"Why does he go so fast?" he asked. He felt the smart of Emmanuel's abruptness in his chest.

"He has his own mother," the woman replied. "Maybe he feels bad for leaving her all day."

Alfredo thought about this, about how he would feel if he had left his mother alone in the hostel, and he understood his mother's words. He said, "We will... When... When will we go to the glass hotel?" The words emerged so quickly from him in his agitation they fell over one another.

"We will go one day," the father said as they entered the room. "You will see." It was his secret plan to take his family to the hotel one weekend, when a person could eat a two-course meal at a special rate. He would work on the construction site until he was able to pay for the things they needed, for the money he would send back home. Then they would all spend the day at the glass hotel. Perhaps there would be a swimming pool for his sons. He touched the boy on his head so he would not feel bad about the place they were in, the unfriendly Emmanuel, the people they had left behind.

At night the father dreamed he was in his old kitchen, with the heat and flies and the cries of chickens outside. The mother flew to the beach on their coast and noticed how the moonlight glinted off the waves. Ernesto dreamed of his school friends before they had been forced to scatter, before the fighting had begun. Only Alfredo remained in the new country in his sleep; he was in the glass hotel, in his own room.

The night moved on and then other dreams began, the ones of violence, of rebels and rape and cutlasses arcing through the air. The father began to shudder in his sleep, and then his wife woke. When she realised it was happening again, she reached out and petted him with her club, her smooth paw. She did not know she was doing so; it was instinctive. Ordinarily she concealed the damaged limb. They had severed her hand in the conflict, but she could still feel the life of her fingers as she comforted her man. In the new country, they had offered her a place to go, for the trauma, but she did not want that; she had her boys, her quiet husband. There was a way to function in the world when the world was devastating, everyone careless of each other and of themselves. She knew that now. She had been forced to learn. In a moment her husband was still again and she lay back with her eyes closed, but she did not sleep.

It was a simple thing, a misunderstanding, that caused the confusion the next day. The father travelled to the south to the construction site. By the end of the week he was certain he would have earned enough to send several packages home. But mid-morning the inspectors arrived.

A foreman took him aside. "You have the correct papers?" he asked.

The father looked at him and nodded. He did not understand what was happening. He continued to work as the inspectors spread out. He could not see the other men from the hostel, but he would look for them soon so they could take their lunch break. It was colder today, but he had been working so hard he had been forced to remove his sweater.

They came up the scaffolding, two men with their briefcases and the foreman beside them. From the corner of his eye the father could see the men from the hostel across the road. They were waving to him frantically. The inspectors approached another man and talked quietly with him. They stood where the ladder was situated. The father could not see another way down. He thought, I am in a place I do not understand. The ground is vanishing beneath me. He pictured the boy, his youngest, and he pushed away the fear. He ran to the edge of the platform and grasped the metal pole. He did not look down in case he faltered. He held the pole and allowed gravity to carry him, not knowing how it would end. His hands were cut and then his torso rubbed hard against the brackets. He remembered his sweater lying on the platform. He did not have the strength to manage a smooth descent and his shirt and trousers were torn, but he did not notice these things. His mind was on his folly. If he were caught he would jeopardise everything for his family and he did not know if he could live with himself after that.

He hobbled across the road where the others were waiting for him. He looked behind once to see if he was being followed, but no one was there.

"That was close," one of the men called and clapped him on the shoulder. They all laughed, but he did not laugh with them. He only smiled. His hands and arms were throbbing and the blood had soiled his clothes.

When the mother saw him, she became very quiet. No one spoke. They only fussed around the wounds and the blood and the torn clothing. Their fear was like a fist of bread they could not swallow. The youngest boy began to cry. His brother, Ernesto, was frightened, but excited too. He went and told his friend what had happened. It was like an adventure for him; the blood, the daring escape.

Emmanuel smirked; it only confirmed his thoughts. He said, "He is stupid, your father." He could not help himself. It was the way he was now. Angry. He did not know that he blamed his own father for dying, that it was a wound inside himself that would fail to heal.

Ernesto looked at him, disbelieving, and then he walked away. It was too much, the injured father, the distraught brother, the hurtful friend. Too many things were happening at once and he could make no sense of it. When he returned to the room, his father was resting on his brother's cot. He saw him there, a man who was not slender, a man who hardly spoke. He began to wonder about Emmanuel's words. Was there any truth in them? A seed had been planted now.

Alfredo sat beside his father looking from the carpet to his mother, back to the carpet again. The mother's silence disturbed them all. She tidied the room and soaked the soiled clothes in the bath and seemed not to care about what had happened. Even the father eyed her cautiously, but he did not speak.

"God will help us," the father whispered, so that only the youngest heard.

The boy remained silent. At length he asked, "Where is God, Papa?"

The father sighed and looked at his son. "He is in the room. He is here with us. All around." He lifted his arms and waved his fat fingers to illustrate.

The boy looked around the room, but he did not understand. Ernesto followed his gaze, but he did not know what they were looking at.

"You are a chef, you are not a labourer!" the mother shouted. "You cannot cook with your hands torn like this! Do you understand?" She had gone from silence to blind rage in an instant. She shook her fist, but held the arm where her hand had been severed tight against her stomach. She did not care if other people heard through the thin walls. She was tired of holding everything in. "How can we make a new life if you cannot work because you are injured? Did you think what would happen if they caught you with no papers, what would happen to us, the boys? We cannot go back to that place where they are killing us! Soon they will allow us to stay and you can do whatever job you like. But still you cannot wait! You are ready to risk everything."

The boys looked from their wounded father to their mother as she stood over him. They took in the damp walls, the orange carpet with the kink by the bathroom door, the window that overlooked the street where the girls walked at night and people roared sometimes in their misery.

"I am going to see Emmanuel," Alfredo said after no one had

spoken in minutes. He closed the door quietly and ran along the corridor and down the stairs. He did not stop running when he came to the street or to the busy road where the cars and buses clamoured. A tall man, wrapped in a soiled duvet, strode along the street peering into rubbish bins. Shrieking. Alfredo continued to run. He mingled with people as they waited for permission to cross the road. A woman moved away from him as if he were a street urchin. When he reached the other side he began to run again. He did not look behind for fear of seeing his father or his mother or anyone from the hostel. He ran and ran until he arrived at the hotel and when he was through its glass doors he stood still and breathed deeply.

He said he had been going to see Emmanuel, but ten minutes later, the friend knocked at the door looking for Ernesto. All the anger in the room vanished. They searched the lounge where the television was, and the breakfast room, and the reception, but they could not find him. No one had seen him disappear. The mother was shaking now and the other son was mute with anxiety.

"We must look outside. Alfredo!" the father called. "He cannot go far from here. Where can he go? Alfredo!" He was bellowing now. He was not aware of the strength of his own voice. Ernesto looked at him, his eyes wide with trepidation.

The man at the reception desk said the staff would scour the hostel to ensure Alfredo was not hiding anywhere. "Where could a little boy go?" he asked.

Emmanuel thought suddenly he knew where he was. He said in English, "Maybe he goes to the hotel," and he pointed.

They did not know the boy was already in the elevator of the glass hotel, rising above the street, looking out at the city they had recently arrived in. There seemed to be nothing between him and the world outside except a thin sheet of glass. When he peered down at the retreating traffic he found he was not afraid. He came out on the top floor and approached the long corridor. He began to try the handles of all the rooms he passed. He was looking for his own room, but he knew he needed a key. He did not know whom to ask. A man opened a door he had tried and squinted at him and closed it quickly. Otherwise it was quiet. He saw no people. He was anxious now and tired and he did not know what to do.

A woman opened a door near the end of the corridor and a cloud of light fell across his path. She did not notice him. She removed some objects from a trolley and then re-entered the room. He came to the door and stood for a moment, waiting for her, but he was very tired now. He sat on the carpet in the corridor, trying to remain alert, but his head hung down.

"Who are you?" the woman said to him.

He jerked his head up. He was not sure whether he had fallen asleep, whether time had passed – had she simply come out as soon as he had sat down? He looked at her, but he could not understand all the words she spoke.

"Are you lost?" she asked. "Are you looking for someone?" She did not seem angry, but he did not know how to make her understand.

He said, "The room," with all the English he could muster, but he knew it was not enough.

The woman gazed at him and spoke some words in her own language and he was amazed he could understand her completely. He had thought his family were the only ones in this new place.

"Come," she said. She pushed open the door of the room she had been cleaning and showed him in: the wide bed so perfectly made, the large face of the television set, the gleaming marble in the bathroom. He walked to the window and knelt on a chair and looked out at the vast city. He could not hear the sounds of traffic far below, he could not see the river of people entering the railway stations, he could not see the lost ones shuffling to and fro on the street. He saw only rooftops and sunlight and all the space in the world between the earth and the sky that seemed like emptiness, that was untouched and beautiful. He turned and climbed on to the bed. He did not worry about the woman or his mother and father or when he should return to the hostel. He was too tired for any of that. The boy slept. Again, he did not have bad dreams. He did not even dream of his own country. He saw the green grass in the park that Sunday afternoon, his mother's five fingers searching for his face, his father and brother, even the angry friend, Emmanuel, sitting on the bed in the hotel room, looking for the face of God.

Segun Afolabi is a Nigerian whose collection of short stories *A Life Elsewhere* was shortlisted for the 2006 Commonwealth Writers' Prize. His novel *Goodbye Lucille* was published in 2007 by Jonathan Cape. 'Monday Morning' was first published in *Wasafiri*, issue 41, spring 2004.

Jungfrau

Mary Watson – winner of the 2006 Caine Prize

t was the Virgin Jessica who taught me about wickedness.

I once asked her why she was called the Virgin Jessica. She looked at me with strange eyes and said that it was because she was a special person, like the Blessed Mary.

"A virgin is someone who can do God's work. And if you're very, very clean and pure you can be one of the 144 virgins who will be carried in God's bosom at the end of the world. And if you're not…"

She leaned towards me, her yellow teeth before my eye. I thought she might suck it out, she was so close. She whispered, "If you're not, then God will toss you to the devil who will roast you with his horn. Like toasted marshmallows. You don't want the devil's evil horn to make a hole in your pretty skin, now do you?"

She kissed my nose – my little rabbit's nose, she called it – and walked away, her long white summer dress falling just above her high, high red heels. Her smell, cigarette smoke and last night's perfume, lingered around my eyeball. I wanted to be like the Virgin Jessica. I wanted a name like hers.

We called her Jez for short.

My mother Annette was the Virgin Jessica's adopted sister. She was older and tireder. The Virgin had no children while my mother had 43. She was a schoolteacher in one of those schools where the children wore threadbare jerseys and had hard green snot crystallized around their noses and above their crusty lips – lips that could say *poes* without tasting any bitterness. Or that secret relish of forbidden language.

Sometimes my mother would have them – her other children, her little smelly children – over at our house. They would drape themselves around our furniture like dirty ornamental cherubs and drink hot pea soup. The steam melted the snot, which then ran down into the soup. It did not matter to them because they ate their boogers anyway.

I hated my mother's other children. I glared at them to let them know, but they stared back without much expression. Their faces had nothing to say – I could read nothing there. Jessica found them amusing.

"Sweet little things," she mumbled, and laughed into her coffee. Her shoulders shook epileptically.

After the Virgin told me how important it was to be clean, I tolerated them in the haze of my superiority. I was clean – I bathed every night – and they were filthy, so obviously God wouldn't want to touch them.

The Virgin spent hours in the bathroom every evening. Naked she walked to her bedroom, so lovely and proud she seemed tall; I followed faithfully, to observe a ritual more awesome than church. With creams and powders she made herself even cleaner for God. How he must love her, I thought. She spread his love upon her as she rubbed her skin until it glowed and her smell spread through the house, covering us all with the strength of her devotion. Then she went out, just after my father came home, and stayed out until late.

The Virgin Jessica had a cloud of charm 20 centimetres around her body. Strangers hated her because they thought that anyone that beautiful could only be mean. But it was not her pretty black eyes or her mouth that made her beautiful. She was beautiful because she was wrapped in a cloud of charm. And when you breathed in the air from the cloud, you breathed in the charm and it went down your veins and into your heart and made you love her. If you came close enough, she would smile her skew smile, pretending to love you with her slitted eyes, and the charm would ooze out like fog from a sewer and grab you and sink into your heart and lungs. Even I who had known her all my life would feel the charm with a funny ache. She had a way of leaning forward when she spoke, claiming the space around her with her smell, her charm. And my father, who didn't speak or laugh, he too would be conquered.

"What's the old man up to tonight?" she would say, leaning towards him with a wink, her eyes laughing; and he would fold his newspaper and look pleased, even grunt contentedly.

I tried saying those same words, leaning forward the way Jez did, and he looked at me coldly. So cold that my wink froze halfway and my laugh caught in my throat. Embarrassed, I transformed the laugh into a cough and rubbed my eyes like a tired child. I think it was then that I realised that his love for me was bound to me as his little girl. And my love for him bound me to my little girl's world.

I took pains to keep my girl's world intact after that. When boys teased me at school, I felt the walls of my father's favour tremble. One of them phoned and sang a dirty song into my hot ear. My head burnt for days after that. I felt the fires of hell from that phone call. I feared that the fires would start inside me, catching my hair and eating the strands like candlewick, melting my skin like wax, dripping and staining mommy's carpets (she would be very cross). The fire would eat the horrid children in the schoolroom, then crawl towards my mother, burn her slowly and then finish with her chalk-stained fingers. Her glasses would shrivel up and her mouth crease with silent screams. Unsatisfied, the fire would move towards my father, crackling his newspaper; the smoke would cloud his glasses. Beneath them, his eyes would have that same cold look – but not cold enough to douse the flames. The fire would then stagger towards the Virgin. Leering, it would grab her ankles and eat her white frock, turning it to soot. She would cry out and her head would toss, her hair unravel and she would scream from the force of the flames. The Virgin Jessica's screams in my head made me put a knife on the window-sill of her bedroom so that she could undo the burglar bars and escape.

The image of flames and screams resounded in my head for several days. They surged whenever the other girls in their shortened school dresses lit cigarettes in the toilets. They could not see how the flames would get bigger. I checked all the stubs carelessly tossed into the sink and bin to make sure that the fire did not escape. The slight thrill I had once received from the boys teasing me in the safety of the schoolyard, away from my father's fearsome eyes, faded. I spent my intervals at the far end of the yard, eating sandwiches and talking to the dogs through the wire fence. I had to coax them across the road with my milk and the ham from my bread. I was found one day, squatting on my haunches and telling Nina and Hildegarde about a garden of moss. I felt a shadow; it made me shiver, and I looked up to see if God was angry. Instead I saw Ms Collins above me, her eyes made huge by her glasses. I was scared that she'd be cross. I wanted to pee; some dripped down my leg, so I crouched and shut my eyes tightly, praying fervently that I would not pee. She reached out for my hand and asked me to make some charts for her in exchange for some biscuits and cool drink. From then on I spent my breaks helping Ms Collins in her art room and she would give me yoghurt and fruit and sometimes chocolate. I never ate these. Instead I put them on the steps of the white Kirk on the way home. Ms Collins tried to ask me questions, but I was shy and would only whisper, "I don't know." She would speak relentlessly. She told me about her baby daughter who ate grass.

I preferred just to look at her. I liked looking at her big ugly eyes and her pretty hair. But I think she got tired of me: maybe my silence wore her down; maybe the sound of her own voice scared her, for it must have been like talking to herself. She probably thought she was going mad, talking and talking to still brown eyes. But the day I went into her art room and found a boy from my class helping her with the charts, I remembered the fires of hell and ran away. Maybe she wanted me to burn; maybe she wasn't a virgin either.

It must have been the sound of midnight that woke me. The house without my mother felt unguarded. It seemed her presence warded off a fury of demons. I sat upright in my clean girl's bed, trying to feel the pulse of the night. I slipped my feet over the side of the bed and listened. The darkness is covered by a haze that makes the still corners move.

I knew that my mother had not returned. The wild child with snot streaming from his nose and eyes, he had her still. I sat at the lounge window, watching the sea, hating the wild child. He had come after supper, his little body panting like a steam engine. He ran up the hill in the rain, he had run all the way from the settlement. He sobbed, buried his head in my mother's trousers.

"Please, please, *asseblief*, please," his broken voice scratched.

Wishing so very hard that he hadn't come, I watched the boy cry until my mother barked, "Evelyn, get out of here."

I prayed that the wild child would leave: go back to your plague, I screamed silently. It was too late. He had brought his plague with him. It wandered about our house and muffled my warnings. So she did not hear me, and let the child take her away.

Her trousers soiled with tears and mucus, she rushed into her bedroom, where I was watching one of those endless sitcoms about silly teenagers. She grabbed her car keys.

"Don't wait up for me."

I would not have waited for her. Even now, in the dark hour, I was not waiting for her.

I must have stayed at the window for at least an hour. I saw the sea roar-smash-roar against the rocks. I saw the stillness of the midnight road, the white line running on towards the mountain. The road was empty; but then I saw two people walking up the hill. They walked slowly and closely in their midnight world. The walk was a stagger.

They fell pleasantly against each other. I saw them walk towards the house and only then did I see who they were.

When Jessica and my father entered the house, quietly and with the guilty grace of burglars, they were glowing from the wind and walking and waves and the wildness of the night's beauty. The haze inherent in the darkness was centred around them. I looked on with envy, for I too wished to walk the empty night with them. Jessica let out a startled sound when she saw me curled up on the window-sill.

"Look at you," she fussed, "hanging around dark windows like a sad little ghost."

Her face was close to mine and her breathing deep.

"Have you been watching for your mother? Has she come home yet?"

I shook my head. I had not been waiting for my mother.

She held my hands in her cold, cold fingers. "Your hands are freezing," she said.

"You need some Milo. How long have you been sitting here? Long?

"Your father and I went to see if your mother was coming home. I wish she'd phone, but then they probably don't have one. I really don't understand why Annette involves herself in other people's business. But I suppose you should count your blessings. When we were small, Annette and me, all we had to play with was scrap metal."

Jessica chattered on, repeating the stories I had heard so many times.

My mother came home while I was clutching my Milo. I was playing the mournful ghost, the sick patient, and all the while glowing in the attention of both my father and Jessica. Jessica was chattering brightly, so bright that she made the darkness her own while I huddled in its shadows. My father was silent, his eyes as dark as mine. Jessica's words tripped out of her mouth and drew circles around us.

Then Annette stepped into our enchanted circle. She asked for tea. As Jessica made the tea her words stumbled then stopped. My father went to bed, taking my hand as he left the kitchen. I did not want to go to bed. I wanted to be in the kitchen with just my father and Jessica and me.

I stood on a rock in the garden and stared down at the people watching my sea. They were dotted across the small beach, the wind twisting their hair around their necks and forcing them closer into their jackets. They lifted their fingers to point, just like in a seaside painting.

Their mouths were wide with laughter and their eyes bright, yet all the while I knew that they were posing, as if for an invisible artist. Their minds could sometimes glimpse his black beret, his paint-splattered smock in this idyllic scene.

I went down to the sea. There were too many whale-watchers trampling the sand, my desecrated temple, with their flat feet and stubby toes. I glared at the fat children who clung to their parents, hanging on to their arms and legs.

"Beast with two backs," I muttered.

They smelt suburban. Their odour of white bread and Marmite drifted unpleasantly into the sea air. They huddled into their wind-breakers and yawned at the ocean.

"It's just a dark blob," they whined, their winter-paled faces cracking beneath the noon sun. They shivered from the wind nuzzling their necks.

I sat near the water's edge and buried my pretty toes in the sand. The crowd, the people who came to see the whales, were noisy and their noise ate into my ears as they crunched their chips and the packets crackled in the wind.

"Go home," I hissed to a solitary toddler who wandered near me.

I turned to see a woman scoop him up and pretend to eat his angel curls. My coward's face smiled at her.

I stayed there for a while, watching the people watch the whales. Then I noticed some of my mother's children playing in the water on the other side of the beach. They shrieked and laughed; some played in their dirty clothes, others in varying stages of nakedness.

They sang a ditty with filthy words while roughly shoving and splashing each other with the cold water. They knocked down their friends and made them eat sand. The suburban children's parents shook their heads, pulled their young ones and walked away, still shaking their heads, as though the shaking would dispel the image from their minds. They soon forgot all about those children who haunted the corners of my world, my mother's chosen children.

She came to call me for lunch. She did not see her young ones, who had moved towards the tidal pool, and I did not tell her about them.

I sneaked my mother off the beach, chattering too brightly. We walked towards the hill. Someone came running behind us, but we carried on walking, for my mother didn't seem to hear the footsteps – maybe I was too bright. I walked faster and we crossed Main Road. When we reached the other side, I felt a light strong-hard knock like a spirit just made solid. I turned to see the wild child hugging my mother, her arms wrapped around him. He gave her a flower and ran back. When the wild child crossed the road, he was hit by whale people in a blue car. The driver got out, my mother ran to her child. The driver, annoyed and red, complained that he hadn't seen anyone, there was nobody there.

"Just a shadow flitted across my eyes," his wife wailed. "Just a dark shadow."

The driver said that he would fetch help. He and his wife drove off in their blue car – the dent was slight – and didn't come back. Perhaps to him there really was nobody there: the dent was so very slight, and those children are so thin, after all.

My mother lifted the wild child in her arms. She waited and while she waited, her mouth got tighter and tighter and she wept. When one hundred blue cars had passed by, she slowly got up from the pavement. With the wild child in her arms, she walked up the hill. She did not speak to me, her mouth was tight and her hair unbound from its ponytail.

At our house Jessica and my father hovered awkwardly around her, their legs and arms looking wrong on their bodies, as if they had taken them off and put them back the wrong way. They moved slowly and clumsily, like they had wound down. My mother lay her child on my clean girl's bed and stayed by his side.

"Stephen, get the doctor quickly," she barked at my father.

I ate my Sunday roast. I paid little attention to the doctor's arrival or the child's crying or my mother's pacing. Her tight face had shut me out. I sat in the lounge and watched the sea, picking at the meat. When the violet hour came, the beach was empty and my room smelt of the wild child and the barest hint of my mother's love. But they were both gone.

I stayed in the lounge with my father and the Virgin, who brought us tea. We played cards and laughed the soft, covered laughs of forbidden frivolity. We munched biscuits and watched the Virgin's teasing eyes as she tried to cheat, as she toasted marshmallows over a candle flame, as she spoke, smiled, sighed. The wild child and my mother were forgotten. I did not think of the bruised bundle on my bed.

Then the quiet beneath our laughter became too insistent. It was guilt that sent me in search of her. It was the guilt of the betrayer for the betrayed, because guilt is more binding than passion.

There was not a trace of my mother and the wild child in my bedroom. There was no mark of my mother's care or her chosen child's blood staining the sheets. There were no cup rings on my dressing table, no dent on the pillow. I looked for my mother in my bedroom. I hunted in every corner but could not find the slightest whisper of her smell.

I could find nothing of her in the lounge – that was my father's room. Their bedroom was green and clinical and did not contain either of them. The kitchen was heavy with the Virgin's presence, which smelt of rose water with a burny undertone. I sat down on the floor, perplexed.

Agitated, I realised that I could not remember if her smell had been in the house the day before. Or the previous week. I went to the garage, which she used as a schoolroom. As I opened the door, a fury of smells came screaming towards me. There were the wild children's smells of pain and fear and anger. And she was there, entangled in this foul mix. Nothing of her remained in the house because it was all concentrated here. Delicately it cushioned and enveloped the rawness of the children as it wove itself into them. The force of this beauty, this tenderness made me want to weep with jealousy. Such sadness, such terror. I left the dim garage knowing that my mother had been gone for a long time. I had not noticed because I had been coveting the Virgin. I went back to the house.

Jessica tilted her head slightly and focused her skew eyes on me. I had not seen her standing in the doorway, slim and graceful (she was so beautiful), watching me.

"What are you sniffing around for? Does something smell bad?"

She seemed anxious.

"Not in here," I replied. "I was just smelling. Smelling to see where my mother has gone."

"You funny, funny child," she said, wrapping her precious arms around me. I pretended to squirm. "What else can that incredible snout of yours sniff out? Can you smell where your father is?"

I was surprised, because she didn't understand me at all. I looked at her and saw an odd dullness in her pretty face.

"It doesn't happen with my nose," I tried to explain. "It happens inside somewhere, same as when Daddy and I go to the moss garden. I don't see it with my eyes."

She regarded me with a slight frown shadowing her eyes and making her face sulky.

"What moss garden?"

"Secrets."

I smiled sweetly at her and she lost her frown and said, "Don't you trouble your pretty little head about your inner eyes and ears, you are much too young for such worries."

She coaxed me into helping her make sandwiches, which was easy because I loved doing anything with her. But she still did not know what I meant.

I sought out my mother after that. I lavished attention upon her, for I felt that I had betrayed her. I betrayed her with my unholy, selfish love for the Virgin. I placated her with tokens of love, with tea and wild flowers picked along the road to the beach. I feared that the Blessed Mary would not be pleased that in my heart of hearts I had turned my love from my flesh mother to another. My guilt was augmented by my jealousy of her chosen children, and because I denied her my love yet begrudged her theirs. As my guilt grew so her nocturnal visits to the township increased.

"There's so much fear out there, you couldn't imagine it, Evie. You're a lucky, lucky girl. I remember being so poor that my hunger nearly drove me insane. We were like wild flowers growing on the side of the road."

I resented my mother's childhood poverty. I resented her hunger and I resented being made to feel guilty about not being hungry.

"You could so easily have been one of those children, look at Auntie Carmelita, the way her children run around, that's the inmates ruling the asylum. So you just be grateful that you're not like them. You think about that if it makes you sad when I go out at night."

It did not make me sad when she went out at night. I was jealous but not sad, because her absence set my nights free. I would stare at the midnight sea; I would walk the moss garden with my father.

I sought her greedily with endless cups of tea and awkwardly asked her how her day had been – did she not think the weather was fine for this time of year? – smoothed her hair, kissed her cheek with my Judas lips and fussed about her as much as Jessica did.

And she would be propped in her chair, my mother, my failed heroine, and I would talk and talk and she would say, "Not now, Evie, I'm tired, tired," and my guilt would grow and I would leave unhappy yet relieved. Her eyes would hold mine and she would say, "Thanks Evie," and the guilt grew and grew because there was trust and affection in her eyes, doggy brown eyes that I did not want to love.

Those eyes changed one day and she became cross. Her breath was thin and tinny, like she did not want to take air in, let air out. The tedium of breathing seemed to offend her, so she resisted it. That was when she started smoking cigarettes. She took some of Jessica's cigarettes, shrugged like Jessica and laughed.

"Makes breathing interesting," she tittered. "Besides, we're all going to die anyway," she cackled, looking at the danger signs on the box. She laughed and laughed but it was a cross laugh.

It crept out of the silences, was born between a glance held, then turned away. This guilt would not be contained. It was in the air as plain as the tingling cold of sunny winter days. It kept me awake those cold August nights. So cold that my fingers would ache as I lay awake, feeling the ice in the walls, the breathing of the house, the numbness of my mother's nocturnal absences. I sighed and turned the other cheek, hoping to find sleep with my back to the wall, then my face, then my back again.

There is no rest for the wicked.

"Be a good girl," my father had said as he kissed me that night. "Be a good girl for your old father."

He kissed me again and pulled the covers up to my chin. When he got up from the bed, the mattress rose as the weight lifted. I felt safe then, as the rain and wind struck down on the roof.

It was still raining as I lay staring at the ceiling in the small hours of the morning.

There is no rest for the wicked.

Sighing an old woman's sigh, I kicked my tired sore legs to the right, the side where I always raised myself from the bed. I wandered to the kitchen seeking leftovers from the Virgin's dinner, because I was famished. Trying to be the good child exhausted me and then left me sleepless. I could hear my father snoring. He sounded like a wailing wolf. I was surprised that he slept. When I wandered around the rooms at night, I felt the alertness of a house that did not slumber nor sleep.

I found the Virgin in her kitchen. She was eating. She stuck her fork into the mince and rammed it into her mouth. Again and again she stuffed forkfuls into her mouth, sometimes pausing to mix the mince with spaghetti, her delicate fingers swiftly swirling it around the fork. The apple-pie dish lay empty before her.

When she looked up and saw me, spaghetti was hanging down the side of her mouth, from those sweet red lips. She let go of the fork. She seemed embarrassed, but she had no need to be because I knew that she had been fasting. The Virgin often fasted to deny herself the pleasures of the flesh. I admired her for that because I could not fast no matter how hard I tried. But looking at her with spaghetti on her chin and mince on her white nightgown, I felt ill. Surely she would make herself sick, eating like that. She looked up and saw me, and it frightened me because she looked old. The guilt had etched itself there too. I was frightened because I thought that the Virgin was pure. I chased those naughty thoughts from my mind. I chased them until my beloved Virgin seemed young again. Then unbidden, the words came to my mouth.

"There's no rest for the wicked," I said.

My words hurt her; she placed her head in her hands. The guilt was what made me do it, the guilt, it made words come to my mouth. My secret joy at releasing suppressed words sank into my flesh and I felt my skin tauten. My hands were wet so I wiped my mouth, but it would not be clean. When she left the room, my mind screamed for her mercy, for forgiveness. She did not hear me; she took none of that with her. I sat in her chair and waited and waited.

I longed for my mother then. I longed to press my burning face, my wet nose into her trousers and sob. I wanted her to leave her bed at night and come to me and to choose me as her child and I would choose her as my mother and the guilt would go away and we would be happy. I went to where I knew I would find some of her.

The schoolroom door creaked slightly and my white slippers upon the cold cement floor made a featherlight crunch. I stood in the dark waiting to feel her and the children, waiting for sounds that were long gone. I crossed my arms around myself and waited. And then they came to me – the sighs, the hushed tinkles of laughter, the moans and the whimpers. The room was drenched in sorrow. I listened excitedly as the ghosts of yesterday came to me. The sounds grew less and less faint. They were calling to me. The shadows started taking shape and I saw that everything had fallen into a woven mass, a moving tapestry in the corner of the schoolroom. I saw my mother as a she-wolf, her hair tangled and glowing, licking her young ones, her tongue moving over furry flesh. I wanted to join her pack and have her lick my sins away. I moved towards them, then stopped, for the shadows changed again. My mother now had Jessica's face, an unfamiliar Jessica face with enormous slanted glowing eyes, feral biting teeth that dipped to the whimpering flesh beneath her. My mother was gone.

"Mommy?" I whispered. "Mommy?" It was shrill and anxious. I did not know what magic I had conjured.

"Mommy?"

Everything stopped moving. The tapestry froze and then unravelled.

And then I saw them. I had not imagined the moving tapestry in the corner of the schoolroom, nor had I imagined Jessica licking the furry flesh. As my eyes accustomed themselves to the dim light, I saw that it was my father with Jessica. They were clumsily covering their bodies, hiding themselves, and I thought that was silly – I had seen it all before. But I had not known that he shared the moss garden with her. I left the garage. I heard them calling after me and I walked away.

Mary Watson is a South African writer. 'Jungfrau' was first published in her own anthology of short stories, *Moss*, Kwela Books, Cape Town 2004. She is now working on a novel.

Jambula Tree

Monica Arac de Nyeko – winner of the 2007 Caine Prize

heard of your return home from Mama Atim our next door neighbour. You remember her, don't you? We used to talk about her on our way to school, hand in hand, jumping, skipping, or playing runandcatchme. That woman's mouth worked at words like ants on a cob of maize. Ai! Everyone knows her quack-quack-quack-mouth. But people are still left wordless by just how much she can shoot at and wreck things with her machine-gun mouth. We nicknamed her Lecturer. The woman speaks with the certainty of a lecturer at her podium claiming an uncontested mastery of her subject. I bet you are wondering how she got to know of your return. I could attempt a few guesses. Either way, it would not matter. I would be breaking a promise. I hate that. We made that promise never to mind her or be moved by her. We said that after that night. The one night no one could make us forget. You left without saying goodbye after that. You had to, I reasoned. Perhaps it was good for both of us. Maybe things could die down that way. Things never did die down. Our names became forever associated with the forbidden. Shame.

Anyango – Sanyu.

My mother has gotten over that night. It took a while, but she did. Maybe it is time for your mother to do the same. She should start to hold her head high and scatter dust at the women who laugh after her when she passes by their houses. Nakawa Housing Estates has never changed. Mr Wangolo our SST teacher once said those houses were just planned slums with people with broken dreams and unplanned families for neighbours. Nakawa is still over one thousand families on an acre of land they call an estate. Most of the women don't work. Like Mama Atim they sit and talk, talk, talk and wait for their husbands to bring home a kilo of offal. Those are the kind of women we did not want to become. They bleached their skins with Mekako skin lightening soap till they became tender and pale like a sun-scorched baby. They took over their children's *dool* and *kwepena* catfights till the local councillor had to be called for arbitration. Then they did not talk to each other for a year. Nakawa's women laugh at each other for wearing the cheapest sandals on sale by the hawkers. Sanyu, those women know every love charm by heart and every *juju* man's shrine because they need them to conjure up their husbands' love and penises from drinking places with smoking pipes filled with dried hen's throat artery. These women know that an even number is a bad sign as they watch the cowry shells and coffee beans fall onto cowhide when consulting the spirits about their husbands' fidelity. That's what we fought against when we walked to school each day. Me and you hand in hand, towards school, running away from Nakawa Housing Estate's drifting tide which threatened to engulf us and turn us into noisy, gossiping and frightening housewives.

You said it yourself, we could be anything. Anything coming from your mouth was seasoned and alive. You said it to me, as we sat on a mango tree branch. We were not allowed to climb trees, but we did, and there, inside the green branches, you said – we can be anything. You asked us to pause for a moment to make a wish. I was a nurse in a white dress. I did not frighten children with big injections. You wished for nothing. You just made a wish that you would not become what your father wanted you to be – an engineer, making building plans, for his mansion, for his office, for his railway village. The one he dreamt about when he went to bed at night.

Sanyu, after all these years, I still imagine shame trailing after me tagged onto the hem of my skirt. Other times, I see it, floating into your dreams across the desert and water to remind you of what lines we crossed. The things we should not have done when the brightness of Mama Atim's torch shone upon us – naked. How did she know exactly when to flash the light? Perhaps asking that question is a futile quest for answers. I won't get any! Perhaps it is as simple as accepting that the woman knows everything. I swear if you slept with a crocodile under the ocean, she would know. She is the only one who knows first-hand whose husband is sleeping with whose daughter at the estates inside those one-bedroomed houses. She knows whose son was caught inside the fences at Lugogo Show Grounds; the fancy trade fair centre just across Jinja Road, the main road which meanders its way underneath the estates. Mama Atim knows who is soon dying from gonorrhoea, who got it from someone, who got it from so-and-so who in turn got it from the soldiers who used to guard Lugogo Show Grounds, two years ago. You remember those soldiers, don't you? The way they sat in the sun with their green uniforms and guns hanging carelessly at their shoulders. With them the AK47 looked almost harmless – an object that was meant to be held close to the body – black ornament. They whistled after young girls in tight mini skirts that held onto their bums. At night, they drank Nile Lager, tonto, Mobuku and sung *harambe, Soukous* or *Chaka-Chaka* songs.

> *Eh moto nawaka mama*
> *Eh moto nawaka*
> *I newaka tororo*
> *Nawaka moto*
> *Nawaka moto*
> *Nawaka moto*
> Eh fire, burns mama
> Eh fire, burns
> It is burning in Tororo
> It is burning
> It is burning
> It is burning

Mama Atim never did pass anywhere near where they had camped in their green tents. She twisted her mouth when she talked about them. What were soldiers doing guarding Lugogo? She asked. Was it a frontline? Mama Atim was terrified of soldiers. We never did find out why they instilled such fear in her. Either way it did not matter. Her fear became a secret weapon we used as we imagined ourselves being like goddesses dictating her fate. In our goddess-hands, we turned her into an effigy and had soldiers pelt her with stones. We imagined that pelting stones from a soldier was just enough to scare her into susuing in her XXL mothers' union panties. The ones she got a tailor to hem for her, from left-over materials from her children's nappies. How we wished those materials were green, so that she would see soldiers and stones in between her thighs every time she wore her green soldier colour, stone pelting colour and AK-47 colour. We got used to the sight of green soldiers perched in our football fields. This was the new order. Soldiers doing policemen's work! No questions, *Uganda yetu, hakuna matata*. How strange it was, freedom in forbidden colours. Deep green – the colour of the morning when the dew dries on leaves to announce the arrival of shame and dirt. And everything suddenly seems so uncovered, so exposed, so naked.

Anyanyo – Sanyu.

Mama Atim tells me you have chosen to come back home, to Nakawa Housing Estates. She says you refuse to live in those areas on the bigger hills and terraced roads in Kololo. You are coming to us and to Nakawa Housing Estates, and to our many houses lined one after another on a small hill overlooking the market and Jinja Road, the football field and Lugogo Show Grounds. Sanyu, you have chosen to come here to children running on the red earth, in the morning shouting and yelling as they play *kwepena* and *dool* – familiar and stocked with memory and history. You return to dirt roads filled with thick brown mud on a rainy day, pools of water in every pothole and the sweet fresh smell of rain on hard soil. Sanyu, you have come back to find Mama Atim.

Mama Atim still waits for her husband to bring the food she is to cook each night. We used to say, after having nine sons and one daughter she should try to take care of them. Why doesn't she try to find a job in the industrial area like many other women around the housing estates? Throw her hips and two large buttocks around and play at entrepreneurship. Why doesn't she borrow a little *entandikwa* from the micro-finance unions so she can buy at least a bale of second-hand clothes at Owino market where she can retail them at Nakawa market? Second-hand clothes are in vogue, for sure. The Tommy Hilfiger and Versace labels are the in 'thing' for the young boys and girls who like to hang around the estates at night. Second-hand clothes never stay on the clothes hangers too long, like water during a drought, they sell quickly.

Mummy used to say those second-hand clothes were stripped off corpses in London. That is why they had slogans written on them such as – 'You went to London and all you brought me was this lousy T-shirt!' When Mummy talked of London, we listened with our mouths open. She had travelled there not once, not twice, but three times to visit her sister. Each time she came back with her suitcase filled up with stories. When her sister died, Mummy's trips stopped like that bright sparkle in her eye and the Queen Elizabeth stories, which she lost the urge to retell again and again. By that time we were grown. You were long gone to a different place, a different time and to a new memory. By then, we had grown into two big girls with four large breasts and buttocks like pumpkins and we knew that the stories were not true. Mummy had been to Tanzania – just a boat trip away on Lake Victoria, not London. No Queen Elizabeth.

Mama Atim says you are tired of London. You cannot bear it anymore. London is cold. London is a monster which gives no jobs. London is no cosy exile for the banished. London is no refuge for the immoral. Mama Atim says this word immoral to me – slowly and emphatically in *Japadhola*, so it can sink into my head. She wants me to hear the word in every breath, sniff it in every scent so it can haunt me like that day I first touched you. Like the day you first touched me. Mine was a cold unsure hand placed over your right breast. Yours was a cold scared hand, which held my waist and pressed it closer to you, under the jambula tree in front of her house. Mama Atim says you are returning on the wings of a metallic bird – Kenya Airways. You will land in the hot Kampala heat which bites at the skin like it has a quarrel with everyone. Your mother does not talk to me or my mother. Mama Atim cooks her kilo of offal which she talks about for one week until the next time she cooks the next kilo again, bending over her charcoal stove, her large and long breasts watching over her saucepan like cow udders in space. When someone passes by, she stops cooking. You can hear her whisper. Perhaps that's the source of her gonorrhoea and Lugogo Show Ground stories. Mama Atim commands the world to her kitchen like her nine sons and one daughter. None of them have amounted to anything. The way their mother talks about me and you, Sanyu, after all these years, you would think her sons are priests. You would think at least one of them got a diploma and a low-paying job at a government ministry. You would think one of them could at least bring home a respectable wife. But *wapi!* Their wives are like used bicycles, ridden and exhausted by the entire estate manhood. They say the monkey which is behind should not laugh at the other monkey's tail. Mama Atim laughs with her teeth out and on display like cowries. She laughs loudest and forgets that she, of all people, has no right to urinate at or lecture the entire estate on the gospel according to St Morality.

Sometimes I wonder how much you have changed. How have you have grown? You were much taller than I. Your eyes looked stern; created an air about you – one that made kids stop for a while, unsure if they should trample all over you or take time to see for sure if your eyes would validate their preconceived fears. After they had finally studied, analysed, added, multiplied and subtracted you, they knew you were for real. When the bigger kids tried to bully me, you stood tall and dared them to lay a finger on me. Just a finger, you said grinding your teeth like they were aluminium. They knew you did not mince words and that your anger was worse than a teacher's bamboo whipping. Your anger and rage coiled itself like a python around anyone who dared, anyone who challenged. And that's how you fought, with your teeth and hands but mostly with your feet. You coiled them around Juma when he knocked my tooth out for refusing to let him have his way on the water tap when he tried to cheat me out of my turn.

I wore my deep dark green uniform. At lunch times the lines could be long and boys always jumped the queue. Juma got me just as I put my water container to get some drinking water after lunch. He pushed me away. He was strong, Sanyu. One push like that and I fell down. When I got up, I left my tooth on the ground and rose up with only blood on the green; deep green, the colour of the morning when the dew dries off leaves.

You were standing at a distance. You were not watching. But it did not take you too long to know what was going on. You pushed your way through the crowd and before the teachers could hear the commotion going on, you had your legs coiled around Juma. I don't know how you do it, Sanyu. He could not move.

Juma, passed out? Hahahahahahaha!

I know a lot of pupils who would be pleased with that. Finally his big boy muscles had been crushed, to sand, to earth and to paste. The thought of that tasted sweet and salty like grasshoppers seasoned with onion and *kamulari* – red, red-hot pepper.

Mr Wangolo came with his hand-on-the-knee-limp and a big bamboo cane. It was yellow and must have been freshly broken off from the mother bamboos just outside the school that morning. He pulled and threatened you with indefinite expulsion before you let big sand-earth-paste Juma go. Both you and Juma got off with a two-week suspension. It was explicitly stated in the school rules that no one should fight. You had broken the rules. But that was the lesser of the rules that you broke. That I broke. That we broke.

Much later, at home, your mother was so angry. On our way home, you had said we should not say how the fight started. We should just say he hit you and you hit him back. Your house was two blocks from ours and the school was the nearest primary school to the estate. Most of the kids in the neighbourhood studied at Nakawa Katale Primary School all right, but everyone knew we were great friends. When your mother came and knocked upon our door, my mother had just put the onions on the charcoal stove to fry the goat's meat. Mummy bought goat's meat when she had just got her salary. The end of the month was always goat's meat and maybe some rice if she was in a good mood. Mummy's food smelt good. When she cooked, she joked about it. Mummy said if Papa had any sense in his head, he would not have left her with three kids to raise on her own to settle for that slut he called a wife. Mummy said Papa's new wife could not cook and that she was young enough to be his daughter. They had to do a caesarean on her when she gave birth to her first son. What did he expect? That those wasp hips could let a baby's head pass through them?

When she talked of Papa, she had that voice. Not a 'hate voice' and not a 'like voice', but the kind of voice she would use to open the door for him and tell him welcome back, even after all these years when he never sent us a single cent to buy food, books, soap or Christmas clothes. My Papa is not like your Papa, Sanyu. Your Papa works at the Ministry of Transport. He manages the Uganda railways, which is why he wants you to engineer a railway village for him. You say he has gotten so intoxicated with the railway that every time he talks of it, he rubs his palms together like he is thinking of the best ever memory in his life. Your father has a lot of money. Most of the teachers knew him at school. The kids had heard about him. Perhaps that is why your stern and blank expression was interpreted with slight overtones. They viewed you with a mixture of fear and awe; a rich man's child. Sometimes Mummy spoke about your family with slight ridicule. She said no one with money lived in Nakawa Housing Estates of all places. If your family had so much money, why did you not go to live in Muyenga, Kololo and Kansanga with your Mercedes-Benz lot? But you had new shoes every term. You had two new green uniforms every term. Sanyu, your name was never called out aloud by teachers, like the rest of us whose parents had not paid school tuition on time and we had to be sent back home with circulars.

Dear Parent,
This is to remind you that unless this term's school fees are paid out in full, your daughter/son.......... will not be allowed to sit for end of

term exams....
    Blah blah blah...

Mummy always got those letters and bit her lip as if she just heard that
her house had burnt down. That's when she started staring at the ceiling
with her eyes transfixed on one particular spot on the brown tiles. On
such days, she went searching through her old maroon suitcase. It was
from another time. It was the kind that was not sold in shops anymore.
It had lost its glitter and I wished she never brought it out to dry in the
sun. It would be less embarrassing if she brought out the other ones
she used for her Tanzania trips. At least those ones looked like the ones
your mother brought out to dry in the sun when she did her weekly
house cleaning. That suitcase had all Mummy's letters – the ones Papa
had written her when, as she said, her breasts were firm like green
mangoes. Against a kerosene lamp, she read aloud the letters, reliving
every moment, every word and every promise.
    I will never leave you.
    You are mine forever.
    Stars are for the sky, you are for me.
    Hello my sweet supernatural colours of the rainbow.
    You are the only bee on my flower.
    If loving you is a crime I am the biggest criminal in the world.
    Mummy read them out aloud and laughed as she read the words
on each piece of stained paper. She had stored them in their original
Air Mail envelopes with the green and blue decorations. Sometimes
papa had written to her in aerogramme. Those were opened with the
keenest skill to keep them neat and almost new. He was a prolific
letter-writer, my papa, with a neat handwriting. I know this because
often times I opened her case of memories. I never did get as far as
opening any letter to read; it would have been trespassing. It did not
feel right, even if Mummy had never scolded me for reading her 'To
Josephine Athieno Best' letters.
    I hated to see her like that. She was now a copy-typist at Ramja
Securities. Her salary was not much, but she managed to survive on
it, somehow, somehow. There were people who spoke of her beauty
as if she did not deserve being husbandless. They said with some pity,
"Oh, and she has a long ringed neck, her eyes are large and sad. The
woman has a voice, soft, kind and patient. How could the man leave
her?" Mummy might have been sad sometimes, but she did not deserve

any pity. She lived her life like her own finger nails and temperament: so calm, so sober and level-headed, except of course when it came to reading those Papa letters by the lantern lamp.

I told you about all this, Sanyu. How I wished she could be always happy, like your mother who went to the market and came back with two large boys carrying her load because she had shopped too much for your papa, for you, for your happy family. I did not tell you, but sometimes I stalked her as she made her way to buy things from the noisy market. She never saw me. There were simply too many people. From a distance, she pointed at things, fruit ripe like they had been waiting to be bought by her all along. Your mother went from market stall to market stall, flashing her white Colgate smile and her dimpled cheeks. Sometimes I wished I were like you; with a mother who bought happiness from the market. She looked like someone who summoned joy at her feet and it fell in salutation, humbly, like the *kabaka* subjects who lay prostrate before him. When I went to your house to do homework, I watched her cook. Her hand stirred groundnut soup. I must admit, Mummy told me never to eat at other people's homes. It would make us appear poor and me rather greedy. I often left your home when the food was just about ready. Your mother said, in her summon-joy-voice: "Supper is ready. Please eat." But I, feigning time consciousness always said, "I have to run home, Mummy will be worried." At such times, your father sat in the bedroom. He never came out from that room. Every day, like a ritual, he came home straight from work.

"A perfect husband," Mummy said more times than I can count.

"I hate him," you said more times than I could count. It was not what he didn't do, you said. It was what he did. Those touches, his touches you said. And you could not tell your mother. She would not believe you. She never did. Like that time she came home after the day you taught Juma a good lesson for messing around with me. She spoke to my mother in her voice which sounded like breaking china.

"She is not telling me everything. How can the boy beat her over nothing? At the school tap? These two must know. That is why I am here. To get to the bottom of this! Right now!"

She said this again and again, and Mummy called me from the kitchen where I had escaped just when I saw her knock on our back door holding your hands in hers and pulling you behind her like a goat!

"Anyango, Anyangooooo," Mummy called out.

I came out, avoiding your eyes. Standing with her hands held in front of me with the same kind of embarrassment and fear that overwhelmed me each time I heard my name called by a teacher for school fees default.

They talked for hours. I was terrified, which was why I almost told the truth. You started very quickly and repeated the story we had agreed on our way home. Your mother asked, "What was Anyango going to say again?" I repeated what you had just said, and your mother said, "I know they are both lying. I will get to the bottom of this at school in two weeks' time when I report back with her." And she did. You got a flogging that left you unable to sit down on your bum for a week.

When you left our house that day, they talked in low voices. They had sent us outside to be bitten by mosquitoes for a bit. When they called us back in, they said nothing. Your mother held your hand again, goat style. If Juma had seen you being pulled like that, he would have had a laugh one hundred times the size of your trodden-upon confidence. You never looked back. You avoided looking at me for a while after that.

Mummy had a list of 'don'ts' after that for me too. They were many.

Don't walk back home with Sanyu after school.

Don't pass by their home each morning to pick her up.

Don't sit next to her in class.

Don't borrow her text books. I will buy you your own.

Don't even talk to her.

Don't, don't, don't do anymore Sanyu.

It was like that, but not for long. After we started to talk again and look each other in the eyes, our parents seemed not to notice, which is why our secondary school applications went largely unnoticed. If they complained that we had applied to the same schools and in the same order, we did not hear about them.

1. St Mary's College Namagunga.
2. Nabisunsa Girls' School.
3. City High School.
4. Modern High School.

You got admitted to your first choice. I got my third choice. It was during the holidays that we got a chance to see each other again. I told you about my school. That I hated the orange skirts, white shirts, white socks and black boy's Bata shoes. They made us look like flowers on display. The boys wore white trousers, white shorts, white socks and black shoes. At break time, we trooped like a bunch of moving orange and white flowers to the school canteens, to the drama room, and to the football field.

You said you loved your school. Sister Cephas, your Irish headmistress, wanted to turn you all into Black English girls. The girls there were the prettiest ever and were allowed to keep their hair long and held back in puffs, not one inch only like at my school.

We were seated under the jambula tree. It had grown so tall. The tree had been there for ages with its unreachable fruit. They said it was there even before the estate houses were constructed. In April the tree carried small purple jambula fruit which tasted both sweet and tang and turned our tongues purple. Every April morning when the fruit started to fall, the ground became a blanket of purple.

When you came back during that holiday, your cheeks were bulging like you had hidden oranges inside them. Your eyes had grown small and sat like two short slits on your face. And your breasts, the two things you had watched and persuaded to grow during all your years at Nakawa Katale Primary School, were like two large jambulas on your chest. And that feeling that I had, the one that you had, that we had – never said, never spoken – swelled up inside us like fresh mandazies. I listened to your voice rise and fall. I envied you. I hated you. I could not wait for the next holidays when I could see you again. When I could dare place my itchy hand onto your two jambulas.

That time would be a night, two holidays later. You were not shocked. Not repelled. It did not occur to either of us, to you or me, that these were boundaries we should not cross nor should think of crossing. Your jambulas and mine. Two plus two jambulas equals four jambulas – even numbers should stand for luck. Was this luck pulling us together? You pulled me to yourself and we rolled on the brown earth that stuck to our hair in all its redness and dustiness. There in front of Mama Atim's house. She shone a torch at us. She had been watching, steadily like a dog waiting for a bone it knew it would get; it was just a matter of time.

Sanyu, I went for confession the next day, right after Mass. I made the sign of the cross and smelt the fresh burning incense in St Jude's church. I had this sense of floating on air, confused, weak, and exhausted. I told the priest, 'Forgive me Father for I have sinned. It has been two months since my last confession.' And there in my head, two plus two jambulas equals four jambulas...

I was not sorry. But I was sorry when your father with all his money from the railways got you a passport and sent you on the wing of a bird; hello London, here comes Sanyu.

Mama Atim says your plane will land tomorrow. Sanyu, I don't know what you expect to find here, but you will find my mummy; you'll find that every word she types on her typewriter draws and digs deeper the wrinkles on her face. You will find the Housing Estates. Nothing has changed. The women sit in front of their houses and wait for their husbands to bring them offal. Mama Atim's sons eat her food and bring girls to sleep in her bed. Your mother walks with a stooped back. She has lost the zeal she had for her happiness-buying shopping trips. Your papa returns home every day as soon as he is done with work. My Mummy says, "That is a good husband."

I come home every weekend to see Mummy. She has stopped looking inside her maroon case. But I do; I added the letter you wrote me from London. The only one I ever did get from you, five years after you left. You wrote:

A.
I miss you.
S.

Sanyu, I am a nurse at Mengo Hospital. I have a small room by the hospital, decorated with two chairs, a table from Katwe, a black and white television and two paintings of two big jambula trees which I got a downtown artist to do for me. These trees have purple leaves. I tell you, they smile.

I do mostly night shifts. I like them, I often see clearer at night. In the night you lift yourself up in my eyes each time, again and again. Sanyu, you rise like the sun and stand tall like the jambula tree in front of Mama Atim's house.

Monica Arac de Nyeko is a Ugandan who studied at Makerere University and the University of Groningen. She has just completed her first novel. 'Jambula Tree' was first published in the UK by Ayebia Clarke Publishing Limited (www.ayebia.co.uk) in their *African Love Stories* Anthology edited by Ama Ata Aidoo in 2006.

Poison

Henrietta Rose-Innes – winner of the 2008 Caine Prize

L ynn had almost made it to the petrol station when her old
Toyota ran dry on the highway. Lucky me, she thought as she
pulled on to the verge, seeing the red and yellow flags ahead,
the logo on the tall façade. But it was hopeless, she realised as soon
as she saw the pile-up of cars on the forecourt. A man in blue overalls
caught her eye and made a throat-slitting gesture with the side of his
hand as she came walking up: no petrol here either.

There were 20-odd stranded people, sitting in their cars or
leaning against them. They glanced at her without expression before
turning their eyes again towards the distant city. In a minibus taxi
off to one side, a few travellers sat stiffly, bags on laps. Everyone
was quiet, staring down the highway, back at what they'd all been
driving away from.

An oily cloud hung over Cape Town, concealing Devil's Peak.
It might have been a summer fire, except it was so black, so large.
Even as they watched, it boiled up taller and taller into the sky, a
plume twice as high as the mountain, leaning towards them like an
evil genie.

As afternoon approached, the traffic thinned. Each time a car drew
up, the little ceremony was the same: the crowd's eyes switching to
the new arrival, the overalled man slicing his throat, the moment
of blankness and then comprehension, eyes turning away. Some of
the drivers just stood there, looking accusingly at the petrol pumps;
others got back into their cars and sat for a while with their hands
on the steering wheels, waiting for something to come to them. One
man started up his car again immediately and headed off, only to
coast to a halt a few hundred metres down the drag. He didn't even
bother to pull off on to the shoulder. Another car came in, pushed by
three sweaty black men. They left the vehicle standing in the road and

came closer, exchanging brief words with the petrol attendants. Their forearms were pumped from exertion and they stood for a while with their hands hanging at their sides. There was no traffic at all going into the city.

Over the previous two days, TV news had shown pictures of the N1 and N2 jam-packed for 50 kilometres out of town. It had taken a day for most people to realise the seriousness of the explosion; then everybody who could get out had done so. Now, Lynn supposed, lack of petrol was trapping people in town. She herself had left it terribly late, despite all the warnings. It was typical; she struggled to get things together. The first night she'd got drunk with friends. They'd sat up late, rapt in front of the TV, watching the unfolding news. The second night, she'd done the same, by herself. On the morning of this the third day, she'd woken up with a burning in the back of her throat so horrible that she understood it was no hangover, and that she had to move. By then, everybody she knew had already left.

People were growing fractious, splitting into tribes. The petrol attendants and the car-pushers stood around the taxi. The attendants' body language was ostentatiously off-duty: ignoring the crowd, attending to their own emergency. One, a woman, bent her head into the cab of the taxi, addressing the driver in a low voice. The driver and the *gaardjie* were the only people who seemed relaxed; both were slouched low on the front seats, the driver with a baseball cap tilted down over his eyes. On the other side of the forecourt was a large Afrikaans family group that seemed to have been travelling in convoy: mother, father, a couple of substantial aunts and uncles, half a dozen blonde kids of different sizes. They had set up camp, cooler bags and folding chairs gathered around them. On their skins, Lynn could see speckles of black grime; everybody coming out of the city had picked up a coating of foul stuff, but on the white people it showed up worse. A group of what looked like students – tattoos, dreadlocks – sat in a silent line along the concrete pad that supported the petrol pumps. One, a dark, barefoot girl with messy black hair down her back, kept springing to her feet and walking out into the road, swivelling this way and that with her hands clamped under her armpits, then striding back. She reminded Lynn a little of herself, ten years before. Skinny, impatient. A fit-looking man in a tracksuit hopped out of a huge shiny bakkie with *Adil's IT Bonanza* on its door and started pacing alertly back and forth. Eventually the man – Adil himself? – went over to the family group, squatted on his haunches and conferred.

Lynn stood alone, leaning against the glass wall of the petrol-station shop. The sun stewed in a sulphurous haze. She checked her cellphone, but the service had been down since the day before. Overloaded. There wasn't really anyone she wanted to call. The man in the blue overalls kept staring at her. He had skin the colour and texture of damp clay, a thin, villain's moustache. She looked away.

The black-haired girl jumped up yet again and dashed into the road. A small red car with only one occupant was speeding towards them out of the smoky distance. The others went running out to join their friend, stringing themselves out across the highway to block the car's path. By the time Lynn thought about joining them, it was already too late – the young people had piled in and the car was driving on, wallowing, every window crammed with hands and faces. The girl gave the crowd a thumbs-up as they passed.

A group was clustering around one of the cars. Peering over a woman's shoulder, Lynn could see one of the burly uncles hunkered down in his shorts, expertly wielding a length of hose coming out of the fuel tank. His cheeks hollowed, then he whipped the hose away from his mouth with a practised jerk, stopped the spurt of petrol with his thumb, and plunged the other end of the hose into a jerry-can. He looked up with tense, pale eyes.

"Any more?" he asked in an over-loud voice.

Lynn shook her head. The group moved on to the next car.

She went to sit inside, in the fried-egg smell of the cafeteria. The seats were red plastic, the table-tops marbled yellow, just as she remembered them from childhood road trips. Tomato sauce and mustard in squeezy plastic bottles crusted around the nozzle. She was alone in the gloom of the place. There were racks of chips over the counter, shelves of sweets, display fridges. She pulled down two packets of chips, helped herself to a Coke and made her way to a window booth. She wished strongly for a beer. The sun came through the tinted glass in an end-of-the-world shade of pewter, but that was nothing new; that had always been the colour of the light in places like this.

Through the glass wall, she watched absently as the petrol scavengers filled up the tank of *Adil's IT Bonanza*. They'd taken the canopy off the gleaming bakkie to let more people climb on. The uncles and aunts sat around the edge, turning their broad backs on those left behind, with small children and bags piled in the middle and a couple of older children standing up, clinging to the cab. What she'd thought was a group had been split: part of the white family was left behind on the tar, revealing itself as a young couple with a single toddler, and one of the sweaty car-pushers was on board. The blue-overalled guy was up front, next to Adil. How wrong she'd been, then, in her reading of alliances. Perhaps she might have scored a berth, if she'd pushed. She sipped her Coke thoughtfully as the bakkie pulled away.

Warm Coke: it seemed the electricity had gone too, now.

Lynn started distractedly picking at the strip of aluminium that bound the edge of the table. It could be used for something. In an emergency. She opened a packet of cheese and onion chips, surprised by her hunger. Lynn realised she was feeling happy, in a secret, volatile way. It was like bunking school: sitting here where nobody knew who she was, where no one could find her, on a day cut out of the normal passage of days. Nothing was required of her except to wait. All she wanted to do was sit for another hour, and then another hour after that, at which point she might lie down on the sticky vinyl seat in the tainted sunlight and sleep. She hadn't eaten a packet of chips for years. They were excellent. Crunching them up, she felt the salt and fat repairing her headache. Lynn pushed off her heeled shoes, which were hurting, and untucked her fitted shirt. She hadn't dressed practically for mass evacuation.

The female petrol attendant pushed open the glass door with a clang, then smacked through the wooden counter-flap to go behind the till. She was a plump, pretty young woman with complexly braided hair. Her skin, Lynn noticed, was clear brown, free from the soot that flecked the motorists. She took a small key on a chain from her bosom and opened the till, whacking the side of her fist against the drawer to jump it out. Flicking a glance across at Lynn, she pulled a handful of 50-rand notes from the till, then hundreds.

"Taxi's going," she said.

"Really? With what petrol?"

"He's got petrol. He was just waiting to fill the seats. We arranged a price – for you, too, if you want."

"You're kidding. He was just waiting for people to *pay*? He could have taken us any time?"

The woman shrugged, as if to say, *taxi-drivers*. She stroked a thumb across the edge of the wad of notes. "Are you coming?"

Lynn shrugged back at her.

"You don't want to come in a taxi?"

"No, it's not that – it's just, where would we go? I'm sure someone will come soon. The police will come. Rescue services."

The woman gave a snort and exited the shop, bumping the door open with her hip. The door sucked slowly shut, and then it was quiet again.

Lynn watched through the tinted window as the money was handed over, which seemed to activate the inert *gaardjie*. He straightened up and started striding back and forth, clapping his hands, shouting and hustling like it was Main Road rush hour. The people inside the taxi edged up in the seats and everyone else started pushing in. The driver spotted Lynn through the window and raised his eyebrows, pointing with both forefingers first at her and then at the kombi and then back at her again: *coming?* When she just smiled, he snapped his fingers and turned his attention elsewhere. People were being made to leave their bags and bundles on the tar.

Lynn realised she was gripping the edge of the table tightly. Her stomach hurt. Getting up this morning, packing her few things, driving all this way... it seemed impossible for her to start it all again. Decision, action, motion. She wanted to curl up on the seat, put her head down. But the taxi was filling up.

Her body delivered her from decision. All at once her digestion seemed to have speeded up dramatically. Guts whining, she trotted to the bathroom.

Earlier, there'd been a queue for the toilets, but now the stalls were empty. In the basin mirror, Lynn's face was startlingly grimed. Her choppy dark hair was greasy, her eyes as pink as if she'd been weeping. Contamination. Sitting on the black plastic toilet seat, she felt the poisons gush out of her. She wiped her face with paper and looked closely at the black specks smeared on to the tissue. Her skin was oozing it. She held the wadded paper to her nose. A faint coppery smell. What was this shit? The explosion had been at a chemical plant, but which chemical? She couldn't remember what they'd said on the news.

She noticed the silence. It was the slightly reverberating stillness of a place from which people have recently departed.

There was nobody left on the forecourt. The battered white taxi was pulling out, everyone crammed inside. The sliding door was open, three men hanging out the side with their fingers hooked into the roof rim. Lynn ran after it on to the highway, but the only person who saw her was the blond toddler crushed against the back windscreen, one hand spread against the glass. He held her gaze as the taxi picked up speed.

The cloud was creeping higher behind her back, casting a dull murk, not solid enough to be shadow. She could see veils of dirty rain bleeding from its near edge. Earlier, in the city, she had heard sirens, helicopters in the sky; but there were none out here. It was silent.

Standing alone on the highway was unnerving. This was for cars. The road surface was not meant to be touched with hands or feet, to be examined too closely or in stillness. The four lanes were so wide. Even the white lines and the gaps between them were much longer than they appeared from the car: the length of her whole body, were she to lie down in the road. She had to stop herself looking over her shoulder, flinching from invisible cars coming up from behind.

She thought of the people she'd seen so many times on the side of the highway, walking, walking along verges not designed for human passage, covering incomprehensible distances, toiling from one obscure spot to another. Their bent heads dusty, cowed by the iron ring of the horizon. In all her years of driving at speed along highways, Cape Town, Jo'burg, Durban, she'd never once stopped at a random spot, walked into the veld. Why would she? The highways were tracks through an indecipherable terrain of dun and grey, a blur in which one only fleetingly glimpsed the sleepy eyes of people standing on its edge. To leave the car would be to disintegrate, to merge with that shifting world. How far could she walk, anyway, before weakness made her stumble? Before the air thickened into some alien gel, impossible to wade through, to breathe?

It was mid-afternoon but it felt much later. Towards the city, the sky was thick with bloody light. It was possible to stare straight at the sun – a pink bleached disk, like the moon of a different planet. The cloud was growing. As she watched, a deep rose-coloured occlusion extended towards her, pulling a wash of darkness across the sky. A strange horizontal rain came with it, and reflexively she ducked and put her hands to her hair. But the droplets were too big and distinct, and she realised that they were in fact birds, thousands of birds, sprinting away from the mountain. They flew above her and around her ears: swift starlings, labouring geese. Some small rapid birds were tossed up against the sky, smuts from a burning book.

As they passed overhead, for the first time Lynn was filled with fear.

Approximately 50 packets of potato chips, assorted flavours. Eighty or so chocolate bars, different kinds. Liquorice, wine-gums, Smarties. Maybe 30 bottles of Coke and Fanta in the fridges, different sizes. Water, fizzy and plain: 15 big bottles, 10 small. No alcohol of any kind. How much fluid did you need to drink per day? The women's magazines said two litres. To flush out the toxins. Would drinking Coke be enough? Surely. So: two weeks, maybe three. The survival arithmetic was easy. Two weeks was more than enough time; rescue would come long before then. She felt confident, prepared.

Boldly, she pushed through the wooden flap and went behind the counter. The till stood open. Beyond were two swing doors with head-high windows, and through them a sterile steel-fitted kitchen, gloomy without overhead lighting. Two hamburger patties, part-cooked, lay abandoned on the flat steel plate of the griller, and a basket of chips sat in a vat of opaque oil. To the right was a back door with a broad metal pushbar. She shoved it.

The door swung open on to a sudden patch of domesticity: three or four black bins, a metal skip, sunlight, some scruffy bluegums and an old two-wire fence with wooden posts holding back the veld. A shed with a tilted corrugated-iron roof leaned up against the back wall. The change in scale and atmosphere was startling. Lynn had not imagined that these big franchised petrol stations hid modest homesteads. She'd had the vague sense that they were modular, shipped out in sections, everything in company colours. Extraneous elements – employees – were presumably spirited away somewhere convenient and invisible at the end of their shifts. But this was clearly somebody's backyard. It smelt of smoke and sweat and dishwater, overlaying the burnt grease of the kitchen. Through the doorway of the shed she could see the end of an iron bed and mattress. On the ground was a red plastic tub of the kind used to wash dishes or babies. Two plastic garden chairs, one missing a leg. A rusted car on bricks.

Lynn laughed out loud. Her car! Her own car, 20 years on: the same model blue Toyota, but reduced to a shell. The remaining patches of crackled paint had faded to the colour of a long-ago summer sky. The roof had rusted clean through in places, and the bottom edges of the doors were rotten with corrosion. Old carpeting was piled on the back seat and all the doors were open. Seeing the smooth finish gone scabrous and raw gave Lynn a twinge at the back of her teeth.

She walked past the car. There was a stringy cow on the other side of the fence, its pelt like mud daubed over the muscles. A goat came avidly up to the wire, watching her with its slotted eyes, and she put her arm through and scratched between its horns. The cow also mooched over in an interested way. Smelling its grassy breath, Lynn felt a tremor of adventure. She could be here for *days*. She felt no fear at the prospect: nobody else was here, nobody for miles around (although briefly she saw again: the hand sliding across the throat...).

Out back here, the sky looked completely clear, as if the petrol station marked the limit of the zone of contamination. She shot her fingers at the goat and snapped them like the taxi-man, and spun round in a circle, humming.

She breathed in sharply, stepping back hard against the wire. "Jesus Christ."

Someone was in the car. The pile of rugs had reconstituted itself into an old lady, sitting on the backseat as if waiting to be chauffeured away.

Lynn coughed out a laugh, slapping her chest. "Oh god, sorry," she said. "You surprised me."

The old lady worked her gums, staring straight ahead. She wore a faded green button-up dress, a hand-knitted cardigan, elasticised knee stockings and slippers. Grey hair caught in a meagre bun.

Lynn came closer. "Um," she began. *"Hello?"* Afrikaans? Lynn's Afrikaans was embarrassingly weak. "Hallo?" she said again, giving the word a different inflection. Ridiculous.

No response. Poor thing, she thought, someone just left her here. Would the old lady even know about the explosion? "Sorry... *tannie*?" she tried again. She'd never seriously called anyone "*tannie*" before. But it seemed to have some effect: the old lady looked at her with mild curiosity. Small, filmed black eyes, almost no whites visible. A creased face shrunken on to fine bones. An ancient mouse.

"Hi. I'm Lynn. Sorry to disturb you. Ah, I don't know if anyone's told you – about the accident? In Cape Town."

The woman's mouth moved in a fumbling way. Lynn bent closer to hear.

"My grandson," the old lady enunciated, slowly but clearly. Then she smiled faintly and looked away, having concluded a piece of necessary small talk.

"He told you about it?"

No answer.

So. Now there was another person to consider, an old frail person, someone in need of her help. Lynn felt her heaviness return. "*Tannie*," she said – having begun with it she might as well continue – "There's been an accident, an explosion. There's chemicals in the air. Poison, *gif*. It might be coming this way. I think we should go out front. There might be people coming past who can help us. Cars. Ambulances."

The old lady seemed not averse to the idea, and allowed Lynn to take her arm and raise her from her seat. Although very light, she leaned hard; Lynn felt she was lugging the woman's entire weight with one arm, like a suitcase. Rather than negotiate the complex series of doors back through the station, they took the longer route, clockwise around the building on a narrow track that squeezed between the back corner of the garage and the wire fence. Past the ladies, the gents, the café. As they walked, it started to rain, sudden and heavy. The rain shut down the horizon; its sound on the forecourt canopy was loud static. Lynn wondered how tainted the falling water was. She sat the old lady down on a sheltered bench outside the shop, and fetched some bottles of water and packets of chips from inside. Then she urgently had to use the bathroom again.

The toilet was no longer flushing. Her empty guts felt liquid, but strained to force anything out. The headache was back. When she got back outside, the rain had stopped again, as abruptly as it started, leaving a rusty tang in the air. The old lady had vanished.

Then Lynn spotted movement out on the road: her car door was open. Coming closer, she saw that the woman was calmly eating tomato chips in the back seat. Having transferred herself from the wreck in the backyard to the superior vehicle out front, she was now waiting for the journey to commence. A neat old lady, Lynn noted: there were no crumbs down her front. She seemed restored by the chips. Her eyes gleamed as she whipped a small plastic tortoiseshell comb out of a pocket and started snatching back wisps of hair, repinning the bun into place with black U-bend pins that Lynn hadn't seen since her own grandmother died. In contrast, she felt increasingly dishevelled, and embarrassed about her tip of a car: the empty Heineken bottles on the floor, the tissues in the cubbyhole. She should have kept things cleaner, looked after things better.

"My grandson," the woman said to Lynn, with a nod of reassurance.

"Of course," said Lynn.

Evening was coming. The clouds had retreated somewhat and were boiling grumpily over the mountain. The brief rain had activated an awful odour: like burnt plastic but with a metallic bite, and a whiff of sourness like rotten meat in it too. Lynn sat in the front seat, put the keys into the ignition and gripped the steering wheel. She had no plan. The sky ahead was darkening to a luminous blue. The silent little woman was an expectant presence in her rear-view mirror. Feeling oppressed, Lynn got out of the car again and stood with her hands on her hips, staring east, west, willing sirens, flashing lights. She ducked back into the car. "I'll be back in a sec. Okay? You're all right there?"

The old woman looked at her with polite incomprehension.

She just needed to walk around a bit. She headed off towards the sun, which was melting messily into smears of red and purple. The mountain was no longer visible. The road was discoloured, splattered with lumps of some tarry black precipitate. She counted five small bodies of birds, feathers damp and stuck together. Blades of grass at the side of the road were streaked with black, and the ground seemed to be smoking, a layer of foul steam around her ankles. It got worse the further she walked, and so she turned around.

There was someone standing next to her car. At once she recognised the moustache, the blue overalls.

Her first impulse was to hide. She stood completely still, watching. He hadn't seen her.

The clay-faced man was holding something... a box. No, a can. He had a white jerry-can in his hands and he was filling her car with petrol. Suddenly her stomach roiled and she crouched down at the side of the road, vomiting a small quantity of cheese-and-onion mulch into the stinking grass. When she raised her chin, the man was standing looking back at the petrol station.

Deciding, she made herself stand, raising her hand to wave – but in that moment he opened the door and got in; the motor turned immediately and the car was rolling forward. She could see the back of the old woman's head, briefly silver as the car turned out into the lane, before the reflection of the sunset blanked out the rear windscreen. The Toyota headed out into the clear evening.

Lynn sat in the back of the rusted car and watched the sky turn navy and the stars come out. She loved the way the spaces between the stars had no texture, softer than water; they were pure depth. She sat in the hollow the old lady had worn in the seat, ankles crossed in the space where the handbrake used to be. She sipped Coke; it helped with the nausea.

She'd been here three days and her head felt clear. While there'd been a few bursts of strange rain, the chemical storm had not progressed further down the highway. It seemed the pollution had created its own weather system over the mountain, a knot of ugly cloud. She felt washed up on the edge of it, resting her oil-clogged wings on a quiet shore.

Sooner or later, rescue would come. The ambulances with flashing lights, the men in luminous vests with equipment and supplies. Or maybe just a stream of people driving back home. But if rescue took too long, then there was always the black bicycle that she'd found leaned up against the petrol pump. The woman's grandson must have ridden here, with the petrol can, from some place not too far down the road. It was an old postman's bike, heavy but hardy, and she felt sure that if he had cycled the distance, so could she. Maybe tomorrow, or the day after. And when this was all over, she was definitely going to go on a proper detox. Give up all junk food, alcohol. Some time soon.

Lynn snapped open a packet of salt-'n'-vinegar chips. Behind her, the last of the sunset lingered, poison violet and puce, but she didn't turn to look. She wanted to face clear skies, sweet-smelling veld. If she closed her eyes, she might hear a frog, just one, starting its evening song beyond the fence.

Henrietta Rose-Innes was born in 1971 in Cape Town, South Africa. She is the author of two novels, *Shark's Egg* (2000) and *The Rock Alphabet* (2004). In addition to winning the 2008 Caine Prize for African Writing, she was shortlisted in 2007, and was also awarded the 2007 Southern African PEN short story award, judged by J.M. Coetzee. She has also compiled an anthology of South African writing, *Nice Times! A Book of South African Pleasures and Delights* (2006).

G.C. Osondu

Waiting

E.C. Osondu – winner of the 2009 Caine Prize

My name is Orlando Zaki. *Orlando* is taken from Orlando, Florida, which is what is written on the t-shirt given to me by the Red Cross. *Zaki* is the name of the town where I was found and from which I was brought to this refugee camp. My friends in the camp are known by the inscriptions written on their t-shirts. Acapulco wears a t-shirt with the inscription, *Acapulco*. Sexy's t-shirt has the inscription *Tell Me I'm Sexy*. Paris's t-shirt says *See Paris And Die*. When she is coming toward me, I close my eyes because I don't want to die.

Even when one gets a new t-shirt, your old name stays with you. Paris just got a new t-shirt that says *Ask Me About Jesus*, but we still call her Paris and we are not asking her about anybody. There was a girl in the camp once whose t-shirt said *Got Milk?* She threw the t-shirt away because some of the boys in the camp were always pressing her breasts forcefully to see if they had milk. You cannot know what will be written on your t-shirt. We struggle and fight for them and count ourselves lucky that we get anything at all. Take Lousy, for instance; his t-shirt says *My Dad Went To Yellowstone And Got Me This Lousy T-shirt*. He cannot fight, so he's not been able to get another one and has been wearing the same t-shirt since he came to the camp. Though what is written on it is now faded, the name has stuck. Some people are lucky: London had a t-shirt that said *London* and is now in London. He's been adopted by a family over there. Maybe I will find a family in Orlando, Florida that will adopt me.

Sister Nora is the one who told me to start writing this book, she says *the best way to forget is to remember and the best way to remember is to forget*. That is the way Sister Nora talks, in a roundabout way. I think because she is a Reverend Sister she likes to speak in parables like Jesus. She is the one who has been giving me books to read. She says I have a gift for telling stories. This is why she thinks I will become a writer one day.

The first book she gave me to read was *Waiting For Godot*. She says the people in the book are waiting for God to come and help them. Here in the camp, we wait and wait and then wait some more. It is the only thing we do. We wait for the food trucks to come and then we form a straight line and then we wait a few minutes for the line to scatter, then we wait for the fight to begin, and then we fight and struggle and bite and kick and curse and tear and grab and run. And then we begin to watch the road and wait to see if the water trucks are coming, we watch for the dust trail, and then we go and fetch our containers and start waiting and then the trucks come and the first few containers are filled and the fight and struggle and tearing and scratching begin because someone has whispered to someone that the water tanker only has little water in it. That is, if we are lucky and the water tanker comes; oftentimes, we just bring out our containers and start waiting and praying for rain to fall.

Today we are waiting for the photographer to come and take our pictures. It is these pictures that the Red Cross people send to their people abroad who show them to different people in foreign countries and, after looking at them, the foreign families will choose those they like to come and live with them. This is the third week we have been waiting for the photographer, but he has to pass through the war zone so he may not even make it today. After taking the photographs, we have to wait for him to print it and bring it back. We then give it to the Red Cross people and start waiting for a response from abroad.

I want to go and join my friend under the only tree still standing in the camp. Acapulco is raising a handful of red dust into the air to test for breeze; the air is stagnant and the red earth falls back in a straight line.

"Orlando, do you think the photographer will come today?" he asks.

"Maybe he will come."

"Do you think an American family will adopt me?"

"Maybe, if you are lucky."

"Will they find a cure for my bedwetting?"

"There is a tablet for every sickness in America."

"I am not sick, I only wet myself in my sleep because I always dream that I am urinating outside and then I wake up and my knickers are wet because it was only a dream, but the piss is real."

"The same dream every night?"

"Yes."

"Do you think that if I go to America, my parents will hear about me and write to me and I will write to them and tell my new family to let them come over and join me?"

"When the war ends, your parents will find you."

"When will the war end?"

"I don't know, but it will end soon."

"If the war will end soon, why are the Red Cross people sending us to America?"

"Because they don't want us to join the Youth Brigade and shoot and kill and rape and loot and burn and steal and destroy and fight to the finish and die and not go to school."

This was why Acapulco was always sitting alone under the tree: because he always asked a lot of questions. Sister Nora says it is good to ask questions, that if you ask questions you will never get lost. Acapulco begins to throw the sand once more, testing for breeze. Pus is coming out of his ears and this gives him the smell of an egg that is a little rotten. This was another reason people kept away from him. A fly is buzzing around his ear; he ignores it for some time and at the exact moment the fly is about to perch, he waves it away furiously.

"I wish I had a dog," he said.

"What do you want to do with the dog?"

"I will pose with the dog in my photograph that they are sending to America because white people love dogs."

"But they also like people."

"Yes, but they like people who like dogs."

"London did not take a picture with a dog."

"Yes, London is now in London."

"Maybe you will soon be in Acapulco," I said laughing.

"Where is Acapulco?"

"They have a big ocean there, it is blue and beautiful."

"I don't like the ocean, I don't know how to swim, I want to go to America."

"Everyone in America knows how to swim; all the houses have swimming pools."

"I will like to swim in a swimming pool, not the ocean. I hear swimming pool water is sweet and clean and blue and is good for the skin."

We are silent. We can hear the sound of the aluminium sheets with which the houses are built. They make an angry noise like pin-sized

195

bullets when going off. The houses built with tarpaulin and plastic sheets are fluttering in the breeze like a thousand plastic kites going off. Acapulco raises a handful of dust in the air. The breeze carries it away. Some of it blows into our faces and Acapulco smiles.

"God is not asleep," he says. I say nothing.

"There used to be dogs here in the camp." He had been in the camp before me. He is one of the oldest people in the camp.

There were lots of black dogs. They were our friends, they were our protectors. Even though food was scarce, the dogs never went hungry. The women would call them whenever a child squatted down to shit and the dogs would come running. They would wait for the child to finish and lick the child's buttocks clean before they ate the shit. People threw them scraps of food. The dogs were useful in other ways too. In those days, the enemy still used to raid the camp frequently. We would bury ourselves in a hole and the dogs would gather leaves and other stuff and spread it atop the hole where we hid. The enemy would pass by the hole and not know we were hiding there.

But there was a time the Red Cross people could not bring food to the camp for two weeks because the enemy would not let their plane land. We were so hungry we killed a few of the dogs and used them to make pepper-soup. A few days later, the Red Cross people were let through and food came. The dogs were a bit wary, but they seemed to understand it was not our fault.

And then, for the second time, there was no food for a very long time. We were only able to catch some of the dogs this time. Some of them ran away as we approached, but we still caught some and cooked and ate them. After that we did not see the dogs again; the ones that ran away kept off. One day, a little child was squatting and having a shit. When the mother looked up, half a dozen of the dogs that had disappeared emerged from nowhere and attacked the little child. While the mother screamed, they tore the child to pieces and fled with parts of the child's body dangling between their jaws. Some of the men began to lay ambush for the dogs and killed a few of them. They say the dogs had become as tough as lions. We don't see the dogs any more. People say it is the war.

I decided I was going to ask Sister Nora. As if reading my mind, Acapulco told me not to mention it to anyone. He said people in the camp did not like talking about the dogs.

"I am not sure the photographer will still come today," I said.

"Sometimes I think there is a bullet lodged in my brain," Acapulco said.

"If you had a bullet in your brain, you would be dead."

"It went in through my bad ear. I hear explosions in my head, bullets popping, voices screaming, *banza, banza bastard, come out we will drink your blood today*, and then I smell carbide, gun-smoke, burning thatch. I don't like smelling smoke from fires when the women are cooking with firewood; it makes the bullets in my brain begin to go off."

"You will be fine when you get to America. They don't cook with firewood; they use electricity."

"You know everything, Zaki. How do you know all these things though you have never been to these places?"

"I read a lot of books, books contain a lot of information, sometimes they tell stories too," I say.

"I don't like books without pictures; I like books with big, beautiful, colourful pictures."

"Not all books have pictures. Only books for children have pictures."

"I am tired of taking pictures and sending them abroad to families that don't want me, almost all the people I came to the camp with have found families and are now living abroad. One of my friends sent me a letter from a place called Dakota. Why have no family adopted me? Do you think they don't like my face?"

"It is luck; you have not found your luck yet."

"Sometimes I want to join the Youth Brigade but I am afraid; they say they give them we-we to smoke and they drink blood and swear an oath to have no mercy on any soul, including their parents."

"Sister Nora will be angry with you if she hears you talking like that. You know she is doing her best for us, and the Red Cross people too, they are trying to get a family for you."

"That place called Dakota must be full of rocks."

"Why do you say that?"

"Just from the way it sounds, like many giant pieces of rock falling on each other at once."

"I'd like to go to that place with angels."

"You mean Los Angeles."

"They killed most of my people who could not pronounce the name of the rebel leader properly, they said we could not say *Tsofo*, we kept

197

saying *Tofo* and they kept shooting us. My friend here in the camp taught me to say Tsofo, he said I should say it like there is sand in my mouth. Like there is gravel on my tongue. Now I can say it either way."

"That's good. When you get to America, you will learn to speak like them. You will try to swallow your tongue with every word, you will say *larer, berrer, merre, ferre, herrer*."

"We should go. It is getting to lunch time."

"I don't have the power to fight. Whenever it is time for food, I get scared. If only my mother was here, then I would not be *Displaced*. She would be cooking for me; I wouldn't have to fight to eat all the time."

We both looked up at the smoke curling upwards from shacks where some of the women were cooking *dawa*. You could tell the people that had mothers because smoke always rose from their shacks in the afternoon. I wondered if Acapulco and I were yet to find people to adopt us because we were displaced and did not have families. Most of the people that have gone abroad are people with families. I did not mention this to Acapulco; I did not want him to start thinking of his parents who could not say *Tsofo*. I had once heard someone in the camp say that if God wanted us to say *Tsofo* he would have given us tongues that could say *Tsofo*.

"Come with me, I will help you fight for food," I say to Acapulco.

"You don't need to fight, Orlando. All the other kids respect you, they say you are not afraid of anybody or anything and they say Sister Nora likes you and they say you have a book where you record all the bad, bad, things that people do and you give it to Sister Nora to read and when you are both reading the book both of you will be shaking your heads and laughing like *amariya* and *ango*, like husband and wife."

We stood up and started walking towards the corrugated-sheet shack where we got our lunch. I could smell the *dawa*, it was always the same *dawa*, and the same green-bottle flies and the same bent and half-crumpled aluminium plates and yet we still fought over it.

Kimono saw me first and began to call out to me, he was soon joined by Aruba and Jerusalem and Lousy and I'm Loving It and Majorca and the rest. Chief Cook was standing in front of the plates of *dawa* and green soup. She had that look on her face, the face of a man about to witness two beautiful women disgrace themselves by fighting and stripping themselves naked over him. She wagged her finger at us and said: No fighting today, boys. That was the signal we needed to go at it; we dived. *Dawa* and soup were spilling on the floor.

Some tried to grab some into their mouth as they fought to grab a plate in case they did not get anything to eat at the end of the fight. I grabbed a lump of *dawa* and tossed it to Acapulco and made for a plate of soup but as my fingers grabbed it, Lousy kicked it away and the soup poured on the floor. He laughed his crazy hyena laugh and hissed saying: the leper may not know how to milk a cow, but he sure knows how to spill the milk in the pail. Chief Cook kept screaming, hey no fighting, one by one, form a line, the *dawa* is enough to go round. I managed to grab a half-spilled plate of soup and began to weave my way out as I signalled to Acapulco to head out. We squatted behind the food shack and began dipping our fingers into the food, driving away large flies with our free hand. We had two hard lumps of *dawa* and very little soup. I ate a few handfuls and wiped my hands on my shorts, leaving the rest for Acapulco. He was having a hard time driving away the flies from his bad ear and from the plate of food, and he thanked me with his eyes.

I remembered a book Sister Nora once gave me to read about a poor boy living in England in the olden days who asked for more from his chief cook. From the picture of the boy in the book, he did not look so poor to me. The boys in the book all wore coats and caps and they were even served. We had to fight, and if you asked the chief cook for more, she would point at the lumps of *dawa* and the spilled soup on the floor and say we loved to waste food. I once spoke to Sister Nora about the food and fights but she said she did not want to get involved. It was the first time I had seen her refuse to find a solution to any problem. She explained that she did not work for the Red Cross and was their guest like me.

I was wondering how to get away from Acapulco. I needed some time alone but I did not want to hurt his feelings. I told him to take the plates back to the food shack. We did not need to wash them because we had already licked them clean with our tongues.

As Acapulco walked away to the food shack with the plates, I slipped away quietly.

E.C. Osondu was born in Nigeria. He worked as an advertising copywriter for many years before moving to New York to attend Syracuse University, where he gained an MFA for Creative Writing and is now a Fellow. He has won the Nirelle Galson Prize for Fiction and was also shortlisted for the 2007 Caine Prize.

An Emissary

Nadine Gordimer

*'... how few Westerners grasp malaria's devastation.
That said, its global toll remains staggering. In the last
20 years, it has killed nearly twice as many people as
AIDS... Malarial mosquitoes can even stow away on
international flights – just ask recent unsuspecting
victims near airports in Germany, Paris and São
Paulo.'*

All impurity hazing away, middleage evanescing,
you can't really make out their jowls and eye-
pouches in the steam, and your own face if
you could see it would be smudged, all that you've
done to it, the wriggles of red veins down the nose,
wafted from view. Underneath is you as you were.

This place calls itself Fredo's Sauna and Health
Club. But when you're lying here you're a senator
among senators and nobles in a Roman bath. It's
winter now – no need to worry, no dangerous ultra-
violet striking you, nothing noxious survives. Winter
now but there's no shivering here! Never any winter.
In the humidity summer lives on; and there's some
tiny thing floating out off the misty heat – can't be –
no, must be a shred of someone's towel – but it lands
on a plump wet pectoral, just above the hair-forest
there, it's alive – and now dead, smack! A deformed
punctuation mark of black, a scrap of wing, sliding
on sweat.

Winter outside but there's water and privacy for
breeding, eggs to lie low where no-one could imagine
it, a place in which to emerge as you were, sloping

back, transparent wings and special proboscis feature, in Fredo's Sauna and Health Club.

The musical conversation of the orchestra, tuning up rather like athletes running-on-the-spot and shadow-punching, before performance; it even includes the pitch of anticipation in the low interchange of human voices. A diminuendo from this audience, as the musicians come from the wings, and a rallentando when the guest conductor, a famous young Czech or whatever, appears to bow, turn his back, mount the podium and settle his shoulders in readiness to enter the symphony with raised baton.

HEAVENLY
CHORUS
OF THE
SPHERES

It's winter, but nobody coughs. The sonority of wind, strings and keyboard calms all, the following tempest of brass sweeps away all reactions but the aural. The cello and viola file into the temple of each ear with the intoning of monks, there's the query of the flute, the double-stopping grunt of the bass, the berating of drums and an answering ping of a triangle. All these creatures produce the beauty of the invisible life of sound. They dive, they soar, they ripple and glide almost beyond the reach of reception, and swell to return; some overwhelm others and then in turn are subsumed, but all are there somewhere in the layers of empyrean they ravishingly invade and transmute. They weave in and out of it, steal through it, flow into eight hundred sets of ears – it's a full house when this conductor comes out on tour from one of those dangerous benighted Balkan countries that are always seceding and fighting and changing their names.

The auditorium is kept welcomingly heated by artificial means and by the pleasant warmth of human breath. A minute manifestation of being flies with the music, contributing a high, long-drawn fiddle-note. Nobody hears this Ariel materialise round their heads.

On the other hemisphere – Southern – it is summer, not simulation that makes all the year a summer.

They are not here officially, driving on a rutted

muddy road between baobab trees, if officially means that your whereabouts are known to close collaterals – wives, husbands, and professional partners. An irresistible mutual impulse – like the original unlikely one that brought them together – to take to themselves something more than two hours once a week under an assumed name in an obscure hotel, had discovered in each the ability to devise unbelievably believable absences, the call of professional commitments. They took a plane, carefully not travelling even in the same class (how clever passion makes even those who have been honest and open all their lives). They chose an unlikely destination – they hoped; in their circles people travel a lot and quite adventurously, so long as the camps are luxury ones with open-air bars and helicopter service.

The baobabs are mythical animals turned to stone.

Whenever before would he have found himself beside a woman who would come out with such delightful fantasies! She's a writer, and sees everywhere what he has never seen; he's an economist, privy to so much about the workings of the world she always has felt herself ignorant of, and here he is, listening with admiration to her trivial knack of imagery.

This adventure of theirs can only last a few days – the credibility of the alibis won't allow longer – and it has come late and totally unexpected, to both of them. Husband, wife, half-grown children, reputation – now a last chance: of what? Something missed, now to be urgently claimed. He loves her to speak poetry to him as he drives. It's her poetry, appropriated by her to accompany her life, the poets knowing always better than she does what is happening to her; now, to them. What they have done is crazy, the final destination a bad end; the realisation comes silently to each with a bump in the rutted road. Then she's saying for them both, as the medium possessed by a dead poet, the lines don't all reach her in the right sequence – at my back I always hear, Time's wingèd chariot hurrying near... let us roll

WINGED
CHARIOT

all our strength and all our sweetness up... and tear our pleasures with rough strife through the iron gates of life... the grave's a fine and private place but none I think do there embrace...

He swerves to the side of the deserted road and turns off the ignition. They stare at each other and he breaks the spell with a smile and slow-moving head, side-to-side. There's no-one, nothing to witness the embrace, the struggle of each not to let go. Then he suddenly frees himself, gets out of the car, opens the passenger door and takes her by the hand. There are old puddles, soupy with stagnation, to step across. The sagging remains of a broken fence: whose land was this, once. No-one, nothing. The sun rests on their backs as a benign hand, they walk a little while over stubble, viscous hollows bleary with past rain, and cannot walk farther, are arrested by need. And there is some tree that really is a tree, in leaf over a low mound of tender grass grown in its moist shelter.

Lying there they find their way to each other through their clothes like any teenagers making love wherever they can hide. It doesn't matter. Now they lie, breathing each other in, diastole and systole, and nothing draws near, there is only that indefinable supersonic humming of organic and insect life, the sap rising in the tree, grass sprouting, gauze of gnats hovering, and a silent shrike swoops from a branch to catch some kind of flying prey in mid-air.

He is stirred, eventually, by past reality, in concern for her – remembering the hazards of hunting trips he has taken: I hope there're no ticks. She moves her head, eyes closed, no. Nothing. Safe. Opens her eyes to see him, nothing else. One of the flying specks has landed on the lobe of his ear, lingering there, while she blows at it. He starts with a faint exclamation, she frees a hand and flicks whatever it is, so small, nothing, away.

The rave is in one of those four-walls-and-roof with creaky boards that has housed all kinds of purposes

– a church or school hall where there isn't, in this neighbourhood, a church or school anymore, and the toilets are across a yard that in the daytime is used by some guys to repair exhausts. Dismembered vehicle parts and gas cylinders have to be navigated to reach where he's gone off to. There he is, sitting on the broken seat, but he has his trousers on, he's sure not having a shit, and his sweat-shirt sleeve is rolled back on his bare white arm, he's got an arm pale and hairless as a girl's. And just look at it.

I thought you'd kicked the habit.

He laughs. You want to use this seat?

But he allows the arm to be grasped.

Just see your arm.

What's one more prick? How can you tell one from another, high yourself on booze.

So what's that on your arm?

Mosquito bite.

Very funny. Hahaha.

Summer, winter, Northern Hemisphere, Southern Hemisphere. There's nothing to be afraid of, nothing! A speck hovering, landing, you can swat with the palm of a hand. It's not the Reaper with the scythe.

It's his emissary, Anopheles.

Nadine Gordimer is a South African who won the 1974 Booker Prize for her novel *The Conservationist*. She has published 14 novels and 17 volumes of short stories. She was awarded the Nobel Prize for literature in 1991. 'An Emissary' was originally published in *Loot*, Bloomsbury, London 2004, and is reprinted with permission of A P Watt Ltd on behalf of Felix Licensing BV.

SHOOTING
UP

About the **New Internationalist**

The **New Internationalist** is an independent not-for-profit publishing co-operative. Our mission is to report on issues of world poverty and inequality; to focus attention on the unjust relationship between the powerful and the powerless worldwide; to debate and campaign for the radical changes necessary if the needs of all are to be met.

We publish informative current affairs titles and popular reference, like the *No-Nonsense Guides* series, complemented by world food, fiction, photography and alternative gift books, as well as calendars and diaries, maps and posters – all with a global justice world view.

We also publish the monthly **New Internationalist** magazine. Each month tackles a range of subjects, such as Afghanistan, Climate Justice, or the Economic Meltdown, exploring each issue in a concise way which is easy to understand. The main articles are packed full of photos, charts and graphs and each magazine also contains music, film and book reviews, country profiles, interviews and news.

To find out more about the New Internationalist, subscribe to the magazine, or buy any of our books take a look at:
www.newint.org

Other titles from the Caine Prize collection

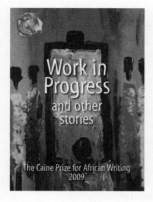

Work In Progress and other stories
The Caine Prize for African Writing 2009
This edition collects the five 2009 shortlisted stories: 'The End of Skill', by Mamle Kabu (Ghana); 'You Wreck Her' by Parselelo Kantai (Kenya); 'Icebergs' by Alistair Morgan (South Africa); 'How Kamau wa Mwangi Escaped into Exile' by Mukoma wa Ngugi (Kenya); and the eventual winner 'Waiting' by EC Osondu (Nigeria). The book also contains 12 stories written at the Caine Prize Writers' Workshop, which took place in Ghana, in spring 2009 – including 'Work in Progress' by 2008 winner Henrietta Rose-Innes.

ISBN: 978-1906523-14-5

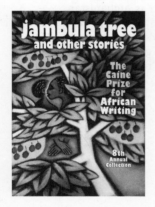

Jambula Tree and other stories
8th annual collection
The winner of the 8th Caine Prize for African Writing was 'Jambula Tree' by Monica Arac de Nyeko from Uganda. Her story leads this stimulating anthology from some of the best new writers across the continent. This book also contains the five shortlisted stories that competed for the 9th prize, which was won by Henrietta Rose-Innes from South Africa for her story 'Poison'.

ISBN: 978-1904456-73-5

Jungfrau and other stories
7th annual collection
The 7th winner was Mary Watson from South Africa for 'Jungfrau', which Dr Nana Wilson-Tagoe, who chaired the judges, said was "a powerfully written narrative that works skilfully through a child's imagination to suggest a world of insights about familial and social relationships in the new South Africa".

ISBN: 978-1904456-62-9

All New Internationalist titles are available on our website on www.newint.org/shop

ONE WORLD

A GLOBAL ANTHOLOGY OF SHORT STORIES

CHIMAMANDA NGOZI ADICHIE

JHUMPA LAHIRI

AND 21 OTHER AUTHORS

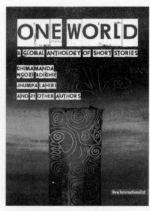

A teenage Nigerian girl struggles to shed her cultural roots in the US...

An Inuit girl is rowed by her parents to the shore, unaware of the fate that awaits her...

ISBN: 978-1906523-13-8

A Filipina maid in Hong Kong gets entangled with her employer...

The lover of an African freedom fighter has to choose between fidelity and survival...

ONE WORLD is a collection that speaks with the clarity and intensity of the human experience. The swift transition from story to story, from continent to continent, from child's perspective to adult's: together, these evoke the complex but balanced texture of the world we live in. The diversity of subject, style and perspective results in vivid and poignant stories that will haunt the reader.

All authors' royalties from the sale of ONE WORLD will be donated to Médecins Sans Frontières.

All New Internationalist titles are available on our website on
www.newint.org/shop